Vina's Quest

Irene Lebeter

Vina's Quest

By **Irene Lebeter**

Published by Author Way Limited through CreateSpace
Copyright 2014 author

Author **way**

This book has been brought to you by -

Discover other Author Way Limited titles at -
http://www.authorway.net
Or to contact the author mailto:info@authorway.net

ISBN-10 1503205657
ISBN-13:978-1503205659

Dedicated to the memory of my beloved

Alan and Peter

Acknowledgements

With thanks to

Elaine and Gerry Mann, Authors and Publishers.
David Neilson, Creative Writing Tutor.
David Pettigrew, Creative Writing Tutor.
Andrea McNicoll, Creative Writing Tutor.
Margaret Thomson Davis, Author and Honorary President of Strathkelvin Writers' Group, for introducing me to the group.
All Members of Strathkelvin Writers' Group for their inspiration.
Mary Edward, Author, Past President of the Scottish Association of Writers and Past President of Strathkelvin Writers' Group, for being my mentor, inspiration and friend.
Kate McDougall, Birthlink Co-ordinator, Birthlink, Edinburgh.
The late Greg Gillen, for his brilliant idea of the scarf.
Alan Fraser, for advice about characters' health issues.
The Organisers of the Arctic Convoy Exhibition, Edinburgh.
Alma Ross, for information about Melbourne.
Kathleen Fraser, for information about Penguin.
The late Des McDougall, for all his helpful critiques.
Frank Muir, Author, for his valuable critique.
Rosemary Gemmell, Author, for her valuable critique.
Campbell Thomson and Agnes McEwan, for proofreading my work.
Robert Garrity, James Scott and Yvonne Chapman for their patience with my lack of I.T. skills.
Jane Garrity, Elma Wilson, Ellen Pender, Helen Hodge and Jeanette Tallan, for their faith in me.

Prologue

Scotland - May 1945

Sandwiched between the brooding, weighted clouds and the colourless pavement slabs, the miserable atmosphere twinned the young woman's mood as she pushed the pram along Glenburgh's High Street.

Casting her dark-circled eyes down, she caressed her baby's soft cheek and murmured, 'I can't tell him about you, my darling, he'll kill me.' The infant made sleepy humming noises as the pram wheels bumped across the cobblestones in Castle Street, so named when Glenburgh boasted a castle. The castle, built in the thirteenth century, had long since been demolished.

She steered the pram around the barrels that were being rolled towards the Black Bear pub, beer to quench the thirst of the steelworkers and employees of the local chemical factory. Above the pub sign, a torn piece of red, white and blue cloth fluttered in the dank breeze, a remnant from the Union Jacks strung across High Street for the V.E. day celebrations three weeks ago. The joy and excitement of that day brought a smile to her face but her current fears soon returned and the smile vanished as quickly as it had come.

Dark thoughts had whirled around her mind since the telegram arrived three weeks ago informing her that her husband had been found alive in a POW camp. He could be home any day now. She shivered when she recalled his threats of what he'd do if she was unfaithful. Even her terror in the early years of the war when she'd hunkered down beside her mother and neighbours in the rear of their tenement close during air raids was nothing to her present fear.

The No 10 tramcar appeared out of the grey murk, rounding the corner from Stonefield Road into High Street. She had a vision of her husband's face, leering, threatening. Her heart began to pound and her throat tightened as a black

3

mist surrounded her.

The dark blue tram swayed along the tracks, its mast sparking on the electric cables. With the baby now fast asleep, a strange calmness came over the young woman. She carefully applied the brakes and tied her green silk scarf round the pram handle. Then she ran on to the tramlines.

A pedestrian screamed and, too late, the tram driver plunged his foot pedal down hard and jammed on the hand brake. The young woman's haunted eyes met his for a second before she disappeared beneath his wheels.

Part I - Scotland

Chapter One

January 1944

'If only your father was still alive,' Agnes McQueen yelled. Her eyes were bulging and there were angry red circles on her cheeks as she glared at her teenage daughter. 'Maybe he would have made you see sense, but then again perhaps not as he was always too soft with you.'

'Dad wanted me to have fun. Not like you, always spoiling things for me,' Jean Morrow shouted back. 'And anyway you can't stop me. I'm nearly 20 and a married woman.'

'Married woman or not, you are no match for the sorts of men who frequent these city centre dance halls. I'm telling you, no good comes to women who go there.'

Jean put on her coat and stood in front of the kitchen mirror to fix her beret. 'Well, whether you like it or not, I'm going. I've told Brenda I'll get her at the Locarno and I'm not going to let my best friend down.' She picked up her bag and gloves and stormed out on to the landing, almost pulling the door off its hinges.

The door opened again and her mother's angry outbursts continued as she made her way down the stone steps to wait at the tram stop in front of their tenement building. When the tram arrived she climbed aboard, still reeling from the ferocious row. 'A return to Hope Street,' she said to the driver, and took a seat inside the dimly lit vehicle.

It was during the first few days of 1944 that she'd met her sailor boyfriend, Bill Prior, at the Locarno ballroom in Sauchiehall Street. They'd dated regularly since, but on each occasion she'd told her mother she was going out with Brenda.

On the night she'd met Bill, she really had been out with Brenda. She smiled at the memory. She'd worn her favourite green dress, one that highlighted her green/grey eyes, and for once her hair had fallen into place perfectly.

Jean pulled off her knitted gloves, grey to match her

beret. She flicked her long black hair out of her coat collar and in the dim light re-applied her lipstick. Amber Rose was the shade, a cross between pink and orange. She only used lipstick on special occasions with such commodities hard to come by in wartime.

Lifting the blackout blind a little she peered through the crack, her breath drawing a mosaic on the glass. As her eyes gradually adjusted to the intense darkness outside, she spied the ghostly outline of pillars. If her hunch was correct they were on the King George V Bridge, which spanned the River Clyde, and she had only two more stops to wait until she saw him. The usual butterflies started at the thought of being with her handsome sailor again.

Bill pulled her into his arms when she alighted in Hope Street, at the side of Central Station. Even with three-inch heels she only came up to his shoulder. She leant her cheek against the warmth of his uniform, trying to believe it was only three weeks and three days since she'd first met him. It felt like she'd known him forever.

They walked up Hope Street hand in hand, Jean picking her way carefully over the paving stones. When she slipped on a broken slab, Bill's arm tightened around her waist and he drew her into a shop doorway. They kissed, their bodies pulsing with pleasure. 'I've had word to report back to the ship tomorrow morning,' he whispered, his voice hoarse with emotion. 'I wasn't going to tell you yet, didn't want to spoil our last night together.' He began to kiss her again, a more probing kiss this time until she felt the desire swelling up in him. 'We could go to the Regent Hotel in Bath Street, instead of the Locarno. If you want to?'

They both knew her answer and a few minutes later the porter at the Regent showed them to their room and reminded them of the blackout restrictions. Alone again, they sat down on the eiderdown and he pulled her into his arms.

'We haven't enough time to marry, Jean, even with a special licence. This is the best we can have meantime, darling.' As he was speaking, Bill undid her bra and fondled her breast. Her heart pounded and her breath came in short bursts when he slid his other hand up the inside of her leg. She struggled to pull down the zip on her black taffeta skirt and raised herself up off the bed while he eased the rustling material over her hips and let the skirt drop on to the floor at the side of the bed, to be followed by her underwear.

Bill's breathing matched her own as Jean unbuttoned his shirt and he shrugged himself out of it. Naked, their passion heightened; she moaned quietly as he explored her body, giving herself up to her desire for him.

When she touched him, he responded immediately until, by mutual consent, he entered her. Jean had never before found sex so pleasurable, culminating in such a joyous surrender; so different from the aggressive lovemaking she'd experienced with her late husband, Frank, which had left her cold and empty.

Bill rolled off her and lay beside her on the eiderdown. He raised himself up, leaning on his elbow, and looked into her face. 'I hope I didn't hurt you, darling,' he murmured, the anxiety to please evident in his voice.

'Absolutely not,' she smiled, and traced her finger round the fish tattoo on his forearm, chosen to match his zodiac sign. Happiness rippled through her as she gazed into his clear blue eyes. They got into the bed proper and snuggled down under the blankets. She laid her head against his chest, drawing her fingers down its hairy front. 'I don't want to go home yet,' she whispered.

Bill stroked her long hair, spread out across the white pillowcase. 'We could spend the night here. I've already said my farewells to my parents, as they've gone up to visit my grandmother in Aberdeen for a few days. But what about your mother?'

'I'll say I missed the last tram and stayed overnight with Brenda. She thinks that's who I'm with tonight.'

'Is Brenda the girl you were with the night I met you at the Locarno?'

'Yes, we work together. Mum knows Brenda lives within walking distance of the dance hall so she won't suspect anything.'

'You're sure Brenda will cover for you?'

'I know she will.'

'Sounds good to me,' he smiled and began to caress her once more.

* * *

The morning dawned crisp, with a bright blue sky.

Their steps slowed the nearer they got to the Central Station. It was time for parting, Bill on his train to Portsmouth and Jean to return to her work in Hamilton's grocery store in Glenburgh.

They arrived at Jean's tram stop in Union Street. 'That colour brings out the green of your eyes,' he said, cradling her in his arms.

She held the silk scarf with its Paisley pattern against her cheek, savouring the feel of it. 'Thanks for buying it for me, darling. I love it. I could never have afforded to pay for it myself.'

'I save lots of money when I'm away at sea; there's nothing to spend it on except booze. You will write to me, darling, won't you? I'll miss you like mad but I can face anything if I know you're waiting for me.'

'You know I'll wait and I'll write every day.'

He pulled his kit bag further up on his shoulder. 'The war will be over soon, darling, and then we can be together forever.' The Glenburgh tram drew up, its brakes squealing to a halt, and Bill kissed her again before she went on board.

From the tram window she watched the winter sun strike his reddish/fair hair, turning it to burnished gold. She waved until the tram turned a corner, praying that he would be returned to her safely.

She got off the tram in Glenburgh High Street and bumped into Brenda. The two girls walked, arm in arm, towards Hamilton's grocery store.

'Brenda, will you say I stayed with you last night? I'll explain later.'

'Sure,' Brenda said, turning the door handle. The door opened with its familiar jangling ring. 'Hope he was worth it,' she giggled once they got inside but she was silenced by

Jean's warning look.

'Mr Green, I missed the last tram home and stayed overnight at Brenda's house. Can I go and let my mother know?' Bob Green was a fair man and a good boss; Jean felt guilty about lying to him but she convinced herself it was in a good cause.

Putting his pen into the top pocket of his white coat, her silver-haired manager looked at Jean over the top of his horn-rimmed glasses. 'Of course, Jean, you must do that straight away. Your mother has already come into the shop this morning. She's very worried about you. Pity you couldn't have contacted her.'

'We don't have a phone, Mr Green, nor does anyone else who lives in our tenement. The only phone in the building belongs to Mr Maxwell, the baker, but his shop was closed overnight.' That at least was the truth, she thought, and hurried across the road to their tenement flat at No 80 where she told her well-rehearsed lie.

'You should've watched the time for the last tram,' Agnes McQueen roared at her daughter, more from relief than anger. 'I've been worried all night, was going to contact the police this morning. How was I to know you were at Brenda's?'

'I couldn't contact you. Brenda's mum doesn't have a phone, nor do we. Anyway, I'm nearly twenty and I can look after myself. You worry too much.'

'Any mother worth her salt would have been anxious. There are lots of evil men out there looking for decent young girls. I don't like you frequenting those dance halls. If only your dad was still alive.'

Jean shook her head at these words she'd heard so often since her father passed away ten years ago, but she kissed her mother's cheek. 'Mum, I'm fine,' she said and a few minutes later emerged from her bedroom dressed in her work clothes.

Back in the shop Mary Paterson, little dinky curlers peeping out from under her red tartan headscarf, was in full flow. The elderly housewife lived alone above the shop and came in daily to relay some piece of gossip she'd heard.

'That John Baxter says he's a conscientious objector but he's leaving other boys to go into the services to die for him,' she said, taking her bacon ration from Brenda. 'He's a coward and that's an end to it.'

Later, as Jean attended to customers, she brooded about Bill becoming a conscientious objector. But Bill would always do his duty by his country, and Jean loved him all the more for it.

'Please, please, keep him safe for me,' she prayed to the God she had once believed in.

Chapter Two

March 1944

'Damn and blast.' Bill Prior's words echoed back to him in the stiff breeze as he stood on the deserted dock in Gibraltar where MV. Ontario had lain for the past eight days while essential repairs were carried out. It wasn't Bill's first time in this densely populated city, overshadowed by the massive rock. Despite such a mix of nationalities, the people were fiercely proud of their British sovereignty.

He'd little memory of yesterday's bender, drinking until he was almost unconscious. Too intoxicated to make his way safely back to the ship, he'd checked into a hotel to sleep it off. This morning the winter sun was bright after the dimness of his dingy, wood-panelled hotel room. Blinded by the sun, he didn't see his attackers. By the time he did, his arm was twisted up his back and a punch landed on his nose.

Stunned, but quickly recovering his senses, Bill lashed out at the two men. He struck one of his assailants a blow that knocked the man to the ground and was wrestling his wallet away from the second when a police car appeared, its siren blazing. The thug released his grasp and ran off.

Next thing Bill knew he was arrested for causing a disturbance and bundled into the police car. Forced to spend a couple of hours in a cell despite his protestations of innocence, he was released only after some guests from the hotel, who had witnessed the assault, came forward to speak in his defence.

Bloody hell, he thought, I'll have to report DBS. As a Distressed British Seaman he'd be escorted back to Portsmouth and assigned to another ship.

* * *

Gerry King stood on the starboard side of MV. Ontario and looked down at the unusually dark and sullen Mediterranean, sea and horizon merging together in a ghostly greyness. These stormy conditions had raged since they left Gibraltar early this morning and the mighty Ontario was being tossed about like a toy by the furious waves that crashed around them.

At the beginning of February they'd joined a convoy heading for the Med. The Bay of Biscay had been tempestuous to say the least and even the most experienced seamen turned green during the crossing. The ship sustained major damage and they fell behind, limping their way along the sheltered Strait of Gibraltar to have repairs carried out.

Gerry's thoughts drifted to his shipmate, Bill Prior. He and Bill had been classmates at school in Riverdale before the war and had met up again at the Merchant Navy Training School in Liverpool. They were both assigned to serve on the Ontario early on in the war. Yesterday morning, having completed their duties, Bill and some others kicked their heels on board before requesting a shore pass for twenty-four hours. The ship had sailed before Gerry discovered that Bill was missing.

Where the hell was he? Gerry knew his friend had fallen in love with a girl called Jean during his recent home leave and was obsessed about going back to marry her. But surely his old pal wasn't idiotic enough to go AWOL in order to do so.

'Attention all crew, mail is now ready for collection. I repeat, mail is now ready for collection.' The loudspeaker message pulled Gerry out of his reverie and he squelched his way across the sodden deck to the stairway.

'Hi, Angus, any letters for me?'

Angus Campbell, another Glaswegian, looked up from the pile of mail he was sifting through. 'Yep, think I saw one. There you go, she still loves you,' he grinned.

Gerry was halfway to the door when Angus called after him. 'Know anything about your pal Bill Prior? His name's been deleted from the register.'

Gerry shrugged. 'He went ashore in Gib. and that's the last I saw of him.'

'Thanks, mate.' Angus pushed a letter addressed to Leading Electrician William Prior back into the mailbag to be returned to Portsmouth.

Gerry was in his cabin reading his wife's letter when a muffled thump came from below decks. The shaving mirror toppled off its ledge and crashed into the washbasin. He was clearing up the broken glass when another bang, louder this time, threw him off his feet. 'Hell, we've been hit,' he said aloud and grabbed his life jacket as the warning alarm sounded.

Up on deck Gerry joined in the scramble to release the lifeboats and fifteen minutes later he was aboard one, hanging on to its side as the lifeboat swung haphazardly halfway between deck and water. But the damage inflicted by the German submarine was immense and with a shudder the ship started to list. Gerry heard some mumbled prayers from sailors in his lifeboat. His own lips began to move and he closed his eyes as the great hulk that had been his home came towards them. Very quickly the Ontario slipped under the waves, taking the lifeboats and their crew with her.

Chapter Three

'Come and help me lift this box up on to the table, Jean,' Agnes called through to the front room where her daughter was putting the last of the ornaments into a case before the removal men arrived. Mr Green had given Jean a few days off work so that she could help her mother with the move.

Jean pocketed the letter and wiped her eyes, keen not to let Mum see she'd been crying. Three letters had come from Bill since he left Glasgow at the end of January but she'd heard nothing for weeks now. She dreaded the thought that something had happened to him or, even worse, that he no longer loved her.

'I packed more into this box than I'd realised,' Agnes said when Jean joined her in the kitchen.

Jean felt her mother's eyes boring a line around her girth. Mum seemed to be giving her strange looks lately. She deflected her mother's thoughts elsewhere. 'Will the removal men not lift it for us? After all that's their job.'

'I suppose so,' Agnes nodded, hurrying into the lobby when the doorbell rang.

Betty Black, their next door neighbour's daughter, held out a box. 'Mum's made up some sandwiches to keep you and Jean going until you get all your kitchen stuff sorted out.' The teenager sniffed back the tears. 'I'll miss you and Jean, Mrs McQueen, it won't be the same without you next door.'

Agnes threw her arms around the 13-year-old and hugged her. 'Don't worry, Betty, we aren't going far, just to Queen Street. You can come round and see us whenever you want.'

After the constant bombing Glenburgh had experienced earlier on in the war, their tenement had been deemed unsafe and the residents were all being rehoused as quickly as possible.

Jean came into the hallway behind her mother. 'And you know your mum and dad are due to get a new flat soon,' she reminded Betty. 'Like us, you'll have an inside toilet there and not have to share the one on the landing.'

'That sounds like the removers now,' Agnes said, when heavy footsteps came up the tenement stairs, and she hurried back to the kitchen with the sandwich box.

Agnes and Jean spent the next half-hour directing the men which boxes to put into the van in the first load and which ones were to be left for the second. Once the van was loaded, Agnes put on her coat and hat. 'I'll go with the men in the van and you can wait here with the second load. And make sure nothing is left behind before you lock up,' she instructed her daughter.

* * *

Jean felt numb as she stared at the picture of Bill's ship, the Ontario, on the front page of the newspaper the following afternoon.

Agnes had gone to the shops, leaving her daughter to unpack and sort out the rest of the linen and china. When she'd finished her chores, Jean made herself a cup of tea and sat down with the newspaper.

'It can't be true,' she sobbed, 'not Bill.' Casualties were often kept secret to boost public morale but the report of the sinking had leaked out pretty quickly after the event with the headline clearly stating MV. ONTARIO SUNK WITH ALL HANDS. Her tears fell on to the newsprint, dampening and distorting the words. Jean's sorrow was accompanied by a gripping fear. She'd only missed one period so far but with her regular 28-day cycle it had to be more than coincidence.

There had already been some changes in her breasts in recent days and she could deny it no longer; she was pregnant. In her most recent letter to Bill, she'd told him of her suspicions.

Her clothes had become tighter and she was finding it harder to hide this from her mother. At first her fear at being pregnant was mixed with excitement about carrying Bill's child. But now, reading that he was dead, her overriding emotion was fear, anxiety and guilt about becoming an unmarried mother.

Chapter Four

It was with a heavy heart that Bill had boarded MV. Dalmarnock in Portsmouth a few days after being left stranded in Gibraltar. He was still mourning the loss of his mates on the Ontario, especially Gerry. It was strange to think that the two pickpockets had saved his life.

The Captain of the British Warship that picked him up in Gibraltar had assigned him tasks and on reaching Portsmouth he was transferred immediately to the Dalmarnock, part of an Arctic Convoy due to sail a couple of hours later.

He'd had no time to write to Jean or his mother before he sailed. He'd written since to say he hadn't gone down with his ship and these letters would be mailed tomorrow when they docked in Murmansk. He hoped the authorities had already informed them that he wasn't on board the Ontario when it sank.

They'd left Iceland in clear weather but conditions had deteriorated during the last nine days going round the tip of occupied Norway, skirting around Bear Island. For the past few days they'd sailed through treacherous fogs, affording them little or no visibility and increasing the risk of icebergs and enemy attacks.

On deck, crew members followed the ship's course through the ice floes and shouted directions to the man at the wheel. 'There are bergs alright, if the screeching down below is anything to go by,' Bill yelled to the man at his side.

'You can smell them,' the other man agreed.

The intense cold on deck caused Bill's eyes to weep. He wiped away the moisture with his gloved fingers to avoid it freezing on his eyelashes.

His eyes and nose were the only parts of him that were exposed; a helmet covered his head, ears and cheeks. He drew the collar of his coarse duffel coat tighter around his neck, grateful that he was coming to the end of his long hours on duty. He looked forward to the rest period that would follow; the companionship and laughter below decks well outweighed the hardships experienced on duty.

Minutes later the alarm sounded and Bill heard the drone of enemy planes overhead. Long before the torpedo planes were visible, he'd joined the throng racing to their action stations. In the ensuing battle, involving over twenty enemy aircraft, the sky bled brightly coloured cracks and bangs. Bill's eyes stung with the acrid smoke and the noise was horrendous. When the Dalmarnock took a direct hit, the order was given to abandon ship. The lifeboat Bill got into was packed, as were the others around them. He and his fellow seamen watched in silence as their ship went down, many of its crew still trapped inside.

In the hours that followed the sinking, many men died and were pushed overboard. Some others remained alive in the water; by this time most of them were suffering from gangrene. Bill had never feared death but the two injuries he was terrified of was being left minus a limb or losing his sight.

He survived long enough for their lifeboat to be picked up by a German battleship. He could no longer feel his fingers or toes and was overcome with sleepiness. He began to lose consciousness and sensed rather than saw a figure bending over him.

For Bill the fighting was over.

It was dark when he wakened up. Absolute silence surrounded him. There was a strong smell of something he couldn't quite name. He was stiff and cold and found it difficult to move until he realised that he was wound tightly in a blanket.

Wrenching his arms free, he stared into the gloomy darkness. A faint light came from what looked like a stained glass window. He must be in a church, he decided, becoming aware of the high vaulted ceiling. He turned his head and could just make out a narrow niche in the wall behind. The strange smell he now identified as incense; it wafted across from the altar at the opposite end of the building.

As his eyes grew more accustomed to the dim light, he

noticed the other guys lying on the floor on either side of him. 'Anyone else awake?' His voice reverberated around the walls and came back to him but the silence remained as before.

Eventually he got himself into a kneeling position and pushed his neighbour on the left, prodding him on his side. 'Are you awake, pal?' he asked, but got no response; the man seemed to be out cold. He was turning to speak to the guy on his right when the heavy wooden door was pushed open, creaking in protest.

Blinded by torchlight, he heard guttural tones and when the light was lowered a little, two German stretcher-bearers came into his line of vision. 'Turn off that bloody light,' he yelled as loud as he could through parched lips.

The soldiers dropped the stretcher they were carrying, the clatter echoing in this large, cavernous building. The two men stared at him, terror etched on their faces. The eerie silence continued until he finally realised that the other guys lying beside him had gone to their Maker.

Bill broke into hysterical laughter. If he survived the war, at least he could say he almost attended his own funeral.

Chapter Five

April 1944

In total silence Jean and Brenda made their way through the hushed, blacked out Glasgow streets, the bright April sunshine having long since given way to darkness.

They stopped outside a rundown tenement in Canal Street, paint peeling off the close walls. A piece of cardboard which covered the broken glass panel in the back door had come loose and was blowing in the wind, making a slapping sound each time it touched the door frame.

The concrete stairs were littered with discarded paper and dog mess and the girls had to weave their way through the debris to reach the top floor flat.

Brenda rang the doorbell.

'I'm scared, Brenda. I could die as well as the baby.' Now Jean knew Bill wouldn't be coming back, she couldn't wait any longer; she needed an abortion. She wanted to keep the baby but was terrified to tell her mother of her condition.

'Of course you're not going to die, Mrs Brown's done it many times.' There was the sound of shuffling feet and the door opened. Mrs Brown wore a floral overall, her grey hair pulled off her face tightly and tied in a bun at the back of her head. Under her slippers, she wore thick black knitted socks.

They were ushered into her kitchen, where a kettle sat on the black leaded range. 'Money first,' Mrs Brown held out her hand.

Jean handed over the amount she'd been told by Brenda when they'd arranged this visit.

On Mrs Brown's instructions she removed her underclothing and lay up on the scrubbed wooden kitchen table, a towel placed under the lower part of her torso.

Thoughts swirled around in her head as she lay there. She tried to still the pounding in her chest. What was she doing, getting rid of Bill's child? Why hadn't she confessed to her mother and pleaded for her help? Would she be sent to Hell's fire for this action she was about to undergo?

When the water in the kettle reached boiling point, Mrs Brown sterilised an instrument in it and filled a container with what looked like soapy water. Jean averted her gaze, unable to look into the woman's eyes for fear of seeing either pity or disdain in them. Mrs Brown inserted the instrument into Jean and pushed down on the plunger. Jean grimaced as the liquid stung her insides.

'Lie there for five or ten minutes,' Mrs Brown instructed her, then went over to the sink to wash out the equipment she'd used.

'You can get dressed now,' she said to Jean, once she'd put her equipment away. 'You should get home before the bleeding starts.'

Brenda got up from her chair in the corner, her face almost as white as Jean's. She took her friend's arm and helped her down the stairs and out into the pitch black of the night.

* * *

Their German captors kept Bill and his fellow prisoners in a holding camp for a week before force marching them to another one. For days, with little sleep and only the howling of distant wolves for company, they trudged through deep snow in sub zero temperatures, at times coming across deep pits with rotting corpses. If any of the exhausted prisoners stopped to stare, they were despatched to join the band of dead.

Finally they dragged themselves into their new camp.

'Thank God,' a voice at Bill's side whispered but Bill didn't respond, concentrating his remaining energy on putting one foot in front of the other.

He'd no idea where they were, except that it was bloody perishing. A rumour had spread round the prisoners that they were in eastern Germany, close to the Russian border.

'Schnell,' a German guard barked, hammering his rifle butt into Bill's shoulder when he slowed to look at the low-roofed building ahead. Once inside, the prisoners were ordered to undress for delousing before being issued with dry prison garments. Bill, like many of his fellow prisoners, was suffering from severe frostbite and he felt sick when he looked at his bright red, blistered feet, with two toes on his right foot worst affected. His feet were dead to feeling any pain but the sight of them brought on revulsion.

The medical orderly eventually issued Bill with crutches. They had obviously been made for a much shorter man but no others were forthcoming.

Chapter Six

May 1944

Jean's confession couldn't be put off any longer. Mrs Brown's treatment had brought on sickness and dreadful stomach pains but no bleeding and now, a month on and still pregnant, she had to tell her mum. And she had to do it tonight after work. By the time she got home, she felt hollow and empty inside. 'I'm pregnant Mum,' she blurted out when she walked into the kitchen, where the potatoes were cooking on a low gas.

Agnes looked up from her chair, startled, and yelped when she stabbed her finger with the embroidery needle. 'You're what?' she asked, her tone icy.

'It was only one time and I didn't think I'd get pregnant so easily.'

Agnes dropped the teacloth she was embroidering on to the floor and held her head in her hands. When she looked up again, the expression on her face made Jean cringe with shame. 'You dirty wee whore,' she shouted in a voice shrill with anger. 'I knew all your lying, saying you stayed overnight with Brenda, would lead to trouble. Now look where it's got you.'

'I'm sorry,' Jean sobbed, standing in front of the fireplace.

'It's too late for tears,' Agnes ranted on, getting to her feet and folding her arms across her buxom frame. 'I thought when you married that scumbag, Frank Morrow, you demeaned yourself but marriage to him has nothing on this.'

Agnes fell silent, her face like stone as she stared out of the window. The only sounds were the ticking of the clock above the mantle piece and Jean sniffing back the tears.

When Agnes finally spoke again, Jean could hear the loathing in her tone.

'What on earth were you thinking of, you stupid girl? You surely didn't think that sailor would marry you, not when you gave it to him on a plate.'

'But Bill … how … how did you know about him?' Jean looked aghast at her mother.

'Oh, I knew all about your romance,' Agnes spat out, 'word gets around you know. And you've lost any respect he had for you; no man would take on a woman who acts as you've done.'

'But it wasn't like that with Bill, we love each other.'

'Lust more like it.'

Jean had never heard her mother speak like this before and drew back instinctively from all the venom.

'I didn't think I'd become pregnant, not right away,' she wept.

'No point in being sorry now, the damage is done. Sit down,' Agnes demanded, going over to the cooker to drain the water from the potatoes. Jean sat down at the table and a plate of sausage and mash was flung down in front of her. The two of them ate in stony silence, broken only by an occasional sob from Jean.

After helping with the washing up, when not a word passed between them, Jean felt the need to escape from her mother's wrath and went into the front room. She pushed the blind aside and stared out into the velvety, star-sprinkled sky.

She was sure that her mother would put her out to fend for herself. She had no idea where she would go; perhaps Brenda's mother would let her stay with them? But as soon as the thought entered her head, she dismissed it, knowing that Mrs Duncan had sufficient mouths to feed already.

Agnes came into the room a short time later, carrying two mugs of tea.

'Sit down and drink this,' she said, directing Jean to the armchair beside the window. Her tone of voice had softened a shade. 'We'll get a doctor to check you out.'

* * *

A cheer went up when it was announced that mail was ready for collection.

Bill dropped the piece of wood he was carving on to his mattress and hobbled over to the administration block.

He'd discarded his crutches a week ago but the pain in his badly affected toes still throbbed and hindered his progress. Hungry for news of home, Bill grabbed his only letter, one from his mother; still no letter from Jean.

He went back to his hut and lay down on his bunk. His mother had used the regulation Red Cross Letter Form, with very little writing space and the usual selection of official stamps all over it. Because of this her writing was tiny and quite difficult to read.

31st May 1944

My Dear Son

Your last letter took a few weeks to reach us so I hope you'll get this one quicker. Dad and I were so relieved to get the telegram telling us of your capture. We thought you'd been on the Ontario when it went down so it was wonderful news to hear that you were alive.

From a selfish point of view we are glad that at least you are out of the action now. Gerry King's parents are distraught over his death and his young wife is left to bring up their two kids alone.

I cried my eyes out when I read of how much you were missing home cooking but I'm glad you've made some pals in the camp and you're enjoying the occasional game of cards with them. Is there anything you need us to send you, Son?

I know how sad you were at not receiving a response from your letter to Jean Morrow. I wrote to her at the address you gave me but I had the letter returned marked 'gone away'. Since you'd told us how much she meant to you, Dad and I went over to Glenburgh to try and speak to her.

Unfortunately, due to some residual damage left by the bombing earlier in the war, the building she lived in needs some structural work and the tenants have all been re-housed. We contacted the factor concerned but they wouldn't release any information to us about where the people have gone. We will continue to try and find her, Son, and will let you know immediately if we do.

Uncle John's leg is much improved now and the bandaging has been removed. As you can imagine, he's been running Aunt Grace ragged with all his demands. Gran is coping well in her new abode and has good neighbours.

Everyone sends you love, Son, and we hope to hear from you again soon.

Love from Mum and Dad

Chapter Seven

November 1944

Jean's baby was almost a month late.

Mr Green had agreed to Jean working in the shop until the beginning of October to leave her a month's rest before the delivery. In the event it became nearer two months, as the baby seemed in no hurry to make an entrance.

Friday 24th November started with Jean still a lady in waiting.

'I need to go shopping, Jean, but I won't be long. Will you be all right till I get back?' Agnes' initial anger about the pregnancy had quickly gone and over the succeeding months she'd shown kindness and concern to her only daughter.

Jean shooed her away. 'I'm fine Mum, don't think this baby wants to come into the world, it's too snug where it is.'

'Just sit down and put your feet up, you need as much rest as possible at this time,' Agnes advised, as she left the house, her shopping bag over her arm.

Taking Bill's letters from the drawer beside her bed, Jean sat down in the kitchen beside the coal fire. She read over the dog-eared letters, still unable to believe that there would be no more.

She got up to make a cup of tea and gasped when her first contraction started. Trying to get her breath back, she stood, feet apart, as a pool of fluid splashed on to the kitchen floor. Her mother had told her that if the water broke you were open to infection and the midwife was needed at once.

She crawled upstairs to alert Mrs Black, who'd moved into the tenement a few weeks after Agnes and Jean and was once again their neighbour.

'Go round to Mrs McGregor's and ask her to come here immediately,' Mrs Black told Betty, who was off school with a cold and sore throat.

Mrs Black helped Jean downstairs again and got her

into bed. 'Try and rest between contractions, hen,' she told Jean, when she saw the girl's white, scared face. She bustled off to get towels from the kitchen cupboard and then she boiled water in the kettle.

When Betty arrived with the midwife, her mother gave her further instructions. 'Away over to the Co-op, Betty, and see if Mrs McQueen's in there. If not, try Williamson's dairy. When you find her, tell her what's happened.'

By the time Mrs McGregor got into the bedroom, Jean's contractions were increasing in frequency. Things moved on swiftly, with Jean screaming, sure her insides were being ripped apart. The more the midwife told her not to push yet, the more she wanted to push. She was already exhausted by the time she was allowed to push and, after a supreme effort, she delivered her baby.

Afterwards she lay back in the bed, weepy and sweaty. 'Is the baby all right?' she asked, and then smiled when she heard the loud cries.

'You have a beautiful, healthy daughter,' the midwife told her, laying the baby, wrapped in a sheet, into Jean's arms.

Jean kissed her child's forehead. 'Hello, little one,' she cooed, all pain forgotten as she held her precious bundle.

'That'll be your mum now,' Mrs Black smiled at Jean, as the door of the flat opened. 'Come in Agnes and meet your new granddaughter,' she called, poking her head round the bedroom door.

Tears of joy poured down Agnes' face as she viewed the scene; Jean propped up on her pillows, cradling her baby daughter.

'She's gorgeous, love, and looks just like you when you were born.' Agnes touched the baby's mop of dark hair and drew her fingertip along her rosebud shaped mouth. All the while the tiny limbs were working like mad. 'What will you call her?'

Jean smiled up at her mother. 'Why Nancy, of course, after you?'

Agnes stroked Nancy's face and placed gentle lips on the tiny brow. Then she turned away, her shoulders heaving.

Chapter Eight

May 1945

Jean hummed a little tune while she washed the shelves on the glass fronted counter, certain that the gibberish that 5-month-old Nancy had said this morning was 'Mama'.

She'd returned to work shortly after Nancy's birth, leaving the baby in the care of her doting grandmother. Mum had given her great support during her pregnancy and she knew she'd never have managed without that help. And she's still helping, Jean thought, by looking after Nancy to let me earn some money.

Jean's thoughts were halted when Mary Paterson raced into the shop, her curlers underneath her scarf as usual. 'The war's over,' she shouted. 'A German General somewhere in France has signed an unconditional surrender.'

Wet cloth in hand, Jean looked up at Mary. 'Are you sure?' She was aware that the woman got her stories mixed up from time to time, although the general feeling was that the war would be over any day now.

'Of course I'm sure, I've just heard it on the radio, haven't I?'

'Did you hear that, Mr Green?' Jean called through to her boss in the back shop. 'The peace has come at last.'

'Thank God, it's been a long six years,' Bob Green said, joining them.

'No more war or rationing.' Mary grabbed Tom, the delivery boy, and danced him round the shop. When Mary's slipper fell off and she bent to pick it up, he dived into the back shop. Undaunted, Mary danced alone.

'We won't get rid of rationing for a while yet, Mary,' Bob Green cautioned. 'Think you'll be using your ration book for a wee bit longer.'

'I'll take my butter and cheese ration today as you'll be closed tomorrow.'

'How do you mean, we'll be closed?' Jean queried.

'Because tomorrow has been declared a national holiday. It's to be known as V.E. day, stands for Victory in Europe.'

'Oh.' Jean went over to the large slab of butter sitting on the cold marble ledge in the corner and used the wooden butter pats to make up Mary's ration.

'You'll make sure you give me the strong cheese, won't you, hen?' Mary asked, once Jean had finished with the butter.

'Yes, Mary.' Jean sighed and raised her eyebrows at Brenda; it annoyed the girls that Mary treated them like idiots, after all they'd been selling the woman strong cheese for years. Jean laid the wire at the correct mark and sliced through the cheese. Having cut cheese so often, she could almost do it with her eyes closed. 'So, will everyone get a holiday then?' she asked Mary while she weighed the cheese and wrapped it in greaseproof paper.

Mary handed her ration book to Jean for stamping. 'Yes, the whole nation will down tools and celebrate our victory over the Nazis. Of course, the Japs haven't surrendered yet so the war in the Far East is still going on.'

Bob's eyes were moist. 'At least the conflict in Europe is over and our boys can come home.'

Before he was required to dance again Tom quietly pushed his bike, its basket full of customers' orders, out of the shop behind Mary's back.

* * *

The excitement next day was palpable, Glenburgh awash with singing, hugging, laughing and crying. Leaving Nancy with her grandmother, Jean rushed down their tenement stairs, her heels ringing on the treads.

When she got into High Street, the shops were closed and shuttered, their owners out on the streets celebrating. She pushed her way into the crush. The circle stretched right along High Street with a smaller circle forming inside. She sang 'Rule Britannia' and 'Jerusalem' until her throat was sore and later joined the street parties, some of which went on well into the night.

Thank God, she thought, when most of the revellers had gone and she made her way home, at least now Nancy will be able to grow up in a country at peace.

* * *

A few days later all the joy of V.E. day vanished for Jean.

She was putting on her jacket to go to work when there was a knock at the door. A telegram boy handed her a yellow envelope, with its War Office stamp, and made his way downstairs again.

The envelope reminded Jean of the one that had brought the news in 1943 that Frank was missing at Montecassino, presumed dead. At the time she'd felt relief surge through her at the thought that he wouldn't be coming back. But now, as she read the contents of this second telegram, the words engulfed her with fear.

I am pleased to inform you that your husband, Private Frank Morrow, Service No 1435511, of the Royal Army Infantry Corps, has been found alive in a German POW camp and will be returning home within the next few weeks.

Jean threw her face into her hands. She'd married Frank against her mother's wishes in 1942 and had suffered nothing but abuse at his hands. She shivered, recalling the black eyes, bruised cheeks and broken limbs that she'd endured during her short time as his wife.

'Was that the postman?' Agnes called to her daughter as she came out of the bedroom carrying a still sleepy Nancy in her arms.

Jean kissed Nancy's cheek and, without a word, handed her mother the telegram. By the time Agnes had digested its contents, the front door was closing behind her daughter.

Chapter Nine

June 1945

Bill and his fellow prisoners had been ecstatic to receive the news of the German surrender. Here in eastern Germany, they were rescued by Russian troops. The Russian soldiers had executed many of the German guards in revenge for the treatment meted out to their comrades. Along with his fellow prisoners, Bill now awaited transportation back to the Mother country.

He'd written Jean many letters since he'd been a prisoner but had given up sending them as he already knew from his mother that she'd moved house and her old tenement was under renovation. This didn't stop his longing for her and her picture remained in his pocket, crumpled, torn and sweat-marked.

The contents of his mother's letter that morning dashed his hopes of ever seeing Jean again. Despite the heartache it brought, he read it over and over.

31st May 1945

My Dear Son

Dad and I pray that you are well and will be home soon. Thank God the war is over at last. I hope you received my last letter written just after V.E. day. We are keeping our spirits up and although we still have a lack of decent food we know that compared to the suffering of others this is nothing.

Son, I hate to add to your troubles by giving you bad news but I feel I have to tell you that Jean Morrow is dead. I know you said you hadn't heard from her for a long time and I also know how much she meant to you.

I won't say any more until you are home with us again and when you feel able I will tell you about her death. Meantime I can't write any more.

We long to see you again. Come home safely.
Love from Mum and Dad.

Tears poured down Bill's face as he folded the letter. His lovely Jean gone, their dreams of a future together shattered. He had a vision of her beautiful body lying cold in a grave and, choking, his head fell into his hands.

* * *

Nancy had been irritable all morning and now she began to cry again.

Agnes sighed and sponged the little girl down for the third time that day. Agnes wore the black cotton dress she'd run up on her old Singer machine for Jean's funeral two weeks ago but the material was sticking to her skin. What a Godsend her sewing machine had been over the years. She'd tried to encourage Jean in the craft but her daughter preferred to buy garments off the peg.

Was it only two weeks since she'd said farewell to her daughter? What a death it had been too, she still couldn't quite believe what had happened. She caught her breath sharply, determined not to cry in front of Nancy.

She sat the infant down on the rug at her feet and opened the kitchen window wider. It was one of the hottest June days they'd had for years, if not the hottest on record. Nancy's crying had eased a little since she'd been cooled down and, wiping away some dribbles from around her mouth, Agnes gave her a dummy. Happier now, Nancy played with her toys.

'Dinner will soon be ready,' Agnes smiled at her granddaughter and began to chop the meagre supply of meat finely for Nancy. Thanks to the produce from Mr Black's allotment, the child could enjoy mashed potatoes and finely grated carrots.

Agnes put a knob of butter and some milk into the potatoes, her thoughts going back to Jean's funeral. She fought back the tears as she pictured the coffin being carried out of the hearse. It looked so small when the undertaker's men carried it towards the grave, and she'd been thankful that she'd seen Jean's body laid out in it. Otherwise she'd have been sure they'd squashed her up to get her to fit into the coffin.

Mrs Smyth, her downstairs neighbour, had looked

after Nancy while Agnes was at the service. Despite their own feelings of grief and loss, the Blacks had given Agnes tremendous support on the day and in the weeks that had followed.

Lifting Nancy up on to her knee to feed her, she stifled a sob and forced her mind to leave the funeral and concentrate on this little girl in her care. She'd only given Nancy a few spoonfuls when the doorbell rang. She held the child in her arms as she went to answer it.

Frank Morrow stood on the doorstep, the usual leering smile on his face. For a moment, Agnes couldn't breathe. 'What do you want?' she demanded.

'Well that's a nice way to treat a conquering hero returning to his wife and home,' he said, a puzzled look on his face when he saw Nancy, wearing only a nappy, in her grandmother's arms.

'Jean's dead,' she told him, no interest in trying to soften it for him. Even the hateful Frank had the grace to look shocked for a moment, but Agnes hardened her heart. 'And there's no need to appear sad, not after the way you treated her. You're not welcome here, so please go and don't come back.'

'Who's the brat?'

Little Nancy pulled back from his harsh tone and cowered into Agnes' neck.

'She isn't yours. That's all **you** need to know. Now get going,' Agnes shouted, pushing the door partly closed against him.

He didn't resist and she heard him pound his way downstairs again.

'Might have known that slag of yours would get herself in the family way while I was away fighting for my country. Don't worry, I don't want anything to do with that bastard of hers,' he yelled up from the stair landing.

'Good riddance,' Agnes roared after him, closing the door with a bang.

Chapter Ten

November 1945

'Do you need any shopping?' Betty Black asked when Agnes opened the door.

'No thanks, Betty, I got everything I needed yesterday.' Seeing the girl's face fall, Agnes quickly added, 'I could do with another pint of milk though.'

'No bother,' Betty smiled happily, moving into the hallway, or lobby as the tenement dwellers called it, while Agnes went into the kitchen for her purse.

Agnes was fond of Betty who often took Nancy out in her pram so that she could get on with her household chores, just like Jean used to do for Mrs Black when Betty was a baby. She dismissed that thought, unwilling to let her mood drop, not today, Nancy's first birthday.

Nancy peeked out of the open kitchen door, saw Betty, and crawled into the lobby. Gurgling with delight, she held up her arms for Betty to lift her.

'Happy birthday,' Betty smiled and cuddled her head against Nancy's, her own ash-blonde plaits contrasting with the younger girl's thick black curls. 'What lovely curls you have Nancy,' Betty cooed as Agnes came back into the lobby.

'Lovely they might be but she screams blue murder every morning when I try to comb the tangles out of her hair,' Agnes said, handing a coin to Betty. 'There's a sixpence for the milk. See if Buchanan's have any sweets for you with the change.'

Betty beamed at Agnes. 'Thanks, Mrs McQueen. And after I get the milk I could take Nancy for a walk to let you get things ready for her party.' Being an only child, Betty loved playing with Nancy. With today being Saturday and no school she could spend more time with the little girl.

'Fine, I'll have her washed and dressed when you get back,' Agnes promised Betty, who handed Nancy over to her grandmother.

Once Betty had gone, Agnes stood Nancy in the sink

to wash her down. She pondered on how much she depended on young Betty; without her help with shopping and baby-minding Agnes doubted if she'd have managed after Jean's suicide.

* * *

'And there she is in her wee bed, just like you, Nancy.'

Agnes closed the picture book, a birthday gift for Nancy. The little girl had fallen asleep a couple of pages ago but Agnes had continued reading, yearning for a happy ending to her own story. The pink party dress she'd made for Nancy lay in a heap at the bottom of the cot and she hung it up in the wardrobe.

'Sweet dreams, pet.' She pulled the infant's thumb out of her mouth. Nancy murmured in her sleep but didn't waken. Agnes put up the sides of the cot and switched off the lamp, leaving the door ajar to let the lobby light shine in.

The memory of Nancy's joy at blowing out the single candle on her birthday cake brought a smile to Agnes' face. All the months of saving the coupons needed for the cake ingredients had been worthwhile.

Back in the kitchen she opened the cupboard and took out an old tin box that had contained biscuits before the war. Carrying it over to the table, she sat down and placed a cushion in between her aching back and the spars of the wooden chair.

The pain gripped her again, accompanied by the usual dragging sensation. She grimaced and leant on the edge of the table for a few moments. She was more worried by these pains than she admitted. They were increasing in frequency and severity, and she'd lost some more blood in the past few days. She hadn't consulted a doctor, afraid that he would send her into hospital and the authorities would put Nancy into care.

She leaned back and took some deep breaths and after a while the pain eased.

Taking a green silk scarf out of the box, she held it close and sniffed Jean's perfume. When she'd untied it from the pram handle that awful day, she'd known she'd never wash it.

A picture of Bill Prior in his naval uniform had the words 'All my love, darling' written on the bottom right hand corner and on the back of the picture Jean had written the name and address of his shipping company. She'd been unable to read Bill's three letters or Jean's diaries, written up faithfully every day, afraid of what they might say.

When the doorbell rang, she slowly made her way out into the lobby. 'It's only me,' Betty called through the letterbox.

At Agnes' invitation, Betty followed her into the kitchen. 'I didn't ring the bell until I knew Nancy would be asleep.' Betty glanced at the open tin box but said nothing. She handed Agnes a paper bag. 'These potatoes are from Dad's allotment.'

'Thanks. I've only a couple of spuds left and the ones in the fruit shop yesterday weren't worth buying. Your dad's are always so lovely and floury.'

'He's very proud of the stuff he grows.'

'He kept us going all during the war.'

'Are you alright, Mrs McQueen? You look tired.'

'Och, I'm fine Betty. Why don't you make us a wee cup of tea, lass?' Agnes suggested and sat down while Betty did that. It never ceased to amaze her how perceptive young Betty was. That was probably why she confided in the girl so much. 'I was feeling a wee bit sad tonight after all the excitement.'

'Were you thinking about Jean?' Betty asked, as she brought over the tea and sat down at the table facing her old friend.

Agnes nodded, the tears welling up. 'I feel so guilty lass about the way she died. I was so angry you see when she told me she was going to have a baby. I'm sorry Betty I shouldn't be talking to you like this, you're just a wee girl.'

'No,' Betty took Agnes' hands, 'it's better to talk about things and you've no need to feel guilty. It's Frank Morrow to blame for causing Jean's death, him and all his treatment of her. My mum says it's a blessing that you're here for Nancy.'

Agnes' face brightened. 'You always cheer me up, lass.'

They chatted on for a wee while longer and then Betty got to her feet and washed the cups. 'I'll need to go now Mrs McQueen, I'm going to help Mum get my uniform ready for tomorrow's parade. I'm carrying the Company flag. We had a rehearsal in the church last night.'

'So you are,' Agnes smiled, aware of how happy Betty was to be a Girl Guide and her pride at achieving her cook's badge recently. 'You can tell me all about the parade later. You know I always enjoy a blether with you, lass.'

* * *

When Mrs Black and Betty returned from church next morning, they heard Nancy crying before they reached the middle landing. The noise followed them upstairs and by the time they reached their own flat she was still crying and quite sorely too. Mrs Black hesitated; Agnes never left Nancy crying for long. She went downstairs and rang Agnes' doorbell but got no reply. Sure something was wrong, she went back to her flat and collected Agnes' spare key.

When she entered, the flat was cold and the lobby light was on although it was broad daylight. Going into the bedroom, she lifted Nancy from her cot, feeling the wetness of the child's sodden nappy against her arm. Nancy stopped crying for a minute and looked at her, then started again, louder this time.

Mrs Black peered round the kitchen door. Agnes' set-in bed had not been used and the fire had long since gone out, leaving a pile of grey ashes in the nest. A tin box lay open on the scrubbed table with various items strewn around it. Then she screamed, her arms tightening around little Nancy.

Agnes lay on the floor near the cooker, fully clothed, a pool of blood visible in the space between her legs.

Praying that she wasn't too late, Mrs Brown raced downstairs to the phone box on the corner of the street. She balanced Nancy on her hip while her shaky hand lifted the receiver off its cradle and she dialled 999.

Part II - Australia

Chapter Eleven

January 1957

'That ball wasn't out,' Fiona Currie yelled over the net at her best friend, Vina West. Fiona's parents were the only people in Laggan Crescent who had a tennis court in their garden and Vina was often invited in next door for a game.

Vina twanged her racket strings. 'We can play the point again.'

But having lost the last two games, one on her own serve, Fiona's frustration brimmed over and she threw down her racket and jumped on it, before storming off the court towards her house. 'I don't want to play with you any more,' she shouted over her shoulder. 'I don't want you as a friend, you aren't like the rest of us. You're adopted.'

Vina's feet seemed to be cemented on to the gravel court. She swallowed deeply. 'Of course I'm like you. You're telling fibs.'

'No I'm not. I heard my mum saying that your mother and father aren't your real parents.' Fiona disappeared into the house, slamming the door behind her.

A few moments later the screen door at No 18 creaked open. Vina rushed inside and let the door close with sufficient force to release a swarm of insects that had been clinging on to the fine mesh.

Hazel West looked up from her pastry making, a smile of pleasure coming on to her round, open face when her elder daughter came in. But her smile froze when she saw the expression on Vina's face.

'Why didn't you tell me?' Vina's glare lashed Hazel, making her draw breath. Hurt puckered the 12-year-old's normally serene face.

'Tell you what, love?'

'That I was adopted. Fiona Currie's mother told her. Tell me it isn't true, you didn't adopt me, Dad and you are my

40

real parents?'

Pain stabbed at Hazel's chest as she wiped her floury hands on her apron. She then made to pull her daughter into an embrace but Vina ran past her to the old settee in the corner of the living room. She threw herself on to it and sobbed into a cushion.

Hazel followed her. 'Darling, Dad and I did mean to tell you but not until you were older,' Hazel whispered, drawing her fingers through Vina's dark curls.

Pushing her mother's hand away, Vina's sobs intensified and she pressed her face deeper into the cushion.

Hazel sighed. The thing she'd always dreaded had happened. Going into the hall, she dialled the number of John's dental surgery in Devonport. He'd been working there since the family came to Tasmania in 1949 and was now the senior partner.

'He's just finishing a scale and polish,' his receptionist told Hazel. 'I'll ask him to ring you before he starts with his next patient.'

'It's Vina,' Hazel told him when he phoned back, 'she's found out that she's adopted. She's breaking her heart, John.'

'How did she find out?'

'She was playing tennis with Fiona next door and, after an argument, Fiona blurted out that she was adopted.'

There was a silence while John digested the news.

'Oh John, you wanted to tell Vina on her birthday last November but I stopped you and now she's heard in this brutal fashion.'

'It's no one's fault, love.'

There was a moment's silence, and Hazel could hear him leaf over the appointment book. 'I've a gap after my next patient and I'll come home.'

When she'd hung up, Hazel returned to the living room and took Vina's cold hand. 'Darling, I'm sorry you had to find out this way. It was very unkind of Fiona.'

Vina finally took her head out of the cushion. 'Are the twins adopted too?' she sniffed.

Hazel shook her head, her hair, neatly cut in a page boy style, swinging around as she did so. 'No, I didn't think I could have children and that was why you were so special to us,' she said, mopping up Vina's tears with her hankie. 'You were nearly four when Sue and Andy were born. We love them dearly but they could never mean more to us than you do.'

The screen door swung open once more and the usual shrieks and giggles heralded the arrival of the twins. 'It's started to rain,' Sue complained, 'and we've left our bikes in the shed until it stops.'

Andy stared at Vina's red eyes. 'What's wrong, Sis?'

'Vina slipped on the tennis court,' Hazel told her son. 'You two go upstairs to play and I'll call you when lunch is ready,' she shooed them away.

'Race you upstairs,' Sue challenged and dived off, closely pursued by Andy.

* * *

On the forty-five minute drive from his surgery, John drove with his car window open to hear the sound of the waves crashing in on the shore to his right. Having come from a large city he still found it a novelty to live beside the sea.

Once he arrived in Penguin, he dropped his speed to weave his way through the crowd of holidaymakers. January was the busiest month for tourists with the long school summer holidays.

He continued along the main road, past the Post Office. Nearing the Methodist Church, a wooden building dating back to the first settlement in Penguin, he turned left at Pascoe Road and took a right into Laggan Crescent.

'Dad, Dad,' Vina threw herself into his arms when he came into the house.

He hugged her tightly, his tall frame stooped over his beloved elder daughter. 'What's this I hear about Fiona upsetting you, poppet? Your adoption makes no difference, you'll always be our daughter and we'll always love you.' He cupped his hands around Vina's chin and kissed her forehead. 'We were shown a lot of babies when we didn't think we could have any and we chose you. You came to us like a precious gift from God.'

'And don't forget,' Hazel added, 'you were specially chosen but with the twins we had to take what we got.'

Vina threw her arms around her mother's waist and hugged her. 'I'm sorry, I do love you and Dad but I can't forgive my real parents.'

'Don't say that darling, I'm sure your mother wouldn't have given you up if there'd been any other way.'

Vina's sobs had eased a little by now and she raised her earnest eyes to Hazel, then on to John. 'Who were my real mother and father? Did you know them?'

'No darling, we knew very little as adoption is a confidential matter, but I'll tell you what I know.'

Hazel pulled Vina gently down on to the settee again and rocked her back and forth. 'You were born in a place called Glenburgh, near Glasgow, and you lived there with your grandmother when you were a baby. When your grandmother died, you came to live with us in Muirbank, on the south side of Glasgow. You were four, nearly five, when we left Scotland to come here.'

John sat down next to them and he stroked Vina's bare arm, his dark brown eyes glistening behind his horn-rimmed glasses. 'From the minute we set eyes on you, poppet, you were ours and we were so glad to have you.'

He put his arm around Vina's shoulder and she laid her head against his chest and sobbed quietly into his shirt.

She was much calmer by the time the twins arrived downstairs again.

'Are you feeling better, Sis?' Andy asked.

Vina nodded and tried to smile at her little brother.

'When's lunch, Mum?' Sue asked. 'I'm starving.'

'Won't be long now.' Hazel looked at her husband. 'Are you staying for some lunch, John?'

'No, I need to get back for my two o'clock patient. I shouldn't be too late home tonight. Ok kids, see you all later,' he said brightly and headed for the door.

Chapter Twelve

Slipping out of her sandals, Vina slung them over her wrists by the strap. The shingle ran in between her toes, tickling them. Her cotton skirt wrapped itself around her bare legs in the soft breeze as she made her way over the warm sand.

It was two weeks since she'd found out she was adopted. She hadn't seen Fiona since that day as her friend had gone to stay with her grandparents in Hobart for two weeks. Although on the surface things seemed back to normal, she'd cried herself to sleep many nights, knowing that Mum and Dad were downstairs and wouldn't hear her. Sue, who shared the room with her, was a sound sleeper and Andy's room was at the other end of the corridor.

She glanced back to where her mum sat on the sand, sheltered by an overhanging bush, reading her novel. She had one eye on the book and the other on the twins, a skill she had developed over the years. The twins were building a fort near Mum's deckchair and Sue's loud tones floated over to Vina.

'No, not like that Andy, we need a moat around it so we can fill it with water.'

Andy was the younger by twenty minutes and was constantly bossed by his more dominant twin. Only his gentle nature saved more fights erupting.

Her dad caught up with her. His trouser legs were folded up to his knees and a hat kept the sun off his bald patch. She took Dad's hand and they looked up at the almost unbroken blue sky, any clouds white and fluffy.

'Can you see any pictures?'

'That looks like a man's head,' she pointed over to her left.

'The fluffy bit on the bottom could be his beard,' Dad smiled.

They walked on, keeping up a companionable silence. Dad always sensed when she wanted to be quiet and she loved him for it.

As she walked, Vina's toes and heel left an indentation in the sand. To her right was a row of very large imprints left by a walking boot. The pattern from the sole of the boot was chiselled into the sand. The prints would remain only for another couple of hours, after which the tide would be in. Ebb and flow, she thought, ebb and flow. The incoming waves looked like the soapsuds that came out of Mum's washing machine.

Dad was first to break the silence. 'We'll need to head back soon, poppet, we promised the twins we'd give them a ride on the train to Burnie.' The little steam train travelled back and forward between Ulverston and Burnie during the summer months and was popular with children and adults alike.

Still staring at the waves, Vina nodded, and next minute the tears were rolling down her cheeks.

'Beautiful, isn't it?' he murmured. 'Beauty that's almost painful.' Dad as ever had caught her mood perfectly. He threw his arm around Vina's shoulder and she laid her head against him just above his waist.

The spell was broken by the train rounding the corner on its way from Ulverston, smoke curling up into the air from its red and black funnel. With a toot-toot, the train drew up at the Penguin station above the beach. 'We've plenty of time,' Dad said, as they walked back across the sand. 'It stops here for fifteen minutes.'

Hazel folded up her deck chair. 'Hurry up you two,' she called to the twins. 'Pick up your towels and don't forget your buckets and spades.'

'The buckets, Andy,' Sue instructed her brother, as she grabbed the towels, 'we don't want to miss the train.'

Dad bought the train tickets and they piled on board. The window was open, letting some welcome air into the compartment. Leucodendron bushes covered the station wall, their lemon flowers sparkling in the sunshine. The twins grabbed the two seats on either side of the window, Sue sitting next to Mum and Andy beside Vina.

Vina smiled and threw an arm round her brother's

neck, pointing to the little bird perched on top of the gatepost near the ticket office. 'Look, Andy, see the blue wren, isn't he gorgeous?'

Blue wrens were tame here in Tasmania and although Andy had seen many in their garden at home he smiled up at Vina. 'Yeah, I love his bright blue chest. They're much prettier than the brown female wrens.'

'And look at the length of his tail,' Vina said, as the bird moved his position.

'Who cares about a stupid wren,' Sue piped up. 'I've seen loads of them.'

Vina made a face at her sister. 'Well I think he's lovely, so there.'

'And so do I,' nodded Andy, shifting his position nearer to Vina.

The guard on the platform blew his whistle and waved a green flag. Then, with a clickity-click, the wheels moved along the track. Andy and Vina craned their necks until they could no longer see the station house.

Chapter Thirteen

February 1957

'Your lunch, darling.' Hazel lifted the blue plastic box and held it out to Vina.

'Thanks, Mum,' she smiled, putting it into her school satchel.

Hazel stood at the family room window and watched the kids waiting on the nature strip for the school bus. They'd grown so much since the last term ended in December. Andy looked smart in his tan-coloured shorts and polo shirt while the two girls wore their green and white checked school dresses.

Hazel heard Vina calling to the twins to stay off the road; she was like a second mother to them. The past month, since Vina discovered the truth about her adoption, had been fraught. She'd sulked for about a week and made little spontaneous conversation, disappearing into her bedroom at every opportunity.

She and John had often heard Vina sobbing in bed at night. As a mother, her first reaction had been to go upstairs to console her daughter but John persuaded her to stay where she was, saying that it was better for Vina to work things out on her own. The situation improved gradually and by now their daughter seemed almost back to her normal self.

A horn sounded and the yellow school bus came into view. As soon as Tim had stopped, Rose jumped down to usher the children into the vehicle. Hazel had known Tim and Rose Parsons for many years as they'd held the bus contract when Vina first started school. The twins turned to wave as they climbed aboard and Vina blew a kiss. After dropping the twins at the local primary school, Vina and the older pupils would be taken to Ulverstone High School, a half-hour drive from Penguin.

Hazel made a cup of coffee and sat down in her

wooden rocking chair. She smiled, recalling how Vina, as a young child, would come home from school and climb on to the chair beside her. She'd then tell Hazel all that had happened at school that day.

Her coffee finished, Hazel roused herself and went into the kitchen. She'd a million things to do before the kids returned from school.

* * *

Finishing the English exercise, Vina checked over her work, then laid her fountain pen in the groove on her desk. She wiped the smear of blue ink off her thumb with her hankie, then stared through the window into the school playground with its ornate iron gates. Over near the bicycle shed were the chalk marks left from their game of hopscotch the previous day.

Her thoughts went back to that awful day when Fiona told her that she was adopted. Fiona, who sat in the row in front laboriously writing, had long since forgotten the argument on the tennis court.

Vina knew she'd given her parents a hard time in recent weeks, transferring her anger at her biological parents on to them. The news had come as such a blow that she had to put the blame somewhere. Her behaviour had improved after hearing the song 'You always hurt the one you love' on the radio one day.

She still didn't understand why her biological parents had given her up for adoption but she'd made a silent vow to find out one day. She had to get answers to her questions, no matter how painful they were but she'd never do it while Mum and Dad lived.

Chapter Fourteen

July 1965

'Come and eat while it's hot,' Hazel called to the family from the dining room. Although the winter had been fairly mild, it wasn't just hot enough to eat outdoors.

She smiled when 17-year-old Andy was first to the table, nothing new there. On Friday nights the usual practice at Laggan Crescent was fish suppers for dinner and tonight was no exception. But Hazel always insisted that they take the food out of the newspaper and put it on plates so that they could sit down as a family at the table. 'I'm not having tray dinners in this house,' was her frequently used phrase.

Once everyone was seated, Hazel poured the tea. 'Do you have football training tomorrow?' she asked Andy, as she handed him his cup.

He swallowed quickly and nodded. 'Is my strip dry, Mum?'

'Yes love, ironed and in your drawer.'

'Thanks, Mum.' Andy squeezed another dollop of tomato sauce over his chips.

'Do put that book away, Sue,' Hazel said, 'you know it's rude to read at the table.'

Sue sighed loudly but closed her paperback and laid it down on the carpet at her feet.

'When do you need to be at the pool tomorrow?' Andy asked her.

'The competition starts at two o'clock but we'll have a practice session for half an hour beforehand.'

Teams from the nearby towns were participating in the fiercely fought annual competition, held this year at the Penguin open-air swimming pool.

'Rather you than me,' Andy said. 'The pool is perishing at this time of year.'

'Thanks,' Sue replied, making a face at him across the table.

'When I finish at the surgery tomorrow, I'll grab a quick lunch and Mum and I can come and cheer you on,' John suggested. He and Hazel were proud of Sue's swimming prowess. 'I'm sure your team will do well in the competition.'

'Hope so. Will you come too, Sis?'

'I said will you come too?' she snapped her fingers to get Vina's attention.

Vina's blank expression told how little she'd taken in of the previous conversation. 'Sorry,' she apologised, 'I was day dreaming.'

Sue's eyebrows raised. 'So we noticed. I asked if you were coming to the pool tomorrow afternoon to watch the competition.'

'Sorry, Sue, I can't. I've arranged to meet a couple of the girls from work.'

Hazel collected the empty plates and carried them into the kitchen, returning shortly afterwards with a bowl of trifle. She spooned some into the dessert dishes and handed them round the table.

They all ate with gusto except Vina, who played with hers. 'I've applied for a secretarial post in Melbourne,' she blurted out to her assembled family.

Four pairs of eyes turned to her.

Hazel was the first one to find her voice.

'But why would you want to work in Melbourne, love, when you've got a perfectly good job at Devonport Hospital?'

Vina laid down her spoon and pushed the plate with her partially eaten dessert away from her. 'I know Mum, I like my work, but Tassie is so dull for someone of my age. There's no night-life and Melbourne has much more to offer.'

'But why don't you go to Hobart if you're looking for a better social life?'

Vina sighed. 'Even though Hobart's our capital city there isn't much more going on there than here in Penguin. Tassie's a beautiful island but I want more. I want some excitement in my life and I'm only going to get that on the mainland.'

'But what about your 21st birthday in November? I

was planning a party.'

'You still can, Mum, I can come home for that. I'm not going to the other side of the world, only to Melbourne.'

'We want you to be happy, poppet,' John stretched out and put his hand over Vina's, 'but it's a big step to leave here and go to a large city like Melbourne on your own. Where would you stay?'

'I thought I could ask Aunt Jenny if I could stay with her in Brighton. Just until I get a flat of my own.'

Vina was in primary school last time she'd seen her great-aunt, when the family had gone over to the mainland for a holiday.

'I'm sure Aunt Jenny would love to have you,' Hazel said, knowing that her aunt could be relied upon to look after Vina, 'but it all seems so sudden. When did you apply for the post? Have you been thinking of going to Melbourne for a while?'

'A list comes round our department every month with vacancies in our hospital and others, both here in Tassie and over on the mainland. The one I've applied for is at the Royal Children's Hospital in Flemington.'

'I know the hospital,' John told her, 'it's quite close to the Melbourne Zoo. Which department would you be in?'

'I'd be working in the Orthopaedic Department.'

Hazel smiled at Vina. 'Your experience in Ortho at Devonport should give you a good chance of success, love.'

'That's what I thought. But I don't know if I'll get the job.'

'I'm going to miss you if you go to Melbourne, Vina,' Andy said.

'And I'll miss you too.' She cuddled against him.

'And what about me?' Sue chipped in.

Vina laughed. 'I'll miss your cheek. But I thought you'd be pleased to get a bedroom to yourself.'

Sue smiled. 'Oh yes, I'd forgotten that.' When the twins were small they'd shared a room but once they were older Sue had to move in beside Vina. 'Will you need to stay overnight if you go to Melbourne for an interview?'

'No, I can travel over on the Princess of Tasmania and sleep on board both going and returning.'

'Will you have to go down to Hobart to get the ferry?'

Vina shook her head. 'No Andy, the ferry goes from Devonport over to Melbourne. It's an overnight crossing.'

John smiled at Hazel. 'I can see our daughter has done her homework. Right, poppet, if it's what you really want to do then you will go with our blessing.'

'Thanks, Dad.'

'Why don't we give Aunt Jenny a ring over the weekend and discuss the chances of you staying with her if you do get the job?' Hazel suggested.

'That's great, Mum. I don't want to leave home but I must look to the future.'

'Of course, love,' Hazel patted her arm and smiled.

'Now that's sorted, let's all settle down to watch the film on the new channel.' Television sets had been quite slow to catch on in Tasmanian households but John had been one of the first people to purchase a set in the early sixties. He'd bought it in Melbourne and brought it over on the ferry. 'I'll open a bottle of bubbly.'

'It's too soon to celebrate, Dad. I haven't got the job yet, or an interview.'

'No worries, we can raise a glass to you making an important decision about your future.'

Chapter Fifteen

September 1965

Vina stood on the deck of the 'Princess of Tasmania' in the spring evening sunshine and waved to her family down below on the dock. Dad had driven them to Devonport in the late afternoon. Being a Friday they stuck to tradition and had a fish and chip tea in a café near the dockyard.

There'd been no tears shed a month ago when she'd gone over to Melbourne for interview but this time it was different as she was moving permanently to the mainland. She'd had a few emotional farewells in the past week, including a night out with some of her old school friends from Ulverston High and yesterday a leaving party at work. She'd been a bit choked at leaving her colleagues but was excited about working in such a large hospital as the Royal Children's.

From her position on deck she watched a glorious sunset over Devonport and had to shield her eyes from the glare to make out her family in the crowd waiting to see off the ferry. By the time they were ready to sail, darkness had descended and it was almost impossible to make anyone out from up here. As the ship drew away from the dock, she waved in the general direction of where she'd last seen the family.

She stayed on deck for some time after they'd sailed, staring into the darkness, broken by the lights on the island that had been her home for almost all her life. The breaking of the umbilical cord brought on tears and she remained alone at the rail, long after the other passengers had gone inside the vessel. It was only when the cold got to her that she roused herself and made her way to her cabin.

* * *

'Hi Vina,' Aunt Jenny called, both hands waving as Vina came up the slipway.

The ferry had docked before six in the morning but

passengers weren't allowed to disembark until eight o'clock. From the deck Vina had seen Aunt Jenny arrive and her great aunt waited patiently until Vina emerged down the ship's ramp on to the slipway.

Vina put down her case and went into Aunt Jenny's lavender-smelling embrace. It was lovely to be with her relative and it hit her now how hard it would have been to arrive in Melbourne among strangers.

'It's lovely to see you, pet,' Aunt Jenny's voice was muffled by cuddling deep into Vina's hair. Then she held her great niece at arm's length to admire how grown up she'd become. 'Welcome to Melbourne,' she said in her strong Scottish brogue, something she'd retained despite living in Australia for almost fifty years.

'Thanks, Aunt Jenny.' Vina noticed that her great aunt didn't look as old as she'd expected. Aunt Jenny was in her mid seventies but could easily have passed for ten years younger. Her grey hair was neatly cut in a bob, her tailored trouser suit was in a dusky pink shade and her manner was bright and bubbly.

'Right, let's get your case to the car and I'll whisk you home in no time,' Aunt Jenny said, and led the way over to her blue Holden.

Vina hadn't expected her great aunt to drive so fast and, had she not been such a confident and skilful driver, it might have been a scary ride back to Brighton. Vina had very little memory of the town of Brighton but when they got to Lansdown Street and Aunt Jenny headed up the driveway she remembered the coloured dwarfs decorating the front garden and the stone boot sitting on the step beside the front door.

'Here we are, pet, home sweet home.' Aunt Jenny opened the car door and got out. 'I've put you in the back bedroom, the one that looks on to the pool.'

Vina smiled. 'I'd forgotten about the pool. I loved it as a child.' Due to the cooler climate in Tassie, they didn't have a pool in Laggan Crescent.

'Yes, thought you might use it more than I do these days.'

Vina carried her case into the back bedroom, with its patio doors opening on to the poolside, and plonked herself down on the bed. The room was decorated in a beige coloured paper with a soft pink carpet. 'It's lovely, Aunt Jenny, thank you.'

'It's cool in here in the morning, pet, but the sun streams in later in the day and you'll be able to swim late at night now the weather's turning warmer. You sort out your belongings and I'll go and get us something to eat while you're doing so.'

'Not too much for me Aunt Jenny, I had breakfast just after we docked.'

'Fine but I'm sure some of my fruit bread and a wee cup of tea won't go amiss,' her great aunt chuckled. 'And once you're ready, we'll ring your mum to let her know you've arrived safely. Then we can sit on the patio while it's cool and you can tell me all about things in Penguin,' she said as she bustled away into the kitchen.

Chapter Sixteen

Vina got off the No 45 tram in Swanston Street near the Town Hall, where she waited each morning for the No 9 to the Children's Hospital.

From Aunt Jenny's house she had only a five-minute walk to the nearest tram stop. Although it had been more of a sprint this morning as she'd overslept. With no time for breakfast, Aunt Jenny gave her some toast to take 'for the journey'.

Now into her second week working in the orthopaedic department at the hospital, she felt quite at home there. The surgeon she worked with was a very pleasant middle-aged man and she shared an office with two other secretaries, Katie and Marion, both in their late forties. She didn't feel any age gap with them and dissolved into hoots of laughter most days at the stories they told.

The No 9 tram arrived a few minutes later, going to Melbourne Zoo. On board, Vina enjoyed her toast, glad after all that Aunt Jenny had thought ahead. She got off the tram at the hospital, leaving the vehicle to continue up through Royal Park to its terminus at the Zoo.

'Morning, kiddo,' Marion greeted her when she walked into the office.

'Morning,' she responded, yawning as she hung her jacket on the coat stand, which resembled the Tower at Pisa. It always amazed her that it stayed upright. She yawned again as she sat down at her desk.

'You look a bit hung over,' Katie said, 'been on the booze last night have we?'

'No, I was sitting outside with Aunt Jenny after dinner and it was so warm I couldn't drag myself indoors until almost midnight. I slept in this morning and haven't properly wakened up yet.'

'That old aunt of yours is quite a live wire,' Marion laughed. 'Wish I'd half her energy. By the time I chase my lot away to their beds, I'm ready for my own.'

'Our Joe is playing up something awful at the moment and staying out until all hours,' Katie told them. 'Didn't come home until almost two o'clock this morning and by that time Danny was ready to commit murder. Kids,' she shrugged, 'who'd have them?'

Before Vina could reply her boss, Mr Westwater, came in to ask about a set of case notes that had gone missing. The rest of the morning was chaotic and there was no chance to ask more about Joe's relationship with his dad.

Chapter Seventeen

November 1965

Vina opened the tram window wider to get the benefit of what little air there was, all the while yearning for the fresh breeze of Tasmania. She was finding the humidity in Melbourne hard to take and sometimes wondered if she'd ever get used to it.

Keeping an eye out for the various landmarks Lucy Graham had given her, she plastered on some more sunscreen. She rummaged in her handbag for the advert she'd cut out of Aunt Jenny's Saturday Sun newspaper this morning and looked at it again.

FEMALE FLATMATE SOUGHT
BY SINGLE BUSINESSWOMAN

Camberwell, quiet location, handy
for tram stop and railway station.
Own bedroom but shared kitchen
and bathroom.

Rent negotiable. Phone to arrange
visit. Tel: Camberwell 9808

After spending two months in Brighton, where she'd been well looked after by Aunt Jenny, she felt ready to move into a flat. To help ease the costs, she decided to share with someone. When she saw the advert this morning, she phoned immediately.

She got off the tram at Camberwell Junction and walked through the shopping area into the residential part beyond, the heat burning through the thin soles of her sandals. Every time a tram passed she was between stops and it was with relief that she saw the sign for Wattle Grove. The door of No 19 opened before Vina had a chance to ring the bell. A slender woman, about 5'5' tall, stood in the doorway. 'Hi, Vina', she smiled, her brown curly hair giving her a tomboyish look.

'Come in,' she invited, standing back to let Vina pass her into the long narrow hallway. 'Will I show you round first and afterwards I'll make us a brew?' Vina didn't recognise Lucy's accent although she guessed it was English.

The venetian blinds in the living room were tightly closed and the drapes hung to a level just under the windowsill. 'The room gets very hot during the day, and with no air-conditioning you have to shut out the sun, else it gets like an oven. Come and I'll show you the spare bedroom.'

When Vina saw the bedroom that would be hers, she screwed up her face at the deep purple flowery wallpaper. 'It's a good size, though not my taste in décor,' she said, then blushed when it struck her that Lucy might have chosen it.

But Lucy laughed. 'The people before me seemed to like gaudy colours, but there's no problem about you changing it. You'd have plenty of hanging space,' she said, opening the doors of the fitted wardrobe. A three-drawer cabinet sat beside the single divan bed, with a beanbag chair in the corner. 'These are some things I borrowed from friends but you can bring your own if you prefer.'

'I don't have anything to bring. I only arrived here two months ago and I stayed with my parents back home in Tassie.'

'You must find it different in Melbourne then after living in such a quiet place. Are you working here?'

'I'm a secretary in the Children's Hospital.'

'I also work in a hospital. I'm a physio at the Austin. Where are you staying at the moment?'

'In Brighton with my great aunt. She's really kind but she tends to fuss me.'

Lucy smiled and nodded. 'And you want a bit of independence. And quite right too.'

Once Vina had seen the bathroom and kitchen, she sat at the kitchen table while Lucy made some tea. She held out the biscuit tin. 'You can see we don't stand on ceremony in this establishment.'

'Did you have a flatmate previously?' Vina asked, taking a custard cream.

'Yes. Jessie and I came over together from Newcastle five years ago.'

'I take it you mean Newcastle in England and not the one here in Oz?'

'Yes, my Geordie accent gives that away, doesn't it?' she laughed. 'Anyway, Jessie was married last month and now lives in Queensland. Up near Cairns, where her husband manages a sugar plantation. I can't afford to pay the rent myself and, as I didn't want to move out of this area with its closeness to the shopping centre, I decided to advertise for a flat mate.'

'When would you want me to move in? If you're willing to have me.'

'I'd be delighted. I was hoping for someone of my own age.' Lucy took the mugs over to the sink and put them into the basin. 'We only do washing up a couple of times a day, to save water. We need to be careful how much we use, with the water restrictions that are in place.' She sat down at the table again. 'A few people have phoned to enquire about the flat but you're first to come and see the place. If we agree the rent, we can call it a deal.'

'How much is the rent?'

'$180 a month so that would be $90 each and then we could chip in another, say $15 each, to cover electricity and phone.'

'What about food?'

'Jessie and I had a kitty for that. We could do that too or, if you prefer, we could buy and cook our own food. Whatever suits you would be fine with me.'

'The kitty would be fine.'

'Great. And you can move in whenever you're ready.'

'I'm going over to Tassie at the weekend as Mum has arranged a 21st party for me but I could move in on my return.'

'Fantastic. Happy birthday. I had my 21st last year.'

'That's settled then,' Vina smiled. She'd liked Lucy

straight away and was sure that they could get on well sharing the flat.

'There's only one thing I must tell you before you decide to come and stay. It's only fair to let you know that we have lodgers sharing with us which might put you off.'

'Lodgers?'

'I've been having a problem with possums nesting under the eaves. You don't hear them in the daytime, but when they run back and forward on the roof during the night it sounds like they're wearing hob-nailed boots. I've sent for Peter the possum catcher and I'm just waiting for him to arrange a visit.'

'No worries, I'm well used to possums back home so I'll share with you and the possums until Peter gets here,' Vina laughed, handing over $105 for her first month's rent and utilities.

'Thanks.' Lucy stuck the rent money under the bread bin and took a yale key out of the kitchen drawer. 'I'll give you this and you can move in whenever it suits you.' She walked Vina to the door, pushing it open for her. 'Where are you parked?'

'I don't have a car. I walked up from Camberwell Junction.'

'What? You must be exhausted.' Lucy pointed to the little Honda sitting outside on the road. 'Give me two minutes to change my shoes and I'll run you down to the Junction,' she said, her offer securing their friendship.

Chapter Eighteen

On Friday Vina took her weekend case with her to work. When she finished about six o'clock, she grabbed a bite to eat in the hospital canteen and arrived at the terminal in plenty of time for the overnight sailing to Devonport.

John was waiting on the dockside when they got in next morning and she rushed down the gangway and into his warm embrace. 'Hi poppet,' he greeted her, 'great to have you home for a couple of days.'

'It's lovely to be home,' she said, her eyes misting up at the sight of her dad. 'I love living in Melbourne but I do miss you all terribly.'

'At least you've had Jenny to look after you, although Mum said the other day that you've got yourself a flat. Hope you won't be too lonely there, poppet.'

She smiled. Dad had called her poppet ever since she could remember. 'No, it's fine Dad, I'll be sharing the flat with another girl, Lucy Graham, from Newcastle in England. She's been in Melbourne for five years. Lucy also works in a hospital, she's a physio at the Austin.'

'I know the Austin,' John said, as they were getting into the car. 'My friend Tom is in the dental department there. It's in Heidelberg, not far from Tom's home in Lower Templestowe.'

'Does she seem alright, this Lucy? You know, a decent type of girl,' he asked as he drove out of the car park towards the highway.

'I don't think I'll have any worries on that score, Dad. I'm really lucky to have found a flat and a flatmate so quickly.'

'Aunt Jenny will miss you around the house, poppet.'

'She said that but I've promised I'll visit her regularly.'

John turned on the radio quietly for the drive home and left her to drink in the sights of Tassie. As they arrived in

Penguin seafront, he switched off the radio again. 'Mum is ecstatic about you coming home, she's been cooking and baking for days,' he laughed.

As soon as they got to the front gate, Hazel was out on the nature strip, waving to Vina through the car window.

Hazel and Vina hugged and hugged, as though they'd been apart for two years instead of two months. They linked arms and walked into the cool hallway. 'Andy has football training this morning and Sue has gone with some of her friends on a school outing but they'll both be back by late afternoon in time for dinner. It's going to be wonderful having the whole family together for a few days.'

John followed them indoors. 'Right, Mrs West, and what about a welcome home cup of tea for our daughter?' he asked, winking at Vina as they both knew that Hazel would have everything organised in that department.

* * *

Hazel and John held Vina's party in the Cape Hotel at Wynyards, along the bay from Penguin and on the other side of the neighbouring town of Burnie. Situated beside Table Cape, a flat-topped piece of land jutting out into the water, the view from the hotel was magnificent.

They'd invited over sixty guests, including close family friends and Vina's friends from both school and her work in Devonport.

'You're looking really glamorous tonight, Vina,' her old school friend Fiona Currie said, when they were standing together at the buffet table. 'Did you buy your dress in Melbourne?'

'I got it in a store in Collins Street.'

The white silk dress was low cut at the front, with a white rose sewn on it at the cleavage. 'It felt right the moment I put it on,' she told Fiona, 'and, although I tried on several others, I always came back to this one.'

Vina felt sorry for Fiona, who was still living in her parents' house in Laggan Crescent. Mrs Currie had suffered a severe stroke in her late thirties and Fiona and her dad were her full-time carers. 'How are things at home at the moment?'

'Just the same as ever. Mum keeps smiling but it must be so difficult for her to be so dependent on Dad and me.'

'You both do very well,' Vina said, noticing the tears welling up in her old friend's eyes. Another of their ex-school friends joined them at that moment and the conversation changed.

'Have you enjoyed yourself, darling?' Hazel asked, an hour or so later when Vina sat down beside her to get her breath back after dancing 'The Dashing White Sergeant'.

'It's been marvellous, Mum. You and Dad have given me such a super birthday. I didn't expect a party in a hotel. I'll never be able to repay your kindness.'

Hazel squeezed her daughter's hand. 'There's no need to repay us, darling. We love doing things for you and the twins and our reward is to see you so happy.' She stroked Vina's cheek. 'We do miss you so, Vina, but we're delighted to see you looking so happy and contented with your life in Melbourne.'

'I do love Melbourne, Mum, but you know I'll always come back here for holidays. You won't get rid of me that easily,' she teased.

Before Hazel could reply, Trevor, one of Vina's old school friends, came over.

'Can I have this dance, Vina?' he asked, as the music started up for 'The Gay Gordons'.

Vina's earlier breathlessness was forgotten as she smiled at him and let him lead her on to the dance floor.

Chapter Nineteen

June 1966

It came as a complete shock, leaving Vina numb with pain and desolation. She'd been doing her hair before heading off to work when Lucy answered the phone.

She looked up when Lucy poked her head round the bedroom door. 'There's a phone call for you, Vina,' she said, and the look on her face told Vina that something was wrong.

'Vina,' Andy's wavering tones came over the line, 'Vina, I'm so sorry to have to do this to you but … but,' and she heard the catch in his voice, 'Vina, it's Dad …'

'What about Dad. Andy, what's happened to Dad?'

After a silence, he said, 'Dad's dead, Vina, he died just over an hour ago.'

By now both Vina and her brother were crying and she sat down on the floor, trying to take in what he'd just told her. 'No, it can't be, I spoke to him last night and he was fine,' she stammered.

'It was a major heart attack and he was dead in seconds. We're all in a state here but Vina he didn't suffer, it was too quick for that. We have to keep that in our minds, Vina, we have to.' Andy's voice sounded stronger now but she knew that he was keeping it together for her sake, being so far from home.

She felt Lucy's touch on her arm and, looking up, took a small glass from her, which the smell told her was brandy.

'Sip that slowly,' Lucy mouthed to her and she did as she was bid.

'Let me speak to Lucy again,' Andy went on and once again, in her trancelike state, Vina obeyed the instruction without question.

She heard the conversation between Lucy and her brother from a distance as she felt she wasn't real. What she'd just heard was a lie and when she came out of her dream it would all have been that, a dream.

After hanging up, Lucy returned and took Vina's hands in her own. 'Now Vina,' Lucy said in a matter-of-fact voice, 'I know this has been a great shock, but we have to make arrangements for you to return home. Your family need you and you need them.'

'I'll get the ferry tonight.'

'No, Vina, we need to get you home sooner than that, so I'll tell you what I've arranged with Andy. I'm going to phone work to cancel my early appointments and I'll also let your office know you won't be in.'

Vina nodded, without speaking.

'Andy has already let your Aunt Jenny know. He phoned her first as she's a very early riser. She wants to go over with you for the funeral, so I'll get on to the airlines and arrange a flight for you both. You'll be there in an hour.'

Vina remained mute.

'While I'm making the phone calls, I want you to keep focused, Vina, and concentrate on packing a case to take with you. And finish that brandy, it'll calm you until you get home.'

Lucy waited until Vina got to her feet and pulled her case down from the top cupboard before she returned to the phone.

* * *

'Close your eyes and try and have a sleep, pet,' Aunt Jenny said once they were settled in their seats on the plane. Lucy had run them both to Tullamarine Airport for their flight over to Devonport, where Andy was to pick them up.

Vina did close her eyes but sleep evaded her so she simply stared out of the window at the water below, trying to convince herself that this was really happening.

Halfway through the flight, the stewardess brought them a cup of tea and a bun. Vina held the cup between her palms without drinking; the bun remained in its paper untouched. Aunt Jenny didn't eat anything either although she did drink her tea.

'How is your mother holding up?' Aunt Jenny asked quietly, when she was sitting beside Andy in the car on the journey from the airport.

'She seems very calm. I think she's still in shock. I guess we all are, just can't believe what's happened.' Andy glanced at Vina, sitting dumbly in the back seat, then he looked round at Aunt Jenny with raised eyebrows.

Jenny sighed and shook her head but said nothing.

Vina gazed blindly out of the car window, unable to bear looking ahead at her brother because of his resemblance to their father. Andy even had a bald patch in exactly the same spot as Dad and he was growing more like him every day. It was wonderful, while at the same time painful, especially at this particular time.

'Oh, my darling girl, I'm so sorry you got the news when you were so far away from us,' Hazel whispered to Vina when she embraced her. 'But rest assured, love, Dad didn't suffer, it was all too quick.'

'Oh Mum, I wish I'd been here with him,' Vina wailed. Both she and her mother let go of their grief and their tears flowed unabated. They sat together on the sofa, trying to comfort one another, while Andy and Aunt Jennie went to join Sue in the kitchen.

'Have you phoned the undertaker and the minister yet?' Aunt Jenny asked.

Sue nodded. 'The undertaker is coming this evening as we wanted to wait until you and Vina got here and the minister's already been in to see Mum.'

'Good. Now is there anything else I can help with?'

'You could help me make some sandwiches. I don't think any of us have eaten anything since last night.'

'Good idea, Sue. You can't think properly on an empty stomach,' Aunt Jenny said, with a sad smile.

* * *

The funeral day dawned overcast and with a likelihood of rain, making the atmosphere even more dismal for the sad occasion.

There was to be a service in the local Methodist church with a committal afterwards in Penguin cemetery. A large turnout was expected, as John was so well known in the area through his work and his connection with the Lyons Club.

After almost no sleep, Vina rose early. The others were still in their rooms so she made herself a mug of coffee and sat in the rocking chair, remembering all the happy times she'd had in this house. Hard though it was, she'd try to keep these memories at the front of her mind today to help her through the dark hours ahead.

'Oh Dad,' she sniffled, rocking back and forth while staring out at the waves crashing in over the rocks down below. You loved this view so much, she thought, and how I wish you were here now to see it. 'And to call me your poppet,' she whispered to the empty room.

When she heard someone moving about upstairs, she went into the kitchen to lay the table for breakfast. They'd decided last night that they needed to eat a proper breakfast before the coming ordeal.

'Morning, Vina,' Andy said, when he came into the kitchen a few moments later and in silence the two of them prepared breakfast for the others.

* * *

'Here's the hearse now,' Andy said, a couple of hours later when they'd gathered downstairs, dressed for the funeral.

They all wore something black but Hazel had insisted they did have some colour too, such as a scarf or gloves to break the grim shade.

'That's what John would have asked us to do,' she said, 'he wouldn't want us to be gloomy and downcast but would prefer we celebrate the good life he had, however short.'

'Will we go then?' Jenny said softly and gently took Hazel's arm, leaving the others to follow them out to the funeral car.

Chapter Twenty

April 1982

Thursday morning clinics were always busy and Vina and Leonie were glad to sit in the staff room with a book at the lunch break. Their peaceful interlude was shattered when the door was flung open.

'God, I'm whacked.' Margo wheezed her way in and dropped her carrier bags on to the floor while she toppled down into the nearest empty seat. Her hair, with its blonde tips done only yesterday, was dripping in sweat. 'Myers was jumping,' she told them once she'd caught her breath.

Vina was at a loss to understand why anyone in their right mind would want to fight their way through a crowded store in such heat. Instead of the autumnal weather they should be having in April, the temperatures had been scorching over the past week, weather like they normally got in January and February. Myer's store in Bourke Street was busy enough at the best of times, but when there was a sale on it didn't bear thinking about. 'Rather you than me,' she said.

Margo grinned and raked her fingers through her damp hair. 'You know me, kid, I'm a sucker for a sale. Tony says they see me coming. But the sale finishes tomorrow and there'll be nothing worth buying by then. Any tea in the pot?'

Vina squeezed out what was left into a spare mug and handed it to her. 'Looks like you've done well,' she said, glancing at Margo's bags.

'Three pairs of shoes and a couple of blouses … and a shirt for Tony. By the way girls, I've decided to have a surprise 40th party for him on Saturday night and you're both invited. Said he didn't want any fuss but I'm not letting him off that easily.'

'You know Mike and I are always there for a knees up,' Leonie grinned.

'I'll give you directions to my place, Vina, and you're

welcome to bring Lucy with you.'

'Lucy's up in Queensland at the moment.'

'Oh yeah, I forgot that.'

'Mike and I could pick you up on our way to Margo's,' Leonie offered. 'That way you won't have to arrive on your own.'

'Great, thanks.' Vina wasn't keen to go, sure that the guests would mainly be in couples, but she didn't want to upset Margo by refusing her invitation. Six months ago, when she'd tired of all the needless changes taking place at the Children's Hospital and when Marion and Katie had both retired, she'd come to work here in Dr Stansfield's dermatology practice. Although Margo and Leonie had worked together for years, they welcomed her into the fold and the three of them worked as a team, covering reception, accounts and correspondence.

She rinsed out her mug and returned to the office. Although the surgery was on the seventh floor, with the desk positioned beside the window she could see pedestrians down on Collins Street and hear the screech of the trams coming up the hill outside the building.

Switching on the fan at the side of the desk, she picked up the case note on the top of the pile and fed some paper into the electronic typewriter.

* * *

Margo staggered up the road on Friday night after work, balancing her heavy load of food shopping. 'Damn,' she muttered as the heel of her left shoe snapped. Putting the bags down on the nature strip, she wrenched off the shoe. A tin of tomato soup fell out of one of the bags and rolled down the street, to land in the gutter.

She limped back to retrieve the tin. As she neared the house, shoe in one hand, soup in the other, Tony emerged from the garage.

'Why didn't you phone me?' he grumbled, running back to pick up the bags scattered across the grass on the nature strip.

'I didn't mean to buy so much,' she told him, when he

followed her indoors.

His eyebrows arched as he helped her unload all the food. 'What the hell is all this tucker for? Looks like we're feeding the five thousand.'

'I took the chance when so much was on special. The tinned goods will keep and most of the rest will freeze,' she lied.

* * *

Vina collected a Chinese carry out that Friday night on the way home from work. With Lucy away, she didn't feel like cooking for herself and anyway it was far too hot to slave over an oven.

While she ate, she watched the ABC news. The main topic was the Falklands War, covering interviews with Margaret Thatcher, the British Prime Minister, and her Defence Secretary, John Nott. The phone rang during the programme and she slid her empty plate on to the coffee table, turning down the volume on her way to answer it.

'Hello,' Lucy's chirpy tones reached her over the wires, with the usual echo that seemed to accompany an Interstate call. 'How're things?'

'Apart from getting sauce down the front of my blouse and breaking our only butter dish, great,' she laughed. 'How's Queensland?'

'We're having a ball. Jessie and Norm have a fabulous place up here with a swimming pool in the garden. It's a necessity because of the heat.' The line began crackling by the time she got to the end of her sentence.

'Bet you've made good use of that,' Vina shouted into the mouthpiece. Her flatmate was committed to her regular morning swim at the gym before work.

'Too right,' Lucy yelled back, as the line began to break up again. 'Can't believe I've been here almost two weeks, the time has whizzed by. What have you been up to since I left?'

'Nothing very exciting, just the usual routine. I've had an invitation to Margo's husband's 40th party tomorrow night. You were invited too.'

The interference increased, with a high pitched buzzing noise, and she was unsure if Lucy heard about her invitation before the line went dead.

* * *

Vina went into town first thing on Saturday morning before the intense heat of the day started. She found it hard to choose a gift for Tony since she'd only met him a couple of times and didn't want to get anything too personal. She settled for an after shave that the assistant in George's assured her sold well with men of Tony's age group.

When she got home, she dropped her bags at her feet and unlocked the mailbox. There was a postcard from Lucy and a letter from Mum. She stepped from the gravel path on to the lawn and walked barefoot towards the deck, almost keeling over in the hot northerly wind. The coarse, corn-coloured grass was rough from lack of moisture. Even after living seventeen years in Melbourne, she still missed the feeling of the soft, lush grass of Tassie brushing the soles of her feet. The recent severe drought had caused bush fires in many suburbs in the Dandenong mountain area, thankfully without loss of life on this occasion.

She felt frazzled after her morning in town. Lifting the cushions off the sun-lounger, she shook them vigorously to get rid of any spiders or other creepy-crawlies that had taken up residence during her absence.

She went indoors for a cool drink and applied some sunscreen, then she lay back on the lounger and ripped open Mum's letter. She and Mum had long telephone chats but there was nothing to beat the time they spent together when Vina was home for holidays. It was at times like now when Lucy was away that she was sorry Mum and the twins didn't live nearby.

Mum gave her news of the twins and said Sue's daughter, Heather, was settling well into her nursery. She asked Vina how life was treating her and Vina knew this meant had she found romance yet?

At 37, she didn't feel on the shelf just yet but Mum was obviously concerned that she hadn't settled down with a husband. Although she'd had lots of boyfriends over the years she'd been in Melbourne, none of them had appealed to Vina as a suitable husband and indeed none had ever proposed to her.

Mum went on to tell Vina that she'd had a bumper crop of peaches this year and had made some peach chutney and jam with them. 'Next time you're home, love, I'll give you some jars to take back with you,' she wrote. Vina drooled as she folded up the letter, almost tasting Mum's gorgeous chutney.

Along the fence-line the sunflowers had grown tall enough for their dark-eyed centres to observe the goings on in next door's garden, from where she could hear the drone of old Ben's lawnmower. From her lounger, if she craned her neck, she could see the bottlebrush with its mass of red flowers half covering the roof of the shed. The branches intertwined with those of the nearby wattle bush. The yellow wattle blossoms were pushing forward, spilling out on to the path.

'Hi, Vina. How's tricks?' She sat up and shaded her eyes with the letter. Ben was grinning at her over the fence. 'Lucy having a good time up north?'

'Yep. Phoned last night. Surely you aren't gardening in this heat, Ben?'

'I was, but it's too hot.'

He removed his wide-brimmed bush hat and used his hankie to mop up the perspiration on his forehead and around his eyes. 'I'm just wishing I could use the sprinkler, the ground is crying out for some rain.' Shaking his head dolefully, he looked down at the bushes on his side of the fence, his scalp showing through his sparse white hair.

'We could do with weeks of constant downpours,' Vina agreed.

'Fat chance of that though,' he snorted. 'Guess we'll have these water restrictions for a while yet.'

'I've noticed the native bushes seem to be able to withstand the heat.'

'Yep,' he nodded, pulling on his hat again. 'They're

tenacious right enough.'

Naomi called to him from the back door that lunch was ready and he winked at Vina. 'I'd better go. The boss summons.'

She smiled after his retreating figure and lay back on the lounger. She quickly fell prey to the soporific effect of the ringing tones from the bell birds in the nearby gum tree and it was not long before her head dropped down on to her chest.

* * *

Leonie and Mike were late picking Vina up that night.

Going out to meet them, she felt dwarfed by the big, burly truck driver, who held out a giant paw. 'Sorry we're late. Leonie is disastrous as a navigator.'

'Hold on, Mike.' Leonie glowered up at him, her thick black tresses threatening to break free of their gold clasps. Her small frame was in sharp contrast to his and even in her high-heeled sandals she barely came up to his shoulders. 'You turned left when I said right and you went your own way instead of following Vina's instructions.'

'Steady on,' he thundered back. 'You couldn't make up your mind so I **had** to find my own way.'

'Never mind.' Vina spoke in her most placatory tone. 'You got here eventually. Would you like a cold drink?'

'Thanks, but we'd better push off in case **she** gets us lost again,' Mike scowled, while Leonie made a face behind his back.

By the time they were driving up Margo's runway, the party was in full swing.

Even with the patio doors wide open, it was stifling in the house and Vina was glad she'd worn flimsy trousers and a sleeveless top. Some nibbles were handed round and someone pushed a glass of wine into Vina's hand.

A while later, when people started to dance, she laid her empty glass on a nearby coffee table and made a hasty exit through the patio doors into the garden. This was the part she hated, once the couples began to dance, and she was left feeling isolated and abandoned. She wandered around the side of the house in the gathering dusk, the stillness broken by the cicadas. She had stopped to admire the purple blossom on the Royal Robe bush, when she heard his voice.

'Magnificent, isn't it?'

She turned to the tall, fair-haired man standing behind her, his smile extending to his grey/blue eyes. She studied his deep blue silk shirt, deciding that the colour suited him, and then reddened, realising he was waiting for her reply.

'Yes, it's a gorgeous colour.' She addressed the bush rather than the man, an adolescent blush moving across her cheeks.

'I have one in my own garden. Are you escaping too?' He moved closer, his hand outstretched. 'Kevin Harte. I go to the footie with Tony.'

'I work with Margo.' She got a whiff of his after-shave. Its spicy fragrance was similar to the one she'd bought for Tony.

'And do you have a name?' the man teased, his eyes twinkling.

She felt the accursed blush return. 'Sorry, I'm…'

'Vina.' She turned as Leonie came into the garden. 'Vina, are you coming indoors? Supper's ready and now's a good time to give Tony his gifts.'

She muttered an apology to Kevin Harte and followed Leonie inside.

Chapter Twenty-One

May 1982

The week beginning Sunday 2nd May was one that, in hindsight, Vina wished she could have re-lived and changed the outcome.

Lucy arrived home about eight o'clock on Sunday evening. 'Hello-o, I'm back from my wanderings,' she called from the hallway where she dumped her case.

Vina rushed out of the living room and hugged her friend. 'How was your flight?'

'Great, no hitches, and thankfully the seat next to mine was empty so I didn't need to listen to some other passenger wittering in my ear. Jessie and Norm have a fabulous life up north, I was quite envious.'

'You wouldn't want to give up your post at the Austin, would you?' Lucy was in a senior position in her department and could suit herself regarding her hours.

'No of course not, my life is here in Melbourne but it was good to get a taste of the relaxed lifestyle in Queensland.' She yawned. 'Think I'll go and soak in the bath for a while.'

'When you're finished I'll toast some raisin bread and make us a brew,' Vina said, returning to her novel meantime.

* * *

After dinner on Monday evening Vina and Lucy listened to the news about the sinking of the Argentine cruiser, the General Belgrano, by a British nuclear submarine. With the time difference between Australia and UK, it hadn't long happened. The programme participants discussed the pros and cons of the legitimacy of the sinking.

Shortly afterwards, Lucy began yawning again. 'Think I'll turn in early tonight, not yet over my jet lag.'

'Sweet dreams,' Vina called to her retreating figure and settled down on the sofa to watch the new detective series about to start on the ABC channel.

* * *

On Tuesday morning Vina got off the tram slightly later than usual at her stop on the corner of Swanston and Collins Streets. The autumn day was already hot for this early in the morning. She ran up Collins Street, wending in between other pedestrians, and turned into No 100. The coolness hit her immediately she stepped into the air-conditioned entrance hall.

She rushed past the milk bar on the ground floor of the building and cursed inwardly when she saw an 'Out of Use' notice hanging from the lift button. It was all she needed when she was already running late; there was nothing else for it but to tackle the stairway up to the surgery on the seventh floor.

She got as far as the fifth and stopped for a breather. A man was coming down from the level above and she stood aside to let him pass, barely glancing in his direction. When they drew level, he smiled briefly and pushed his hair off his face.

He moved on to the next flight down and then stopped and looked up through the stairwell. 'Excuse me, but aren't you a friend of Tony and Margo Greene?'

'Yes.' She peered down over the banister, a puzzled frown on her face. Then the smile he flashed at her brought recognition.

'Kevin Harte. I met you at Tony's fortieth. I spoke to you in the garden although I don't expect you'll remember.'

'Yes, of course I remember,' she said politely. 'I'm Vina West.'

'Your friend took you away just when we were getting acquainted.'

She leaned on the banister, playing with the strap of her shoulder bag. 'Do you work in this building?'

'No, I'm a surveyor in East Melbourne. I was taking measurements in an office on the tenth floor and wanted to get them done before the staff arrived. I think you told me you work with Margo?'

'Yes, in Dr Stansfield's surgery on the seventh floor.' The mention of the surgery reminded her why she'd been on the stairs this morning. 'I'm really sorry, but I'm going to have to shoot because I'm running late. It's been great speaking to you again,' she said, hoping he wouldn't take it as a brush off.

'How about joining me for a meal and a drink sometime? Maybe tomorrow night after work?'

She felt a prickly sensation at the back of her neck, aware that he was watching her. 'That would be nice.'

'What time do you finish at night?'

'Officially we stop at half past five but it's often nearer six by the time we get away.'

'Great. I'll wait for you at six o'clock at the front of the building. Till tomorrow then,' he said, and continued on his way downstairs.

* * *

Vina became nervous as Wednesday evening approached. Fortunately the clinic didn't overrun and she had time to shower in the surgery and change into her blue linen dress. She was pleased that for once her hair sat the way she wanted it to.

Not trusting the lift, which still hadn't been working properly that day, she used the stairway. The butterflies started on her way down. What if the evening turned out to be a dismal failure? Worse still, what if he didn't show up?

She felt a flutter inside when she saw him standing in the doorway, looking even more handsome than yesterday. He stood with his jacket looped on to his finger and slung over his shoulder.

He turned round and smiled at her as she crossed the foyer towards him. The soft breeze wafting in through the open door blew his tie up over his collar to play around his face.

'Hi,' he greeted her, slipping an arm around her waist. 'I know a good place round the corner in Russell Street. You okay with that?'

'Great,' she smiled, and he took her arm and steered her towards the pub.

'What would you like to drink?' he asked, once they were seated in a booth.

'Gin and tonic is my tipple.'

'Gin and tonic it is then. Back in a mo,' he smiled,

heading over to the bar.

She studied the other customers while he was gone. The people in the nearby booths were in pairs, probably like themselves out for a quiet drink after work. There was a large group of women sitting around a table in the corner, adjacent to the bar, and from their excited chatter and laughter it looked like a leaving party or maybe even a pre-wedding do.

Kev returned and sat opposite her. 'Where in Melbourne do you stay, Vina?'

'In Camberwell. I stayed with my late aunt in Brighton for the first few weeks I was living in the city but my friend Lucy and I have shared a unit ever since.'

'You're not so far from me then. I live in Blackburn. And where's home for you originally?'

'I come from Tassie, from Penguin on the north coast.'

'Yeah I know it, my great-grandparents lived in Tassie, a place called Magnet. They lived to a good age and I went often for a holiday when I was a kid.'

'I've heard of Magnet, though I've never been that far to the west.'

'It's out in the sticks, not somewhere you're likely to visit.'

Vina loved his relaxed manner and quiet confidence and she placed every movement and nuance into her memory bank in case this evening proved a never to be repeated experience.

'Did you get into work on time yesterday?'

'Just.'

A passing waitress laid a couple of menus on the table.

'You don't look like a surveyor,' she said, once they'd made their choice.

'And how should a surveyor look?' he teased.

She turned scarlet. 'Don't know exactly. I thought you were a teacher or an artist. Not sure why.' She floundered to a halt, feeling foolish.

'My job can become pretty routine but I've never

regretted choosing it as a career.' He stopped speaking when the waitress came back to take their order. 'A spaghetti for the lady,' Kev pointed to the dish on the menu, 'and I'll have one of your delicious chillis.'

The girl wrote down the order. 'Something to drink?'

'Think we'll have a bottle of Wolf Blass Cabernet Sauvignon, 1971,' he said, without consulting Vina.

With her limited knowledge of wines, this suited Vina fine.

He sat back in his seat and loosened his tie. 'Would you mind if I took this off?' he asked, and when she shook her head he whipped it off, folded it up and put it into his jacket pocket.

'I hate wearing ties but I wanted to make a good impression on our first date,' he smiled, and his eyes crinkled at the sides as he did so.

'Cheers,' he lifted his glass and held it against hers. The waitress brought the wine to the table and put it into an ice bucket on the end of the booth.

'I'll be floating home after this lot,' she laughed.

'No rush, we have all evening. Are you married?' It was more a statement than a question. 'Hope you don't mind me asking?'

'No, I don't mind and no, I'm not married. What about you?'

'My wife, Norma, left me four years ago. We'd been dating since high school and I always thought our relationship was solid. Then, out of the blue, she left a note on the kitchen table and went off with another guy. She'd been having an affair for months and I didn't suspect a thing. We've been divorced for two years now.'

His voice sounded hard and bitter and for a moment he vanished into his thoughts. Then, remembering Vina was facing him across the table, he smiled once more and the light came back into his eyes. 'Sorry, Vina, I shouldn't be giving you all my problems.'

'It's alright, better to get things out rather than bottling them up.' Unsure what else to say, she said no more.

Their food arrived at that moment and he passed her the breadbasket, then poured the wine. 'Enough about me. Tell me about you.'

'Not much to tell. I was born in Scotland and came to Tassie when I was 4. I lived there until I was 20 but found life a bit slow and boring so moved to the mainland just before my 21st birthday. I've been here since.'

'That'll be about ten years ago,' he suggested.

'You must be joking, more like twenty. I'll be 38 in November.'

'I'd never have believed it. I'm 39 and I thought I was years older than you.'

'I'll take that as a compliment then.'

The ice broken, the evening passed in a flash. He drove her home and they sat in the car for a few moments outside the unit. He kissed her, a long lingering kiss, and she responded positively. Before they parted, they arranged another date for Sunday.

* * *

'How did your date go last night?' Lucy asked when she and Vina were having breakfast next morning. 'I didn't hear you come in.'

'I knew you'd likely be asleep so I tried to make as little noise as possible. Took my shoes off before walking up the path.'

'That was thoughtful but no need to worry, Vina, you know I almost die when I go to sleep. It would take more than some crunching on the stones to waken me.'

Vina stretched over for the jar of honey. 'We had a few drinks in a pub in Russell Street and ended up eating there too. Kev's nice, I enjoyed his company.' She poured honey on to her toast and wiped the drips off the rim of the jar with her knife.

Lucy's eyebrows arched, and she smiled. 'Do I sense another date?' she asked, topping up their teacups.

Vina nodded, her mouth full of toast. Once she'd swallowed it she said, 'I'm seeing him again on Sunday. He suggested a drive somewhere if the weather is fine or the cinema if it rains.'

Lucy cradled her cup between her palms. 'Think it'll be the drive. The weekend is forecast to remain hot and sunny.'

'Great,' Vina washed her toast down with a drink of tea. Then she looked at her watch and ate her last piece of toast. 'Must get off,' she said, pushing her chair back and getting to her feet, 'we've a full clinic list today.' She put her used dishes into the sink to soak and went off to brush her teeth.

* * *

After work, the girls had their dinner outside to enjoy the late evening sunshine. They lingered over their coffee and a glass of wine. Their solitude was broken by their next door neighbour, Emma, calling to them over the fence.

'Wonder how Ben and Naomi are enjoying their break up in Sydney. Have you heard from them?' She laid her washing basket on the grass and began unpegging the clothes from the rotary washing line, or a whirley-gig as most folks called it.

'We had a postcard,' Lucy said, 'and they seem to having a great time. It's nice for them to spend time with their son and his family. I think Ben misses the grandchildren since his son took that new job in Sydney.'

'At least you girls have a key. It's good for them to know that you can keep an eye on the place for them.' Emma turned away for a moment. 'You've got a visitor, girls, I've just seen him walking up your front path,' she said as she unpegged her sheets before they became too dry for ironing. The breeze whipped up for a moment and enshrouded her in the white sheet.

'I'll go.' Vina got up and picked her way, barefoot, round the side of the unit. 'Ouch,' she cursed, each time she trod on a sharp stone. Her disgruntled scowl changed to a beaming smile when she reached the front garden and saw Kev standing in the porch holding a book.

'Sorry to call at your mealtime but I was passing this way and thought I'd drop off this book on Aboriginal legends that I promised to lend you.'

'Thanks. Lucy and I are in the back garden. Are you coming round?' she invited, keen to introduce him to her flatmate.

'I won't, Vina, I'm on my way to a footie match with Tony and a couple of other guys. Tell Lucy I'll meet her next time.' And with that he blew her a kiss and got into the car, driving off at speed.

When she got back, Emma and Lucy were engaged in conversation. They stopped speaking and glanced at the parcel in Vina's arms. Lucy took off her sunglasses. 'You certainly got shot of our visitor quickly, whoever it was.'

'Kev brought this book for me but he couldn't wait. He was going to a footie match with some mates.'

Emma grinned from her side of the fence and winked at Vina. 'Handsome looking devil, I'd hang on to him, you could do a lot worse. Right, girls, must get on, some of us don't have time for sunbathing,' she laughed, picking up her basket and heading indoors again.

Chapter Twenty-Two

'Nice car and, from what I can see, not a bad looking driver either,' Lucy grinned on Sunday morning, when she spotted the grey Holden draw up on the road beside their driveway. 'Have a fab day,' she said, giving Vina a quick hug.

Kev had arranged to pick Vina up at ten o'clock and had arrived on the dot. He came across as someone who was in control of every situation. Unlike herself, she thought, aware how she tended to dither about things.

'Thought we'd go to Ballarat,' he said, as she was putting on her seat belt.

'I love Ballarat, haven't been there for ages. Think the last time was when Lucy and I went to the Begonia Festival. We tried panning for gold when we were there, but were unsuccessful in making our fortune,' she laughed.

Later, as they drove into Ballarat, an old gold-mining town just over a hundred kilometres north-west of Melbourne, Kev overtook a truck that seemed to be labouring despite the flat road surface. 'It's one of the biggest tourist attractions in the whole State this place, because of the gold panning.'

'I'm sure it must be,' she agreed, 'especially for overseas visitors.'

He came down a gear and drew to a halt at a crossroads. 'A mate of mine was brought up here and he said it was once Victoria's major city. When the gold rush ended in the 1880s, Melbourne began to overshadow it and became the capital city.'

He released the handbrake when the lights turned to green and took a right off the main highway. 'I know a quiet spot where we can have our picnic,' he said and drove along the forest road for some time, eventually slowing down to a crawl because of the rough track.

He stopped in a clearing, the gum trees tall enough to form an arched roof, shielding them from the sun's strong rays.

She got out of the car. 'This is lovely, so cool after the heat in the car.'

She walked over to a nearby picnic table, while Kev got the eski out of the boot. They quenched their thirst and had no sooner got out the sandwiches and crisps that Kev had packed for them than a dozen or more crimson rosellas joined them.

'Fine, you can have a bite,' Vina laughed, as one of the blue and red birds pecked at the half-eaten sandwich she was holding, while another of its mates landed on her shoulder, with a third perched on the top of her head. 'I meant a bite of my sandwich, not me,' she shrieked, when a few more rosellas landed on her arm and one gave her a nip.

'Once we've tried our hand at gold panning, we could visit the Eureka Stockade museum,' Kev suggested, as they gathered up their belongings and returned to the car, which had been kept cool by the ceiling of trees above it.

Vina hadn't been in the museum before and she found it interesting to read about the rebellion, Australia's only civil uprising, in which about twenty miners died.

Later they sat in a pavement café enjoying an iced coffee in the late afternoon sunshine, directly across the road from the Ballarat railway station, with its well photographed clock tower.

Someone further along the street had a radio turned on low, adding to the atmosphere of peace and tranquillity in this beautiful rural setting.

* * *

Lucy saw the headlights of the Holden through the net curtains of the darkened room where she was watching television. By the time she got up and opened the front door, the car had driven off and Vina was crunching her way up the path.

'We don't need a burglar alarm with these stones,' Vina said, as she began to make out Lucy's figure standing behind the screen door, the door closed to keep out any mosquitoes or other insects.

'Good time?' Lucy stood back to let Vina pass her into the hallway, then closed the screen door again quickly.

'Fabulous. I've learned a lot more about Ballarat.'

She was still talking as they went into the television room. 'We had a picnic lunch and you wouldn't believe how tame the rosellas were. Even more so than the ones we saw down at Wilson's promontory last year.'

'I'd say it was a successful date then,' Lucy smiled at her friend, pleased that she seemed so happy.

Chapter Twenty-Three

September 1982

Vina lay back, with her eyes closed, and listened to the parakeets twittering in the trees above her. She had almost dropped off when she heard the splash of oars and, raising herself on to her elbow, looked over towards the boat sheds on the opposite side of the Yarra. Two lads were already sitting in a canoe near the bank and two more came out of the shed behind them, dressed in wet suits. They made their way down the grassy slope and clambered in beside their mates to position themselves on the narrow seats.

'Peaceful, isn't it?' Kev lay on the tartan rug at her side, the lazy afternoon sounds almost putting him to sleep too. They often came here on a Saturday about this time and this spot under the trees was their favourite. The car was parked on the road just behind them and it too was sitting in the shade.

'Mmm,' Vina sat up properly. She pulled her knees up to her chin and leaned on them. 'Can you pass me a sandwich please?'

He handed her the white plastic box out of the picnic hamper. 'Do you want a knife?'

'No, fingers are fine. Want one?'

He shook his head and lay down on the rug again.

'Have you done any rowing, Kev?'

'Yep, I used to be in the University team. Haven't been out for years now. What about you?'

'Not me. Sue's the water baby in our family. Swam in the school team.'

A galah that had been pecking its way around the dried-up grass nearby was lured closer by the sight of Vina's cheese and ham sandwich and a ripple of anticipation ran down its pink breast. Some of the grated cheese dropped out of the bread on to the grass and she watched the galah swoop down and fly off with a string of the grated cheese hanging from its beak.

She lay down again and soon dozed off. When she wakened, Kev was sitting up, staring down at her. She smiled up at him. 'Have I been asleep for long?'

'Don't know, I've just wakened myself. I love watching you sleep.' He pushed her hair away from her face and brushed his fingers down her cheek. 'Vina,' he said suddenly, 'I'd like to come over to Tassie with you the next time you go.'

She sat up, face to face with him. She was surprised, as he'd never before given any indication that he'd like to go there with her. 'Of course you can, Kev, if you want to.'

'I think it's time I met your family, Vina. You do know that I love you, don't you? And that I want to marry you.'

'You do?'

'I'm not good at showing my feelings, especially after what happened with Norma. Find it hard to trust people nowadays. But I do love you, Vina, and hope you feel the same way about me.'

'I do, Kev,' she smiled, putting her hand into his larger one, and leant against his shoulder. 'And I want to marry you too.'

'Good,' he smiled and gave her a long, passionate kiss, his body pressed firmly against hers. Hearing a wolf whistle behind them, he released her and they laughed over at the young lad who gave them the thumbs up.

'Fancy an ice cream?'

She nodded and they packed their belongings into the boot and strolled, hand in hand, over to the ice cream van parked further along the path.

* * *

'How about a trip down to Philip Island today?' Lucy suggested next morning. 'Unless you've arranged something with Kev.'

'No, he has to work today. That would be lovely, it's a long time since we've been there. And we could wait until after dark and see the penguins.' Philip Island was noted for the fairy penguins that came out of the water when darkness descended and paraded up the beach to their homes in the sand dunes.

'Let's pack up a picnic to take with us,' Lucy said, jumping up and clearing the breakfast things off the table. 'And we can stop off somewhere for dinner on the way home.'

'You shower first and I'll make up some sandwiches. We can use the fresh bread we bought yesterday.' Vina took the butter out of the fridge as she was speaking. 'Cheese or cold meat?'

'Some of both,' Lucy replied, already halfway to the bathroom.

A couple of hours later the two friends lay sunbathing on the cliff top above the beach, the radio playing quietly at their side.

'Beautiful, isn't it?' Sitting on her lilo, Vina felt her words weren't adequate enough to describe the scene below them.

'Mmm,' came the response at her side. When she turned round, Lucy had taken off her t-shirt and was sunning herself in her shorts and bikini top. It was early spring but the temperatures were higher than normal for this time of year. With Lucy working most weekends lately, they hadn't enjoyed too many lazy Sundays like this.

Vina's eyes followed the path twisting and turning its descent down the hillside. She could see and hear the waves crashing in on the rocky shore below. The gulls made crazy circles in the azure blue sky, as if their radar systems were out of control. Their cries competed with the noisy cicadas in the bushes behind them. Up here on the ridge, the earth was cracked and baked dry by the ravages of the long hot spell over the past few weeks.

'When will you be seeing Kev again?' Lucy asked, handing Vina a carton of juice from the eski.

Vina shook it and pushed the straw into the top of the carton. 'We thought of taking a trip on Puffing Billy next weekend.'

'It's a very long time since I was on that train.'

'I love the Dandenongs at this time of year. If it weren't for the bush fires, I'd like to live up there.' The Dandenong mountain range lay on the eastern side of Melbourne and almost every summer bush fires started in the forest areas, the bad ones often involving loss of life in addition to property.

'You've been seeing a lot of each other,' Lucy ventured and looked straight at her friend. 'I take it things are becoming quite serious by this time.'

'Well, until yesterday, I would have said no, we were just friends, but yesterday he spoke about wanting to marry me.'

'So he proposed?'

'Well, not actually proposed, in the sense of getting down on one knee, but he did say he loved me and wanted to marry me.'

'And you agreed?'

'Yes, I love him too. Neither of us is very good at showing our feelings and I think Kev finds it especially hard after what happened with him and his wife, Norma.'

'Yes,' Lucy nodded, 'that sort of thing must be hard to get over. Well,' she smiled, 'I think congratulations are in order. I'm very pleased for you both.'

'Thanks, Lucy, although there's no date set yet. Kev wants to come with me to Tassie to meet Mum and the twins before that.' She was sure deep down that Lucy didn't like Kev much. Her flatmate was always very polite and pleasant in his company but Vina knew her well enough to be certain that Lucy hadn't really warmed to him.

They sat in silence for a while, each with their own thoughts. When Vina roused herself a short time later and glanced round, Lucy had dropped off. Beginning to feel sleepy herself, she folded her anorak into a pillow and lay back on it. When she wakened an hour or so later, she felt stiff and the sun had sunk low in the sky.

Beside her, Lucy now had her t-shirt on again. Her friend yawned and pushed her sun hat off her face. 'It's much cooler now.'

'And the light's fading. Will we make our way down to the beach to see the penguins?'

'Let's do that and afterwards we can find somewhere to eat on the way home.'

Chapter Twenty-Four

December 1982

'Have a lovely Christmas, both of you, and give my love to the family in Tassie.' Lucy hugged Vina and gave Kev a peck on the cheek. She'd run them to Tullamarine airport for their flight to Devonport today and tomorrow, Christmas Eve, she herself was flying to Queensland to spend the Festive Season with Jessie and Norm. A work friend of Lucy's was doing the honours in getting her to the airport tomorrow.

As the months had gone by, Vina was more certain than ever that Kev was not Lucy's favourite person and she sensed that, from Kev's point of view, it was a two way thing. However, as he and Lucy hadn't spent much time in one another's company it was no big deal.

'You enjoy yourself in Queensland, and give my best to Jessie and Norm,' she said as she and Kev moved towards the gate for their departure. 'And remember to keep your pressie until Christmas day,' she called back, knowing how hard Lucy found it not to open her gifts before 25th.

'Same goes for you guys,' Lucy grinned and waved, before turning back towards the exit.

They had a smooth flight and Andy was waiting in the airport terminal when they touched down in Devonport on a gorgeous summer's evening. Andy looked bronzed and healthy in his t-shirt and shorts, his feet pushed into a pair of flip flops.

'Welcome home, Sis,' he embraced Vina, then shook Kev's hand. 'Nice to see you again Kev, glad you could spend Christmas with us.' This was Kev's second visit; he'd been over in October with Vina to meet the family.

'I bet Mum's been busy getting everything organised for Christmas,' Vina said to her brother from the back seat of the car.

'Sure has but you know how much she loves doing it.' He turned towards Kev, sitting in the passenger seat. 'Hope you don't feel too grown up for a Christmas stocking filled with goodies, Kev, as Mum makes one up for us all.'

Kev laughed but made no further comment. 'The weather's a lot better than when we arrived in October. Then it was grey skies and drizzling with rain.'

'We've been having gorgeous weather the past couple of months, although not the high temperatures that Melbourne gets.'

The two men chatted on in the front while Vina remained silent, recalling her first time home after moving to Melbourne and her delight at seeing Dad again.

* * *

'Thanks, Mum,' Vina said, as she pulled the goodies out of her stocking on Christmas morning. 'It's easy to see you know I'm a chocoholic,' she laughed, holding up the Chocolate Santa, Chocolate Christmas Tree and Chocolate Snowman.

'I couldn't get any more into it but there's plenty more chocolate treats hanging on the tree. Now, if you've all opened your stocking, let's start on the gifts proper.' For the next half-hour all that could be heard was paper being ripped open and oohs and aahs when the parcels were opened.

Sue gave a squeal of delight when Vina opened the little velvet box Kev gave her and put on her new engagement ring. 'It's gorgeous, Sis,' she said, examining the ruby stone surrounded by tiny diamonds. 'Do let me try it on.'

Vina gave her the ring and Sue put it on and held out her hand to show it off.

'I chose it in a jewellers' shop in Collins Street before we left Melbourne. Thanks, Kev, I love it,' she said and leaned over to kiss her new fiancé.

Kev had spoken to Hazel in October and she'd given her blessing for the marriage. Although both Vina and Kev were well past the age of consent, they were traditionalists at heart.

'Dinner's ready, to the table everyone,' Hazel called from the dining room an hour later.

'I'm so pleased that you were both here when you announced your engagement so that we could all share in the good news,' Hazel said to her son-in-law to be during dinner.

Kev turned to face her and smiled. 'That was the reason Vina wanted to wait until she came home.'

'And when are you guys planning to get hitched?' Sue, to the point as always, asked. 'At your ages, what's the point in waiting?'

'Thanks a million,' Vina pretended to look offended. 'We thought we'd like to have the wedding over here next Christmas.'

'A whole year's engagement?' Sue's eyebrows arched in surprise.

'I had to sell my house when my first wife and I divorced,' Kev explained, 'and I've just been renting since, so it will give us a bit longer to save before we buy a property.'

'And Lucy and I will have our unit paid off by next year and then Lucy is going to buy my half from me which will release some more capital for us to put towards a house,' Vina told the family members sitting around the table. She and Lucy had taken up the offer to buy the unit a couple of years after they'd begun to flat together.

'Very sensible,' Hazel said, handing round the plate of home-made tablet, a tradition in Laggan Crescent on special occasions.

She looked across at Vina. 'And if you want a Christmas wedding you have to prepare well ahead. Have you got a particular day in mind, love?'

'We thought Christmas Eve next year.' Then she laughed. 'Here we are talking about Christmas 1983 and we're still in the middle of Christmas dinner 1982.'

'Time flies,' Hazel replied, 'it'll be next Christmas before we've had time to blink. Will some of your family members come over for the wedding, Kev?'

'I only have my sister in Melbourne and the relatives over here are long dead.'

'Your grandparents lived in Tassie, didn't they? I remember you telling us last time you were over.'

'It was actually my great-grandparents who were here and my grandma went to school in Tassie. I'm a fifth generation Aussie; my folks were among the first settlers. I used to love hearing my grandmother's tales of when she was growing up in Magnet. She was from real pioneering stock.'

'I don't know Magnet, except that it's out west somewhere,' Hazel said.

'Yep. As I said to Vina, it's out in the sticks, not a place many people visit. I went to Magnet often as a child before my great-grandparents died and there were no proper roads. Might be different now, of course.'

'I wonder what it would've been like at school for your grandmother?'

'Magnet was a silver mining settlement when my grandma was a girl, although the mine's defunct now. The men were all employed there and grandma and her siblings used to go through the valley and around the edge of the mine to get to school. Many of them walked barefoot. No transport in those days,' he laughed.

'Did she stay in Magnet all her life?'

'She went to Melbourne as a teenager to find work. Met my grandfather there and the family have been there since. There's only my sister and myself left.'

'And will she come over for the wedding?'

'I think she and her family will and also some mutual friends Vina and I have, like Margo and Tony Greene.'

'Wasn't it at one of their parties that you and Vina met?'

Kev nodded.

'Just as well you don't have a lot of people to invite Kev,' Andy butted in, 'because we have loads. We don't want poor Mum to be bankrupt,' he said and everyone laughed.

Chapter Twenty-Five

Christmas Eve, 1983

Hazel's statement the previous year about time flying was indeed the case as it seemed no time at all until the Friday of Kev and Vina's wedding dawned. The weather was balmy, with a forecasted top temperature of 28.

All the house windows in Laggan Crescent were open and Vina could hear the waves crashing in on the rocks down on the beach as she stood in front of the long mirror in her parents' bedroom. Her eyes filled for a moment, wishing Dad could have been with her but she dabbed the moisture away immediately, careful not to smudge her mascara. 'No tears today,' she muttered to herself, 'I won't let anything spoil our happiness.'

She turned away from the mirror as Lucy came into the room, magnificent in her purple dress. She and Sue were both bridesmaids today but Sue was still downstairs with the hairdresser.

'Can you fasten this chain for me please?'

'Sure.'

Lucy stood behind Vina and fastened the chain of her gold locket. A 21st gift from her parents, it was even more special to Vina as it was the last gift her dad had bought her. Job done, Lucy looked at her friend in the mirror.

In her white satin and lace gown, Vina looked positively regal. Her shiny black hair was pinned up into a roll at the back of her head, adding to the air of elegance.

'You're beautiful, Vina. I hope Kev appreciates how lucky he is.'

Lucy didn't think Kev was right for Vina but had kept her own counsel, aware her friend loved him.

Sue came into the bedroom at that moment, wearing an identical dress to Lucy's, both girls being a similar height and dress size. Sue's blonde hair was bobbed while Lucy had grown her hair longer than she usually wore it, taking away the tomboyish look and replacing it with a very feminine one.

'Wow, you look fabulous, Sis, the tiara's perfect.'

'And you two have scrubbed up quite well too. Now, this is where your bridesmaids' duties begin, in trying to get me downstairs in this dress.'

A short time later Vina got out of the bridal car at Penguin Methodist Church and walked down the aisle on her brother's arm.

Kev turned round from his place in front of the communion table and smiled at her. The look of admiration and love in his eyes set her heart fluttering and it took all her strength not to collapse in a heap beside him in front of the Pastor.

Her posy of yellow roses gradually ceased shaking and she listened to the Pastor's voice. A shaft of sunlight came in through the stained glass window, surrounding the bride and groom in a glowing halo.

After the service, an excellent meal was laid on at Neptune's Hotel at Table Cape, where the view from the dining room was breath-taking.

'Pity the table wasn't facing the other way with that fantastic view behind us,' Lucy, sitting next to Vina at the top table, said.

Vina nodded, smiling. 'This place holds loads of memories for me. Sue had her wedding reception in Neptune's too.'

'Happy, darling,' Kev asked, taking the hand lying on her lap and lifting it to his lips to kiss it. He smiled at Vina, then turned to Sue on his other side when she spoke to him.

'Andy used to release his pigeons from The Cape,' Vina said, returning to her previous conversation with Lucy. 'I sometimes went with him.' She let her thoughts drift back, while the sun struck her posy and the flowers were reflected on to the silver coffee pot sitting beside them on the table.

'And did they?' she heard Lucy's voice at her side.

'Did they what?'

'Did the pigeons all come back safely?'

'Most did, but some were lost to hawks or vultures. Andy always got really upset when his birds didn't come home. Because of that, I was quite pleased when he sold them and took up another hobby.'

'Ladies and gentlemen,' the MC's voice broke into their conversation, 'pray silence for your bridegroom, Mr Kevin Harte.'

Kev cleared his throat and got to his feet, the legs of his chair scraping across the wooden floor as he did so.

He drank some water and began to speak.

Chapter Twenty-Six

June 1985

'I'm so sorry, darling,' Kev choked on the words as he looked down at Vina and touched her limp, white hand, resting on the bed cover.

But Vina knew he was lying, he wasn't feeling her pain. It was all pretence with him.

'It will get better,' he promised, 'it just wasn't meant to be.' His empty words meant nothing and she continued to stare up at the ceiling. She remained silent, tears sliding out of the corners of her eyes.

He tried again. 'The doctor says a miscarriage is not unusual in women over 40 but it doesn't mean we can't try again.'

When she still made no response, he left her, saying, 'I'll come back this evening, darling, but meantime try and get some sleep. You've been through such an ordeal, Vina, and you need to rest.'

After he'd gone, Vina closed her eyes but no sleep came. She sighed deeply, certain that the pregnancy had been her only chance of becoming a mother. She knew people always said that a miscarriage was nature's way of saying that all was not right with the baby but that was small consolation to her. She'd always loved playing with her niece, Sue's daughter, but she'd yearned to hold her own baby and experience the joy of motherhood. And now she was certain she never would.

Vina stared out of the window at Melbourne's high-rise blocks. She heard the noise of the traffic down below but up here in her single room in the maternity unit, her life was cut off from the rest of the world.

She heard some laughter in the corridor outside her door and turned her head, burying it deep into the pillow. The day she'd discovered about her adoption came to mind and her sobbing increased.

When her crying eventually eased, it was more from weariness than the fact that she was feeling any better.

Kev was trying his best to sound sympathetic but she knew deep down that the loss of the baby didn't upset him as much as it did her. He'd made a good show of being delighted about her pregnancy but she'd sensed that he saw a baby as a threat to her love for him. It was as if he became jealous of anyone else getting her attentions and his behaviour left her feeling stifled.

During the eighteen months they'd been married, he'd become more and more possessive of her, not wanting her to spend time with Lucy and other friends, preferring to be on their own.

'I do love you, Kev, but I need female company at times too. I could understand your complaints if I was seeing other men,' she'd thrown at him from time to time during their marriage.

'But why do you need anyone else when you have me? I've given you everything you wanted,' he grumbled.

'I know that, but I can't stand you being so possessive of me. I need to have friends too.'

The arguments always resulted in him flying off the handle or sulking for days until eventually she'd give in and cancel whatever arrangement was annoying him.

They didn't even see Margo and Tony Greene these days. Nor did she see Margo at work any longer since Kev had insisted that she gave up her full time job and find part time work nearer home.

To keep the peace, she'd given her notice to Dr Stansfield and worked three days a week in a coffee shop in the Camberwell Shopping Centre. She got on well with the other members of staff there but didn't enjoy the work half as much as she'd done in the surgery.

Lucy was forever telling her that she should stand up to Kev, and she knew this was good advice, but it wasn't worth following because of the arguments it caused.

At last, exhausted from her ordeal, she cried herself to sleep.

* * *

'Hello, love,' Lucy kissed her friend and laid some flowers on the table at the side of Vina's armchair. 'I would have come into the hospital but Kev was adamant that he didn't want you to have visitors to tire you.'

Vina smiled wanly and held Lucy's hand for a moment. 'I've done nothing but rest,' she said, 'but it doesn't make the pain go away.'

'I know, Vina,' Lucy whispered, drawing her friend closer in a hug. 'No woman can get over losing a baby but I hope in time the pain well become easier to bear. You know I'll just be at the other end of the phone if you want to talk.'

'Thanks, Lucy, I know that. Do you want to put on the kettle and make us a cup of tea?'

'Of course. Can I make you anything to eat?'

'Some toast would be nice and maybe a little scrambled egg.'

'Coming up,' Lucy said and hurried into the kitchen. Vina could hear her cracking the eggs and pouring water into the kettle. It was nice to hear such everyday sounds. It reminded her of the years they'd lived together.

'It's like old times,' she said when Lucy returned.

Lucy laid the two mugs down on the coffee table and gave Vina her egg and toast served on a tray.

'Will I put your flowers into a vase?' Lucy asked, once they'd finished eating.

'You'll get one in the cupboard next to the cooker.'

'It's good that Kev's at work, gives us time to chat.' Lucy stood back to look at the flowers and made a few changes to their arrangement. 'How've things been since you came home?'

'Not great, he just can't seem to understand that he isn't enough for me, I need my friends too.' She sighed. 'I've lost touch with so many people since we were married.'

'Well, you aren't going to lose touch with me, Vina, because I'll make sure of that. Who does he think he is, trying to take over your life?'

Hearing the anger in her friend's voice, Vina smiled. 'I know you've never really liked Kev, Lucy.'

'It isn't so much I don't like him, as I don't like the way he insists on you living like a hermit. You're such a sociable person, Vina, it isn't right. Why don't you refuse to do everything he wants?'

'Because it's easier to do as he wishes, rather than start an argument. He has quite a temper you know and either goes into a rage and throws things around or goes off in a huff.'

'Just as long as he doesn't throw you around. He doesn't, does he? You would tell me.'

'Of course I would Lucy, no he doesn't cause any physical damage. It's his possessive behaviour that causes so much stress. He didn't seem antisocial before we were married, I don't understand it.'

'I don't think he understands himself.' Lucy's voice was less angry, now that she'd been assured by Vina that Kev hadn't been physically abusive.

Later, when Kev arrived home, Vina was laughing over something Lucy was relating about one of her friends at work. It did not escape Vina's notice, however, that her friend departed swiftly after her husband's return home.

Chapter Twenty-Seven

26th January, 1995

The vast crowd at Kooyong rose to their feet that Thursday as the opening strains of the national anthem came over the loudspeaker and the singing of 'Advance Australia Fair' reverberated around the arena. From their seats in Row E, Vina and Lucy were in good voice.

After everyone was seated again, an announcement came over the tannoy. 'Welcome to Kooyong on this Australia Day. The first match on this court is between Barry Paterson of Great Britain and Australia's Mark Hyland. A cheer rose up at the mention of Mark, the golden boy of Australian tennis, with a great deal expected of him in the Championships. Even more so, as Australian champions had been thin on the ground since the glory days of the 1970s.

A few minutes later both players walked on court to wild applause but Hyland's ovation would have lifted the roof had there been one.

'Don't think the Brit stands a chance against our man,' Lucy grinned.

'Too true,' Vina agreed, happy to be spending time with her best friend today.

Her relationship with Kev had steadily worsened since she'd had the miscarriage almost ten years ago and by now she found his behaviour insufferable. Although their sex life was pretty well non-existent, he still demanded to know where she was going, with whom and when she'd return home.

For the next three hours the spectators gasped, cheered and groaned their way through the long five-setter, sitting on the edge of their seats until the very last shot. Mark won as expected but Barry Paterson had done himself, and his country, proud.

Mark was now due to meet Rudolph Liebermann of Germany in the next round on Saturday.

The mixed doubles that followed was much less of a contest but there were still plenty of entertaining moments during the match.

'What a fantastic day,' Vina said, when they were on their way up the stairs towards the exit.

'Worst part is getting out of here without being mowed down in the stampede,' Lucy laughed.

* * *

'Where have you been?' Kev yelled, when Vina walked in the back door. 'I was ready to send out a search party.'

'What do you mean? You know damned well I've been at the tennis with Lucy. Told you last week we'd both taken the day off work to go to Kooyong. **And** I reminded you last night, just in case it had slipped your memory.'

'You and your bloody tennis,' he grumbled.

'And what about your footie, and the cricket?' she retaliated, her voice rising with every word.

Kev was a keen fan of Australian Rules football and regularly attended cricket matches at the MCG. If either of those games was on television, he sat glued to the screen, whether or not Vina wanted to watch it.

'You're impossible,' she shouted over her shoulder, as she went into the kitchen to make dinner.

She'd cooked the meat and veggies and was mashing the potatoes when he came into the kitchen and started again. 'I don't understand why you can't be content in our life together, instead of traipsing all over the place with your so-called friends.'

Vina felt something snap inside and, leaving the masher standing upright in the potatoes, she stormed out of the room, pushing him aside roughly on her way past.

Upstairs, she packed a case with everything she'd need over the next few days. Downstairs again, she took her car keys off the hook beside the front door.

Kev stood in the hallway and glared at her. 'Where do you think you're going?'

'To Lucy's, not that it's any of your business any more. I should have gone years ago,' was her parting shot as the door slammed behind her.

It wasn't until she was driving to her old home in Camberwell that it occurred to her that Lucy might have gone out this evening. Not likely after a day at the tennis, but she couldn't be certain that Lucy would be at home.

However, as she drove into Lucy's driveway, she saw the venetian blinds being pulled apart and, by the time she got out of the car, the door was open and Lucy was out on the path.

She took one look at the case Vina carried and held her arms out to her best friend.

Chapter Twenty-Eight

April 1995

'Are you sure it's what you want, Vina? Don't feel under any pressure, I'm happy for you to stay as long as you wish,' Lucy said, when Vina told her of her plans to return to Penguin.

'I know that, Lucy, and I really appreciate all your support over the past few months. Without you, I'd have been homeless as there was no way I could have stayed any longer with Kev.'

'What will you do about him?'

'I'll consult a lawyer when I get back to Penguin but as far as I'm aware I can request a divorce after living apart for two years.'

'I think you're right. And with no children, it will be straightforward. But just make sure he sells the house and you get your share of the proceeds.'

Vina nodded and took the mug of coffee that Lucy had freshly brewed. She sat down on the chair in front of the window, facing her friend.

'As you know, Lucy, I've enjoyed living and working in Melbourne so much and feel at home in the city. But I can see a difference in Mum; she's become pretty frail and her memory is causing us some concern.'

'Yes, I could see the deterioration last time I was in Tassie with you.'

'Sue and Andy do their best to support Mum but Andy's job is very demanding and involves him travelling all over the island. And, of course, Sue looks after her grandchildren while Heather is at work. It's been hard for Heather since she was left on her own.'

Lucy nodded. 'I can understand your concern.'

'I'll have more time to support Mum if I go back. I can get myself accommodation near her and be there if she needs any help.'

'It's all very laudable, Vina, but what about a job?'

'You know I keep in touch with Thelma, my ex-colleague from Devonport Hospital?'

Lucy nodded.

'Well, she still works there and says there's a couple of job vacancies I could apply for. I've enjoyed working in the coffee shop in Camberwell but I much prefer the medical work.'

'It all sounds like it's meant to happen, Vina, so go for it and follow your gut instinct. It goes without saying that I'll miss you very much but I'll come to Tassie to visit you once you're settled and you can have holidays over here.'

'You and I will never lose touch, Lucy, we've been friends for too long. I'll wash these before I turn in for the night,' and she lifted the empty coffee mugs from the table and carried them into the kitchen.

'Just put them into the dishwasher,' Lucy said, getting up and switching off the living room lights. 'I'll say goodnight then and we can talk more about your plans later.'

Chapter Twenty-Nine

September 2011

While Vina was clearing out the garden shed at her unit in Baxter Avenue, she thought about Lucy's plan to come over for a long weekend next month. It would be super to spend some time together as it was almost a year since they'd last met.

Over the sixteen years she'd been back in Penguin she and Lucy had talked at least twice a week on the phone and now that they both had more up to date laptops, they could use Skype.

She'd phoned Lucy late last night to finalise their arrangements and had left a message on the answer machine. When the landline rang, she was sure it would be Lucy returning her call, and raced indoors. 'Hi, Lucy,' she gasped, lifting the receiver.

'Good morning, am I speaking to Davina West?'

'Speaking,' she replied, her breath more even now.

'This is Sister Woodford from the Accident and Emergency Department at Devonport Hospital. Your mother, Mrs Hazel West, is with us.'

'What's happened?' Vina sat down and grasped the edge of the table tightly. She mopped her brow with the sleeve of her old gardening sweatshirt. Mum had been exhibiting her usual memory problems but otherwise she seemed very well when Vina saw her yesterday.

'She suffered a stroke and was brought here for assessment. We're trying to arrange a bed for her in Ward 6.' The Sister said more, something about Mum having collapsed at the bus stop, but Vina couldn't take it in.

There was a rushing sound in her ears and the room began to spin. 'What happened … how did … when was she taken to hospital?' The questions flooded out of her. 'I need to see her.'

'Of course, come now. Dr Murchison will give you

more information.'

After she hung up, Vina sat for a few minutes leaning her head on the table. She hadn't been able to ask the questions that were racing through her head. Did Mum take the stroke at a bus stop here in Penguin or had she been in Devonport?

She spoke to Mum on the phone most days but hadn't rung her this morning. Don't be silly, she thought, she'll be back to her normal self in a few weeks. Mum was a very fit 94-year-old and this would help aid her recovery.

Vina roused herself. After leaving a brief message on Lucy's answer machine, letting her know what had happened, she went to the kitchen for her car keys. Thank goodness she'd learned to drive while she was in Melbourne. Kev had always discouraged her from driving lessons, saying she'd be too nervous and she'd stupidly believed him. In the event, she'd taken to driving like a duck to water and often wondered these days how she'd managed when using public transport.

Her car keys were missing from their hook near the kitchen door; she was constantly mislaying them these days. She searched the most likely places but no joy. Where the hell had she left them? She was about to ring for a taxi when she spied them in the fruit bowl resting between an overripe banana and an apple.

Deciding to wait and ring the twins from the hospital, she zoomed off in the direction of Devonport, following the coast road, which had less traffic than the highway at this time of day. She switched on a CD of rainforest music but soon turned it off again. Usually she found the music relaxing but right now it seemed to be increasing her stress level.

Traffic allowing, she should arrive at the hospital in half an hour. She became calmer as she drove; the sound of the sea crashing in on the rocks always had that effect on her. On arrival at A & E she was ushered into a cubicle where her mum was lying on a trolley bed.

'Mum, it's me, Vina,' she said to her unconscious parent, sniffing back the tears.

'Do you think she can hear me?' she asked the nurse

in attendance.

'There's always a chance she does.' The nurse, wearing the pink and white striped uniform of a staff grade, smiled kindly at Vina. She moved away when the phone rang. 'Okay, thanks,' she said and replaced the receiver.

'A bed's ready for your mother in Ward 6. I'll call a porter and you can go with him when he takes her up in the lift.'

* * *

'It's Vina, Mum, I'm staying here to keep you company.' She squeezed the limp hand, desperate to feel a response. It felt strange to be talking to her unconscious mother like this but the Consultant had impressed on them last evening how essential this was in helping the patient to recover from her coma.

Sue and Andy had joined her at the hospital the previous evening, when they brought both her and Mum clean clothes. Still wearing her old gardening togs, she'd felt much better once she'd showered and changed. The family had been allocated a room near the ward for this purpose.

After an overnight vigil, the twins returned home for work and family commitments. Retired over seven years now, Vina was free to stay on at the hospital.

Nurse Martin came in to check the IV fluid bag. 'How's she doing?' Vina asked, while the nurse scanned the machines bleeping at the side of the bed.

'We should know more in the next few days.' Nurse Martin laid a gentle hand on Vina's shoulder before slipping out of the room again.

* * *

'You should have a break and go home for a few hours,' Andy said the following evening, his face wrinkled with concern. 'You can't go on like this indefinitely.'

'Don't worry, I'm fine,' Vina lied. She turned her head away from her siblings to hide the tears sparkling in her eyes.

Dr Murchison came into the room at that moment, his face taut. He spoke in a subdued tone as he imparted the grim news.

'I'm so sorry but the latest scan shows that too many of your mother's brain cells have been destroyed. She's being kept alive by machines meantime but there is now no hope of any recovery.'

'Are you telling us she is brain dead?' Sue asked.

'I'm afraid so. I'm really sorry. I wish I had better news for you.'

'What's the next step?' Andy, his voice a whisper, dared to ask the question that was on all their minds.

'It has to be your decision. She could stay on life support for longer, in the unlikely chance of her regaining consciousness, or you can elect to have the machines switched off.'

Vina looked directly into the doctor's eyes. 'What is her condition likely to be if she does wake up?'

'Extremely poor, unlikely she will have any quality to her life. I know it's a big decision so I'll leave you to talk it through, please take as long as you need and don't hesitate to ask any questions?'

'Thank you,' Vina said, stroking her mother's flaccid hand.

After he'd left, the three of them sat around the bed, too stunned by the news to cry. They stared at one another helplessly and Vina was the first to speak. 'What do you guys think we should do?'

Sue played with her fingers for a few moments, before saying, 'I think we need to do it, for Mum's sake.'

Andy nodded. 'I agree. It's a terrible thought and not what we want to happen. But we all know that Mum would hate being left here existing rather than actually living,' he said, his voice breaking up.

Vina choked, averting her eyes from her beloved mother and clasped her brother's hand tightly. 'You're right, Andy, Mum was such a live wire and she'd hate to be an invalid. I think we should separately say our goodbyes to Mum now and let the machines be switched off.'

When they turned round Sue was crying silently but sorely. She could just manage a brief nod.

They took it in turns to sit with Hazel for a short time and afterwards, still sobbing, they hugged one another tightly before their resolve weakened.

Chapter Thirty

December 2011

'Can you steady the steps?' Vina called down to Sue, as she came out of the loft space in the house at Laggan Crescent.

Sue spread her arms around the wooden ladder positioned dangerously close to the stairwell, keeping her anxious eyes on the black hole above Vina's head. There was a gap between the top of the ladder and the loft opening and Vina had had to pull herself up over the abyss to gain entry to the loft. 'Honestly Sis, I don't know why you didn't wait for Andy to go into the loft. Sometimes you forget you're nearly 70.'

'I'm only 67.' Vina balanced an old brown case on the top step and craned her neck to look down. 'I found this in a corner, hidden by some old paint tins. If I hadn't gone up, it might have been left there forever, unwanted, unloved and undiscovered.' She made her way down each rung, supporting the case as she came, and sneezed from the dust that blew up. 'Watch out,' she said as she neared the bottom and Sue twisted her body aside to dodge being hit when the case dropped on to the landing.

Vina dusted the top with the sleeve of her old sweatshirt. 'By the state of it, this case has given good service and travelled widely,' she pointed to the labels on the lid and sides. When the locks wouldn't budge she carried the case downstairs to the living room.

Sue folded away the stepladder. She said nothing about the loft being left open; she'd ask Andy to close it later.

Downstairs Vina sat on Mum's rocking chair with the case on the carpet at her feet. She looked up when Sue came into the room.

'There's a label here with 'SS. Belle Princess' on it. I remember Dad telling me once that we came over here from Scotland on that ship.'

She pushed the metal locks again with no success.

'Hold on, I think I saw some WD-40 in the garage.' Sue left the room and returned with a rusted can of the oil.

Vina sprayed it liberally around the locks. Allowing the oil time to soak into the mechanism, she tried again and on her third attempt the locks sprang open.

When the lid was lifted, they were hit by a musty smell. The inside of the case was covered in a faded thick paper lining in a brown and orange check. The lining was torn near the top and a strip of loose paper hung down. Inside were bundles of old postcards held together with elastic bands and lots of old letters and papers.

'I'll make us some tea,' Sue suggested and disappeared into the kitchen, leaving Vina to go through the rest of the contents. Near the bottom she found a pile of loose papers. Leafing through them, she saw some papers relating to her adoption in December 1945.

Her hands shook as she held the papers. She'd definitely never seen them before. Mum must have decided not to show them to her when she'd discovered about her adoption. The papers didn't tell her much more than Mum had, other than her birth name, but it felt strange to be holding them.

'What's wrong?' Sue asked on her return, laying the tray on the coffee table.

'It's the papers about my adoption, my previous name was Nancy Morrow.'

Sue placed a mug in front of her. 'Drink some tea, it'll make you feel better.'

The phone rang in the back hall and Sue went to answer it while Vina leaned back in the chair. Mum had told her that it was one of the first pieces of furniture that she and Dad had bought on their arrival in Tasmania.

She rocked backwards and forwards, tears streaming down her face. Drawing her hands gently over the patchwork cushions, she pushed herself deeper into their soft depths.

The memory came back to her of how she'd rush home from school and climb on to Mum's lap in this chair.

She'd cuddle into Mum while she related everything that had happened at school that day.

She rubbed her hands along the wooden arms of the chair, a strong smell of furniture polish wafting up. Mum had polished them regularly and since her death three months ago Vina had taken over the task. A faint smell of Mum's lavender perfume lingered on the cushions.

'That was Andy on the phone,' Sue said when she returned, 'he'll come straight here to help us finish the clearing out.'

'Finding this case has helped me come to a decision, Sue.'

'What's that?'

'I'm going to Scotland to try and trace my biological parents.'

'My God, how long have you been thinking about that?'

'Since I discovered at the age of 12 that I was adopted. I'd never have done it as long as Mum and Dad were alive but I feel I need to do it now before it's too late. And with my share of the proceeds from the house, I'll be covered financially.'

Sue squeezed her hand and they were still discussing Vina's decision when they heard Andy's car tyres driving over the pebbles outside.

Part III - Scotland

Chapter Thirty-One

May 2012

Taking the shortbread out of the oven, Molly Bishop sat it on a wire tray to cool. Dad would get some tomorrow; his eyes always lit up when he saw home baking. Putting Dad into a nursing home had been so stressful and even two years on the memory of one particular home she'd viewed haunted her. The stench of faeces and stale urine were still in her nostrils as she'd driven home, tears pouring down her face.

Hollytrees, the care home she'd finally chosen in Broughty Ferry wasn't far from his old house in Shore Road. Not that poor old Dad knew where he was, the dementia that began a year after Mum's death had progressed rapidly.

Molly wiped her brow with the back of her hand. God it was hot, the worst day she could have chosen to bake, especially after a day in the classroom. She pulled her auburn hair off her face, fastening it with a blue butterfly clasp from her selection in the odds and sods drawer. She'd suffered from these bloody menopausal sweats for about fourteen years now and, at 64, they hadn't eased with age as she'd hoped. The worst time was during the night, with her sheets soaking in the morning. She was glad at such times that she and Ted had stopped sharing a bed.

She slid the casserole dish on to the top shelf; it should be ready when Ted got home from work at Ninewells Hospital. She and Ted had been leading separate lives under the same roof for years now. Her love was for her son, Luke, a final year student in English and History at Dundee University. Luke had gone against Ted's wishes that his son should follow him into medicine, in particular pathology, and decided to enter a course of his own choosing.

Molly admired her son for sticking to his guns and not being bulldozed into doing what his dad wanted.

She was 42 when Luke was born, an easy child to rear,

contented and a hard worker at school. She switched on the plate under the potato pot, remembering his first day as a pupil at Harris Academy. There he was, wearing his maroon-coloured blazer and grey trousers, all fired up and ready for off. Molly, an English teacher at Harris, had constantly received good reports of Luke from his teachers there.

Now almost 22, he'd soon be ready to fly the nest but she didn't want to think of that just yet. This was the reason that she'd continued to work on beyond the retirement age of 60, afraid that she'd become bored being in the house all day. She did have friends, of course, some already retired, but she reasoned that there was a limit to how many times a week she could go out for lunch before boredom set in.

With the dishwasher full to capacity, she hand washed the baking bowls, accompanied by the stirring 1812 Overture, courtesy of Classic FM. Raising her arm, she pretended to conduct the orchestra, splattering the window with soap bubbles.

From here you could see the traffic on the Tay Road Bridge, spanning its way over to Fife. They'd bought this house in Farquhar Drive especially for that view. Ted had called it a back to front house, with the kitchen facing the river. The front of the house was on level ground, with ten steps up to their back door on the riverside.

When Luke was young, they'd enjoyed fantastic family days out but that life had gone forever due to Ted's philandering. His affairs still rankled but the intense hurt had eased and she'd learned to cope with her situation better. It was sad how far he'd distanced himself from Luke; he'd bought the lad a top of the range Peugeot last year but she knew Luke would have preferred having more of his dad's time.

With everything ready in the kitchen, Molly sat down to watch Eggheads, her favourite quiz show, until the potatoes were cooked.

* * *

Ted Bishop finished dictating the report on his latest post mortem examination. He moved away from the slab containing the corpse and stripped off his gloves. He dropped them into the metal bin under the sink and, as he scrubbed his hands and nails, he was anticipating his night of passion with his secretary, Lynn. Desire welled up in him at the thought of her.

Ted picked up his notes and pushed open the swing doors, leaving the smell of formaldehyde behind. As he strode along the hospital corridor, he was aware of the many females who glanced in his direction. His black hair had turned to white but this hadn't lessened his appeal to the opposite sex. Thank God for that, he thought; with the frosty relationship he had with Molly, he needed to seek his pleasures elsewhere.

In his office he dialled Lynn's number. She'd used some flexi hours for shopping today so he wasn't surprised when her answer machine clicked on. 'Hi, gorgeous, bet you've shopped till you dropped but hope you've some energy left for me tonight. See you later.'

Ted lifted his briefcase and hummed 'Pretty Woman' as he made his way to the car park. Seconds later, his black Mercedes, Registration TED4, roared out of the hospital exit.

* * *

'Hi, Mum,' Luke called out as he walked into the living room, where Molly was sitting in front of the TV set. 'Dad not in yet?'

'No, darling,' she said, and pressed the record button on the remote before getting to her feet to follow him into the kitchen where he was washing his hands.

'He mentioned he had a meeting that might go on late. You know Dad, there's always something,' she shrugged. 'Hungry?'

'Ravenous. But I don't mind waiting for Dad.'

Molly laid the casserole dish on the table. 'No need to wait. I'll leave his in the oven. I can give it a zap in the microwave if he's very late.'

Luke helped himself from the dish. 'Mike, Dave and I are moving into a flat in Denham Avenue,' he said as he tucked in.

Having dreaded this moment, Molly tried not to let the

surprise show on her face. 'That's great, Luke. I knew of course that you would do that eventually but hadn't realised your plans were so far on.'

'I'll still be within walking distance of the University if my car's off the road. I hope you don't mind me going, Mum.'

She smiled brightly and turned her head a little to hide her brimming tears. 'Of course I don't mind, it's natural for you to want a place of your own. I'll miss you though.'

'And I'll miss you too but I won't be far away. We paid the first rent today.'

'That's great, darling. I know you three lads all get on so well.'

'And … you … what will you do, Mum?' He was well aware of the fraught situation between his parents, having played pig in the middle for long enough. His sympathies lay with his mother who'd suffered so much by all Dad's affairs over the years but, if he was honest, he was fed up of all the arguments and bad feeling.

She stretched out and squeezed his hand. 'Now don't you worry about me, Luke, I'll be just fine. You know I've only stayed here because of you.'

Neither of them heard the Mercedes come up the driveway until Ted walked into the dining room and eyed them suspiciously. 'What's going on?'

Molly's voice was ice cold when she replied. 'Luke's moving into his own flat.' She turned back to her son. 'I forgot to ask you when, darling?'

'We hope to get it fixed up over the weekend and move in early next week.'

'About time you became more independent.' Throwing the words over his shoulder, Ted went into the hall to hang up his coat, his thoughts already on the evening ahead with Lynn.

Luke left the house shortly after his dad, telling Molly that he was going to stay over at a friend's house and wouldn't be back until late the following evening.

Molly yawned her way through a film on telly and

decided to have an early night.

She knew it would be hot sleeping in this humidity, so she opened her bedroom window wide and didn't put on any nightwear.

She fell asleep immediately.

* * *

'I think you've had enough, mate,' the barman in the Bridge Hotel told the customer who'd just asked for another whisky.

'I said fill it up,' the man repeated. His steely eyes locked on to the barman as he held out a £20 note.

The barman shrugged. 'It's your funeral,' he said, taking the money. He slid a measure of Glenfiddich across the counter, placing the change beside the glass.

The guy downed it fast and asked for another. The barman obliged.

Although not a regular punter, the man had been in a few times, with the same blonde in tow, young enough to be his daughter. They'd sit in the corner booth, with her looking all doe-eyed at him. Tonight though they'd argued, their voices rising; she wanted them to get a flat together and he wasn't playing ball.

Eventually the blonde upped and left, refusing to let lover boy go with her. Since she'd gone, he was on to his fourth half and he'd end up on the floor soon.

Shaking his head, the barman moved away to the opposite end of the counter to serve some new customers. When he looked over again, lover boy had disappeared.

* * *

Molly wakened with a start.

Through half shut eyes the bedside clock finally came into focus. It was ten to two. A sound penetrated her sleep-drenched brain and she became aware of Ted's frame standing in the doorway.

At first she thought she was dreaming as Ted never came into her bedroom nowadays but he staggered towards the bed and dropped on to the mattress beside her.

She yelled out in pain when he grabbed her arm. Once his motives became evident, she shrank away from him and pulled the sheet up under her chin. He yanked it away again, muttering incoherently.

'Stop it, Ted! Get off me!' she shouted, gasping for air. But even in his inebriated state he was too strong for her. He slapped his hand across her mouth and she bit firmly on the fleshy part.

'Bitch,' he yelped and pulled his hand away. 'You'll pay for that,' he raged in a slurred voice, his sweat-drenched face close to hers, his breath reeking of whisky.

Her clammy hands clawed at the arms holding her in a vice-like grip, but he pinioned her to the mattress, his lust fuelled by alcohol. Disgust, fear and anger all bubbled up in her emotional cauldron and, choking with revulsion, she was forced to endure this nightmare until his passion exploded.

He threw her aside and stumbled off to his own bedroom and a few minutes later she heard his loud snores while she hid her face in the pillow and sobbed.

She tossed and turned for hours, unsure if she should report the rape to the police. She decided not to as she couldn't contemplate having to answer their probing questions.

At daybreak she got up and ran a bath. The hot water soothed her tormented body and while she soaked she made the decision to contact her lawyer and start divorce proceedings.

An hour later she stole out of the house, keen to leave for work before she met any of her neighbours. Closing the front door quietly, she used the remote to open their double garage. Walking under the lilac bush, a blossom brushed against her cheek, its gentle touch and pungent scent at odds with what had happened to her just a few hours earlier.

Chapter Thirty-Two

September 2012

Clicking her seat belt into place, Vina leaned back against the cushioned headrest with its Emirates logo. She closed her eyes and tried to slow her breathing. Thick black hair encircled her pale, unblemished face. At 67 Vina still had very few grey hairs, much to the annoyance of Sue, who was almost white by now.

Tears welled up when she thought of the emotional farewell to the twins in the terminal at Devonport last night. Sue had been really upset. Andy held it together better but Vina knew he too was fighting back the tears.

Touching down at Tullamarine Airport in Melbourne a couple of hours later, she'd had a few hours sleep in the airport hotel before boarding this flight for London. She'd worn flat sandals for added comfort during the long flight, in addition to the strong support stockings recommended by her doctor. In readiness for Scotland's cooler temperatures, her heavy woollen sweater was in the hand luggage compartment above her seat.

A stewardess stood in the aisle, demonstrating safety procedures while the plane taxied across the runway. Vina heard the whoosh of engines and stuck her fingers into her ears. She didn't enjoy travelling but her fear of flying had worsened since the dreadful happenings at the Twin Towers in New York in 2001.

They'd been airborne for about ten minutes and the 'fasten seat belt' sign extinguished before she allowed herself to look down from her window seat over the red roofs of a Melbourne suburb. She strained to try and make out a familiar landmark but from this height up it was impossible to recognise anything.

She'd only the vaguest memory of living in Scotland and couldn't imagine a better place to grow up in than

Penguin. Although the seed for this trip had begun to germinate many years ago, it was finding her adoption papers last December that had spurred her on to book her flight.

She settled down with the autobiography of her favourite Aussie tennis player, Ray Marks. Because of his 6'7' height, he was better known as Lofty. Vina had harboured ambitions of becoming a professional tennis player in her school days but, although able to punch a frightening serve, she hadn't made the grade to pursue a career in the game.

* * *

'Tea or coffee, madam?' Vina looked up. 'Tea please,' she smiled up at the stewardess and pulled down her tray from the back of the seat in front. Having been engrossed in her book, she now realised they would soon be at their first stop off in Singapore, where she could get off the plane and stretch her legs.

She used the washrooms in Singapore, spacious after the cramped conditions on the plane. Before she boarded again, she checked her watch and sent a text to Sue. *'Hi, at Singapore, abt to get back on for next leg, will txt once in UK. Luv, V. x'*

Back in her seat, she fished around in her bag and brought out a notebook, reading over the information she'd downloaded from the internet a few months ago.

> FIND YOUR FAMILY,
> POST ADOPTION SERVICES,
> 4 GRANGE ROAD,
> EDINBURGH, EH2 7NZ
> TEL. NO. 0131 222 7990
> email mail@findyourfamily.org.uk.

She needed to trace her origins before she got any older. She was aware that her natural parents may be dead or be unwilling to meet her but she had to try, no matter how painful.

She smiled when she thought of the little pink gingham dress wrapped in tissue paper that nestled in her case down in the hold. It was the dress she had worn when the

Children's Officer brought her to Mum and Dad for adoption. The dress had some tiny pink flowers and bows on the front of the bodice and Vina hoped that her biological mother had sewn it for her.

She yawned and looked at her watch. She calculated it would be nearing three o'clock on Wednesday afternoon in Britain right now and their flight was due in London on Thursday at 5 a.m. UK time.

When the lights were dimmed, she put on her eye mask and settled down to snatch a few hours sleep.

* * *

The phone was still ringing as Molly unlocked the back door and, out of breath, she lifted the receiver just as it was about to switch on to message mode. 'Hello.'

'You sound like you've been running a marathon,' Beth Urquhart's teasing tones rang out over the line.

Molly smiled on hearing her friend's voice. 'I rushed up the back steps. Now that I've stopped working on a Wednesday, I go for a walk along the beach.' She pulled a chair away from the kitchen table and sat down, in preparation for her usual lengthy phone session with Beth. 'How are things with you and Greg?'

'We're both fine. But more to the point, how are you? I worry about you, you know.' Beth had wept when Molly told her about the rape back in May. Molly refused to bring charges but at least the odious Ted had moved out of Farquhar Drive.

'I'm okay, Beth. I prefer being lonely to playing second fiddle to Ted's dolly birds. He's bought a property in Carnoustie and taken that slag of a secretary to live with him. More fool her, if she expects him to be faithful. They deserve each other.'

'It's an absolute disgrace the way that man's treated you.' Beth's voice was full of indignation and Molly was, as ever, grateful for her friend's loyalty. 'But on to a happier subject, Greg and I were hoping you'd come through here soon for a visit.'

'That would be nice. When were you thinking?' The

Urquharts lived in Highfield, about 12 miles from Glasgow, and Molly missed seeing Beth regularly.

'Isn't there a school autumn holiday soon?'

'Yes, in the middle of October. Would that be convenient?'

'Of course, any time is convenient but that would allow you to stay a bit longer. Why don't you spend the week with us?'

'No, I have some commitments mid week,' Molly replied, which wasn't strictly true but Beth tended to neglect Greg when she was there. 'I could come down for a long weekend, perhaps travel on the Friday the school breaks up and return home on Sunday night.'

'That's fine with me although I'll try to persuade you to stay a few days more once you're here,' Beth laughed, before filling Molly in on the news since their last phone conversation.

* * *

Molly smiled at Nan, a staff member at Hollytrees. 'Is Dad in the common room?'

'I tried to coax him to go there but he wasn't for it,' Nan smiled and shrugged.

'I know how difficult it is to get Dad to socialise.'

'We just keep trying,' Nan said, and returned to the dining room to lay the table for dinner.

Molly made her way along the corridor to her father's room. 'Hi, Dad,' she said brightly, kissing his cheek, but he didn't respond to her greeting. Even though she knew to expect this it still hurt.

Each time she visited Dad, his bones seemed to be sticking out more prominently than on the previous occasion. The staff did their best to get him to eat but sometimes he just refused point blank. His pate was covered in freckles and what was left of his burnished gold hair, a colour Molly had inherited from him, had turned white and formed a band at the back of his neck.

She pulled up a chair beside him. 'I've brought you some shortbread Dad. It's Mum's recipe, the one you always liked. Do you want a piece now or would you rather wait until you get your cup of tea?' He didn't answer but continued to stare into space, snapping his fingers constantly while his feet tapped on the floor. She sighed and tried another tack. 'Do you want to come along to the common room with me for a wee while, Dad? We could sit at the window where it's bright.' He looked at her for a few minutes and muttered 'Jean?' Then the tears started, little rivulets running down the tramlines in his face.

She took out a hankie and wiped his face. 'No, Dad, it's me, Molly. I'm your daughter, Molly. Who's Jean, Dad? Was she at school with you?'

He'd mentioned this name a few times recently. There was no Jean among her family members, alive or dead, nor had Mum ever spoken about anyone with that name. She assumed, therefore, that it was someone from Dad's past. When she'd cleared out Dad's house before he moved to Hollytrees, she'd found a crumpled picture of a young girl at the back of the drawer where her parents kept old photographs. Perhaps the girl in the picture was Jean.

He turned away from her and lapsed into silence once more, staring intently at the pattern on the carpet.

Nan came in pushing the tea trolley. 'A cup of tea, Mrs Bishop?'

'That would be lovely thanks, Nan.'

'Dad keeps asking for someone called Jean,' she told Nan, when the tea had been poured. 'Could it be a member of staff?'

Nan shook her head. 'He hasn't mentioned any Jean to me. He doesn't really talk much about people from his past, in fact he doesn't say much at all. Isn't that right, Adam?' she smiled at the old man, putting his cup down on the table at his side. 'You like to keep your life private, don't you?'

Nan's fondness for Adam was apparent in her tone. Molly really appreciated the staff's input in her dad's care.

She fed him the shortbread with his tea and soon afterwards she slipped out, leaving him still sitting in the same position staring at nothing.

Molly's eyes were moist as she went back to the car and she shook her head as she slipped in behind the wheel. Poor Dad, she thought, his condition's deteriorating daily in front of me and there is absolutely nothing I can do to stop it. Finding out who Jean was might be the trigger to get Dad talking again.

Back at home, Molly brought out the pile of old photographs that had come from Dad's house but instead of looking through them she poured a large glass of Merlot and settled down in front of the TV set.

Wednesday nights were usually quite good. She flicked through the channels but decided there was nothing worth watching after all and picked up her book instead, the latest offering by her favourite crime novelist. She read the first three paragraphs and then closed the book and let her mind drift back to her relationship with Ted.

At least under the terms of the divorce she'd still have this house. She would be glad to be permanently free of Ted and his affairs although she was finding it hard to adjust to her solo existence.

Living alone was strange after being part of a family for so many years. But Luke continued to pop in from time to time and of course she had her work and her friends.

She began to yawn and decided to turn in for the night.

Chapter Thirty-Three

Weary from the long journey and the changeover at Heathrow, Vina finally touched down in Glasgow around 8 o'clock on Thursday morning. When she saw all the dark green cases swirling around the carousel, she was grateful for the miniature koala bear tied to her luggage.

She took the shuttle bus into the Buchanan Bus Station in the city centre. Putting her case in the left luggage there, she asked directions to the Information Bureau. The office was only a short walking distance away in George Square. The large square housed a cenotaph and many impressive looking statues and was surrounded by magnificent buildings. She guessed most of the buildings were banks or perhaps Council offices, and all were of superb architecture.

Coming from a small town like Penguin, Vina was struck first by the vastness of this great city and then by the number of pedestrians around her. She didn't remember ever seeing so many people milling about even in the Tasmanian summer when tourists flocked to Penguin for the beaches. The people all seemed friendly and many smiled or nodded to her as they passed by, making her feel at home.

'I was looking for accommodation in Muirbank,' she said to the assistant in the Information Bureau. Mum had once told her that their family home had been in Pond Road, Muirbank, so that seemed the best place from which to start her search.

'I'll just check for you,' the girl smiled brightly and entered some details into her computer. 'This is all we have for Muirbank,' she said, handing Vina a two-page list that had come through her printer. 'I've heard good reports of this guest house,' she said, putting a cross in the margin beside one address.

'Is Glenburgh close to Muirbank?'

'Muirbank is on the south side of the city and Glenburgh is more south-east. Muirbank's about a twenty-minute journey by train or bus from here.'

The assistant consulted a list she had on the desk. 'A No 16 bus will take you, or you could catch a train from Glasgow Central Station. Do you want me to book you a room at the guesthouse I've indicated?'

'No thanks, I'll make my way over to Muirbank and take a look at it first. But thanks for all your help?'

'No trouble,' the girl smiled and turned her attention to the next person in the queue.

Leaving the Bureau, Vina crossed over to the centre of the square and looked at some of the statues. She stopped to read the inscription on one, James Watt, inventor of the steam engine. A seagull perched on top of the great man's head with bird droppings down his front. Many famous Scots featured, including Robert Burns, the Scottish poet, whose work 'Tam o' Shanter' she'd read at school in New Zealand.

Vina had only a fifteen-minute wait before boarding a No 16 bus for Muirbank. A guesthouse at 9 Harwood Drive was the one marked by the girl in the Tourist Office and she noticed on the map that Harwood Drive ran off Pond Road. The bus driver called to her when they reached the stop nearest to Pond Road.

A watery sun had appeared and chased away the grey clouds. She stopped outside No 17 Pond Road, which had once been her home although she had no recollection of living there. No 9 Harwood Drive was a large sandstone villa with a freshly cut lawn bordered by thriving rose bushes. The flowers on one bush looked like velvet and she ran her finger over its surface. Her feet made a crunching sound as she walked up the red chipped path.

She smiled at the woman who opened the door. 'Hello, I was given your address by the Tourist Office and wondered if you had a room to let.'

'There's only one room vacant. I can let you see it,' the woman said, moving back to allow Vina into the entrance hall. The carpet was thick and springy, in the same colour and pattern as her home in Tasmania, making her feel less of a stranger. Ahead of her on the stairwell was a floor to ceiling window, with the most magnificent stained glass patterns that Vina had ever seen in a house.

The landlady led the way up a sturdy wooden staircase to a bedroom overlooking the large garden to the rear of the property. 'It's quite a small room but being at the back you don't have the noise from the traffic that you get in the front rooms, and its en suite. I'm Mrs Heron by the way.'

'Vina West,' she held out her hand. 'It's a lovely room, Mrs Heron, and just what I need. What are your charges?'

'£40 a night for dinner, bed and breakfast, but cheaper by the week.'

'Could I book for a week and perhaps I might want to stay longer once my plans are more definite?'

'That's fine. Breakfast is served between 7 and 9 o'clock in the dining room downstairs and dinner is at 6.30 prompt. Will you come down and sign the register?'

'How many boarders do you have?' Vina asked as they went downstairs.

'I use the four upstairs bedrooms and I sleep downstairs.' Mrs Heron handed Vina a pen and she used her credit card to pay for the first week's accommodation. Mrs Heron gave her the door key. 'I don't have strict rules about when guests come home, but I expect them to keep the noise down late at night.'

Vina unpacked and sent a text to Sue. Feeling hungry, she retraced her steps to 'The Coffee Pot' that she'd noticed when she got off the bus in Pond Road.

'Are you on holiday?' the pretty young waitress asked when she brought Vina's order over to the table.

'Not exactly, sort of. I'm living in a guesthouse nearby.'

'We'll probably see quite a lot of you then,' the waitress smiled. 'Enjoy.'

After a sleep, Vina showered and put on her cream tailored slacks and a crisp, cotton blouse. She had a short walk around the area before dinner. Back at the digs she met a grey haired woman, dressed in a smart navy suit, coming downstairs. The woman smiled at Vina, a lovely open smile. Her eyes were an unusual shade, almost violet. 'Hello, you must be the new boarder. I'm Helen Barclay.'

'Vina West, lovely to meet you.'

'Where are you from?' Helen asked, opening the dining room door for Vina. 'Sorry, I always ask too many questions.'

Vina laughed. 'I don't mind, I'm Australian. What about you?'

'Orkney, but I work with the Bank of Scotland and was transferred to Glasgow last year. Mrs Heron is a far out relation of mine, hence my living here.' Helen followed Vina into the dining room, which looked over the side garden of the house. Decorated with heavily embossed paper, the wall lights with their fringed shades mounted on a wooden plinth suited the age and style of the house. The table was set for four and a young girl was already seated there. 'This is Vina,' Helen told her. 'Vina, Jenni Taylor, Jenni's from Yorkshire,' she completed the introductions.

'I'm at Caledonian University,' Jenni started to tell Vina but broke off when another woman came in. 'Hi, Gwen, how are you?'

'Exhausted,' Gwen replied, sitting down. 'Our sale started this morning and the store was buzzing. Hi,' she looked over at Vina, 'I'm Gwen Hughes. Welcome to our little band.'

'Thanks, the name's Vina West. I'm booked in for a week.'

'You'll be well looked after by Monica,' Gwen told her. 'I'm telling Vina what a treasure you are,' she said when Mrs Heron appeared with the soup.

The landlady laughed. 'Flattery gets you everywhere,' she said and went back into the kitchen.

'Which store do you work in, Gwen?' Vina asked.

'I'm a buyer with the House of Eden in Buchanan Street.'

Jenni piped up. 'A very expensive department store. Not suited to the budget of an impoverished student.'

Their meal over, they moved into the sitting room for

coffee, and soon afterwards gradually drifted up to their own rooms.

* * *

Vina was wakened just after 7 a.m. by the sound of running water in the room next door. Shortly afterwards the floorboards creaked when someone went downstairs. She wasn't sure who occupied which room but guessed they would all have an early start for work and college.

Deciding it would be a convenient time for Andy, she sent him a text.

'Hi Andy, in Glasgow. Luvly guesthouse, very comfortable. No Sue will have 4warded my earlier txts 2 u. From now on will send same txt 2 u both. Lots of luv, Vina. xx

After a leisurely shower, she dressed and ventured downstairs. The dining room was empty, the other boarders gone. Mrs Heron was clearing away the used crockery. 'Good morning,' she greeted Vina. 'I hope you slept well.'

'I think I was asleep before my head hit the pillow. And the bed was so comfy that I didn't want to get out of it.'

'Travelling takes it out of you. I usually suffer jet lag when I go on a long haul flight. Now, would you like a cooked breakfast?'

'No thanks, Mrs Heron. Cereal and toast will do me fine.'

'The name's Monica,' the landlady smiled. She piled the used dishes on to her tray and disappeared through the swing door into the kitchen again.

Back in her room after breakfast, Vina dialled the number of Find Your Family. The first few times she tried, the line was engaged but eventually, when she was just about to give up, it rang. After a few rings, a pleasant voice answered. 'Find Your Family, Sheila speaking, how may I help you?'

'Could you put me through to your After Adoption Service, please?'

'This is the After Adoption Service.'

Vina hesitated a moment and took a deep breath. 'My name's Davina West and I hope you can help me. I'm over here from Australia and I'd like to meet with one of your counsellors.' She kept her voice low in case Monica was in the vicinity. Best to keep her business to herself meantime.

'Are you wanting to do a trace?'

'Yes, I was adopted as a baby and want to find my biological parents.'

'One moment please.' Some music played softly as Vina waited. She recognised the tune but couldn't bring the name to mind. After a fairly long silence, Sheila came back on the line. 'Hello, our counsellor, Frances Gellatly, has had a cancellation for Monday 1st October at two o'clock. Would that be suitable?'

'That's great, thank you.'

'Do you know where we are?'

'Not really. I will be coming by train from Glasgow.'

'Good, we're near Waverley Station. Do you have a pen handy?' When Vina said she had, Sheila continued. 'Come out of the side entrance of the station, turn right and then left on to the main road. Walk past the gardens on your left-hand side, cross over to Grange Road, with Forsyth's department store on the corner.'

'Forsyth's department store,' Vina repeated, jotting down the instructions with her free hand.

'If you go up Grange Road you will see our building on the right near the top of the hill, next door to a pizza parlour. We have a buzzer outside the door.'

'Thanks very much,' Vina said and disconnected the call.

She let out a whoop of joy. She couldn't believe her luck in getting an appointment just three days away. And in the meantime she could do the tourist bit in Glasgow.

Chapter Thirty-Four

On Sunday, following the directions she'd been given, Vina got off the bus in the city centre at the corner of Glassford and Argyle Streets, with a large Marks & Spencer store on the corner. She made her way along Argyle Street, a pedestrian precinct and busy even at this early hour of a Sunday morning. She passed some more department stores and turned left towards St Enoch Underground Station.

Feeling like an excited schoolgirl, Vina stepped on to the underground train, the first time she'd travelled by such a mode of transport. There were only another two people in the compartment she chose. She sat down near the door and followed their route on the map pasted up above the window facing her.

She loved the whoosh of the train as it snaked through the dark underground tunnels and the dank, warm smell that invaded the compartment each time the electronic doors opened when they stopped in a station.

Alighting at Kelvin Hall Underground Station, Vina followed the signs for the Art Gallery and emerged on to Dumbarton Road. She walked past a row of shops and cafès and crossed the road at the traffic lights in Byres Road. Just past the entrance to the Western Infirmary she came to the Kelvin Bridge. She looked down at the River Kelvin which coursed its way from the slope above into a waterfall, before running under the bridge she was standing on.

She raised her eyes to the University of Glasgow, a magnificent edifice high on the hill above the river, its towers pointing heavenwards. Focussing her digital camera on the building, she wondered how many inventors, teachers and healers had been trained and nurtured within its walls.

She moved on and climbed the stairs up to the Art Gallery. She sat down on a bench in front of the red-sandstone building and opened the tourist leaflet she'd picked up in the Information Bureau. According to the leaflet, the Gallery had been built in the Spanish Baroque style. She moved round to the back of the building with its impressive view over Kelvingrove Park and the River Kelvin. This entrance was the main one so, in essence, the building seemed to have been designed back to front.

Yesterday she'd done the city open-topped bus tour, stopping off at a couple of places of interest. She'd been taken on a conducted tour of the Glasgow City Chambers, a really impressive building with a lot of history. Later in the day she'd visited the Glasgow Science Centre, a more modern, glassed structure which also warranted a viewing.

Once inside the art gallery her heels made a clicking sound as she crossed the black and white checkerboard floor. Turning round, she looked back towards the magnificent organ loft but a passing member of staff told her she was here at the wrong time of day to listen to them playing. She made a mental note to come back at the correct time another day.

She made her way towards the massive stone staircase leading up to the floor above. Halfway up the staircase, she turned to take a photograph. She collided with a grey-haired man on his way down the stairs and the book fell out of her hand. Loose sheets of paper flew out and were scattered over the stairway.

The man sprinted down a few steps to gather up the scraps of paper. 'I'm so sorry,' he apologised, 'I should have been watching where I was going.'

'No worries. Some directions on how to get here, of no importance really.'

Forgetting he had been going downstairs the man, who was head and shoulders taller than Vina, turned and accompanied her up to the first floor.

They fell into step. 'Are you a visitor to the city?' and without waiting for an answer, he added, 'I recognise an Aussie accent when I hear one.'

'You're right,' she smiled, 'I'm Tasmanian. Have you been in Australia?'

'I spent a year in Melbourne back in the seventies,' he said, leaning against a stone pillar when they finally came to a halt. 'I'm Philip Dawson by the way.'

'Vina West.' She shook the hand he extended. Clean-shaven, with velvety brown eyes and a kind face, Philip was casually dressed in denims and t-shirt.

'Nice to meet you, Vina. Have you had a look at the paintings already?'

'Not yet.'

'Then perhaps I could show you around.'

He pointed to a section of wall above an archway, leading into one of the viewing areas, where Salvador Dali's painting of 'Christ of Saint John of the Cross' hung. 'This painting was kept in St Mungo's Museum near the Cathedral while renovations were being carried out here,' he explained, 'but it's lovely to see it back where it belongs.'

Philip proved to be a most interesting companion and a mine of information on the collections of armour and natural history exhibits. 'Hope I haven't bored you,' he said. 'I do go on a bit I know.'

'On the contrary,' she shook her head, 'it's been wonderful to have such a knowledgeable guide. My own personal tour,' she smiled.

Philip looked at his watch. 'What about a cup of tea? There's a teashop further along Dumbarton Road from here and I think it should still be open.'

They were shown to a table in 'The Rowan Tree'. Vina admired the single rose vase sitting on top of the starched white teacloth, while a waitress took their order. 'So what line of work are you in?' Philip asked Vina.

'I was a secretary all my working life until I retired at 60. Latterly I worked in Devonport Hospital, along the coast a bit from where I live.'

'Ah, so you arranged your trip over here to coincide with your retirement, good idea.'

Vina laughed and shook her head. 'You must be joking, I've been retired almost eight years now.'

His jaw dropped. 'Good God, you can't be that age. I'm 66 and I thought you were years younger than me.'

'I'll take that as a compliment then.'

His face reddened. 'Sorry, I didn't mean to be so personal.'

'No offence taken.' Vina recalled a similar conversation with Kevin when she first met him. 'My mother was still alive when I retired and she depended on me to offer help when needed. She died last year, hence me travelling now.'

Vina stopped speaking as the waitress brought their tea and laid a cake stand on the table, cakes on the top and scones and fruit bread on the bottom.

Lifting the lid, Vina peeked into the teapot. 'Good, it's real tea, a lovely change from the usual teabags.' She poured the tea into their china cups, using the little strainer that was provided.

'Thanks,' she said, taking the milk jug from Philip.

'So do you have relatives over here that you're staying with?'

Vina lifted a pineapple tart off the plate and cut it in half. 'No relatives that I know of – yet,' she said, biting through the icing and cream down to the pastry base.

He said nothing but his eyebrows arched, waiting.

'I was born in Scotland but was adopted when I was a year old.'

He didn't reply but gave her his full attention.

'I went with my adoptive parents and younger siblings to Tasmania when I was 4.' She swallowed her last piece of cake and wiped her fingers with her serviette. 'I've lived in Australia ever since but now that Mum and Dad are both dead I've come over to try and track down my biological parents.'

'Gosh, that's a brave move, coming all this way on your own. How far have you got in your search?'

'I haven't really started yet. I only arrived in Glasgow a few days ago but I'm due to meet with a counsellor at an adoption agency in Edinburgh tomorrow afternoon to see if she can help me with my search.'

'That's great. Sorry I've been asking so many personal questions. Hope you don't find me intrusive.'

'No problem, it's good to talk to someone. But

enough about me, tell me about yourself.'

'Not a lot to tell really. I'm a lawyer and I work in the city centre. Thought about retiring last year but decided to carry on a bit longer. I enjoy my work and as I live alone I was concerned I might be bored if I had too much time on my hands. My hobby is rugby, but that's mainly at the weekend. My club is in the west-end of Glasgow, near where I live. My playing days are long since over, of course, but I help to train the junior team in my spare time.'

'Doesn't sound like you'll have too much of that. Have you always lived in Glasgow?'

'Yes, I've led a pretty boring life really. Mainly socialise with rugby friends or colleagues.'

'Never been married?'

'No, I was engaged when I was in my twenties but it didn't work out.' He stopped speaking and looked down at his plate, playing with his spoon for a moment.

'Truth is, she was unfaithful and I caught her with another guy .... someone I'd thought was my friend.'

Vina made some sympathetic noises but didn't try to say anything.

'I guess since then I've never trusted any woman. I've had dates but nothing serious.'

'Can't say I'm surprised, considering the circumstances.'

'More tea?' he asked, lifting the teapot and pouring it when she nodded. 'Have you ever been married?'

'Yes I was but we were divorced many years ago. No fuss, it was mutual and we both knew we were better off on our own. There were no children to be hurt by our split. I've no regrets, it was the right decision.'

Vina found Philip very easy to talk to and an hour slipped by without her noticing it. 'I suppose we better make a move,' she said eventually, 'it looks like they're getting ready to close.'

Philip signalled to the waitress for the bill. 'If you give me your phone number, we could meet again soon,' he suggested, 'I'd like to hear how you get on at the adoption agency.'

'That would be nice,' she rummaged in her bag for a pen. 'I'll give you the phone number at the guesthouse and also my mobile number,' and, tearing a sheet out of her diary, she wrote down both numbers.

'Can I drop you somewhere? My car's parked nearby.'

'Thanks very much but I'll be fine. I came by underground but have discovered I can get a bus to Muirbank just outside the gallery.'

'Well at least let me see you to the bus stop.' He insisted on waiting with her until the bus arrived. Once on board, she paid her fare and took a window seat.

From here she could see Philip at the kerbside. He smiled to her and waved as the driver pulled away from the stop.

Chapter Thirty-Five

October 2012

On Monday morning, 5 pm in Tasmania, Sue phoned to wish Vina luck for her appointment in Edinburgh. 'Let me know as soon as you hear anything.'

'I won't get any information this time, this is simply a preliminary appointment to meet the counsellor.' She'd butterflies in her stomach even speaking about her meeting with Frances Gellatly.

The previous evening she'd told Helen Barclay about her plan to spend a day in the capital, without divulging the purpose of her visit.

Vina followed the directions from Waverley Station. It was an old building and she climbed the well-worn treads to the Find Your Family office on the first floor. The office had recently been given a coat of paint and lots of light came in through the large windows. She gave her name to the receptionist. 'Please take a seat,' the girl smiled, 'Frances will be with you shortly.' The receptionist's name badge said Sheila, the name Vina remembered from her phone call last week.

A young man was seated in the waiting room reading a newspaper; Vina nodded to him and picked up a gardening magazine, leafing through it without actually reading anything. She looked up when footsteps approached.

A slim, middle-aged lady in a cinnamon coloured trouser suit smiled at her. The woman's white hair was cut in a neat bob. 'Davina,' she beckoned and held out her hand to Vina. 'I'm Frances Gellatly. If you come through to my office, we can talk. Would you like a tea or a coffee?' she asked, as they were passing the reception desk.

'Coffee, please.'

'Thanks, Sheila,' Frances nodded to the girl behind

the desk, who got up immediately, obviously used to producing refreshment for the clients.

Frances ushered Vina into a large, bright room, with striped paper on the walls and a view of the castle from the window. The net curtains were blowing slightly in the breeze coming through the open window. Frances sat at the desk, her back to the window, with Vina in a bucket chair facing her. There was a red geranium plant on one side of the desk and a framed photograph on the other.

Frances stuck to pleasantries about the weather and Vina's journey by train until Sheila brought in the coffee tray. Only after Sheila left and Frances had poured the coffee did she discuss the reason for Vina's visit. 'First of all Davina, let me assure you that anything we talk about today is entirely confidential and its content will only be known by you and me. I understand you are trying to trace your biological parents.'

Vina nodded. 'I was born in Glenburgh, near Glasgow, on 24th November 1944 and adopted when I was a year old.'

'Do you have your birth certificate?' Frances asked gently.

'Yes, I've brought my birth certificate, the one in the name of Davina West. Davina was the name my adoptive parents, Helen and John West, gave me.' She felt a twinge of guilt but dismissed it immediately, aware that her parents would be happy for her to look into her origins.

'I also have a document I found when clearing out my adoptive mother's house after her death. It gives my original name as Nancy Morrow,' she said, pulling the papers out of a tattered brown envelope. Then she slid her small green Australian passport across the desk to Frances.

Frances scanned the details on the birth certificate before picking up the other document. 'The names of your adoptive parents are sufficient for me to begin my search but before I do so I would ask you to read this advice sheet which includes our 'Self Search Guide'. And this leaflet gives our list of service fees.'

Vina put on her reading glasses but before she began to read the literature Frances spoke again.

'It's our policy not to divulge any information we find with our service users by telephone, we only do that by meeting here or by post. We do, however, phone our service users for a general chat about their search. Are you happy for me to photocopy your birth certificate, adoption document and the back page of your passport?'

Vina nodded.

'Right, I'll leave you to your reading while I go and copy them.'

Once Vina had digested the contents of the leaflets and her documents had been returned to her, Frances sat back, clasping her hands together.

'By law, Davina, your biological parents can't trace you, only you can do a search for them. I will check the records for 1945 and get back to you. I will contact you as soon as I have any information and then you can decide if you definitely want to proceed.'

'I've waited for years and I can't rest now until I've discovered my origins,' Vina sniffed, looking at Frances through a screen of tears. She hoped that she wasn't going to disgrace herself by crying and pulled a tissue out of the box that Frances slid discreetly across the desk to her.

'Do you know how long it will take to find my parents? You see, I'm over here on a holiday and can't stay indefinitely.'

'It depends what course their lives have taken, if they've remained in U.K.?'

Frances hesitated a second. 'If they are still alive?'

'I hope so, I'm desperate to find them.'

'If we do trace them, you may want some counselling Davina, as it's such an emotional road to take. Once you go through the door, it's difficult to turn back.' Her voice dropped a little. 'There's also the possibility that one or both of them might not want to meet you.'

By this time Vina's tears flowed freely and she let them, aware that Frances fully understood how emotional the situation was for her.

'No pressure will be put on you to continue with your search if at any time you find it too stressful. The decisions are always yours to take or reject.'

'I'm glad I've started the search, I'm excited and scared at the same time if that makes sense.'

Frances smiled again. 'Perfect sense, many of our service users feel that way. Any questions? Please feel free to ask me, I am here to help in any way I can.'

'I don't have any other questions right now but probably I'll think of lots once I'm on the train back to Glasgow.'

'Should that happen, Davina, you can telephone me at any time during our search. This is my direct line,' Frances said, handing over her business card.

'Thank you and by the way I'm known as Vina.'

Frances jotted that down on her pad before showing Vina out.

Vina felt light-headed after her meeting with Frances. It struck her then that she had played with her food at breakfast time, unable to eat due to the churning in her stomach, and hadn't ordered any lunch on the train.

She recalled Helen Barclay had recommended the restaurant in Forsyth's department store as a good place to eat.

The lunches were over by the time she got there but the waitress served her with a fruit scone and a pot of tea.

She was drinking her second cup of tea when her mobile rang.

'Hi, Vina, it's Philip Dawson, I was wondering how you got on at the adoption agency this afternoon?'

'Philip, how kind of you to take time to phone. I got on very well. Frances Gellatly was most helpful and encouraging. She seems really efficient and is going to look into it and get back to me.'

'I've been thinking of you all day.'

'I was nervous about coming here but now I've broken the ice I think my next visit will be easier. But I really appreciate your kindness in ringing.'

'I did want to hear how you got on but I also have an ulterior motive for ringing. One of my colleagues has given me two tickets he can't use for the Concert Hall tomorrow night. It's the Scottish Symphony Orchestra who are performing and since you told me you like classical music, I wondered if you would come with me?'

'That would be lovely, thank you. Don't think I've come across the Concert Hall yet, where is it?'

'Not far from here. If you could come to my office about five o'clock, we could eat before the concert.'

'Where is your office?'

'I work with Bates, Williams & Petrie and we're at 182 St Vincent Street.' He gave her directions from the bus station.

'I'll be there,' she agreed and smiled happily as she switched off her mobile phone. Her day was improving by the minute.

Chapter Thirty-Six

That evening Helen and Vina had the dining room to themselves as Gwen was on a night out with her workmates and Jenni had gone home for a few days.

'So how was your day in Edinburgh?' Helen asked during their meal.

'I enjoyed it very much. Such a beautiful city, isn't it? By the way, I was going to ask your advice,' Vina continued, changing the subject before Helen asked her any awkward questions. 'I'm going to the Concert Hall tomorrow night and wondered how formally I need to dress?'

'The Concert Hall, how lovely. You don't need to dress up, I'd say neat but casual would be fine. What's on?'

'It's a concert by the Scottish Symphony Orchestra. A friend has invited me, he has two tickets.'

'Do you mean the man you met at the Art Gallery yesterday?' Helen asked excitedly and, seeing Vina nod, her eyes twinkled. 'He's a fast worker. Only joking,' she laughed, 'do you have an outfit in mind?'

'I don't have a lot of formal clothes with me while I'm travelling so it would have to be a skirt and jumper. If you come up to my room, I'll let you see it?'

Upstairs, she laid her pale lilac jumper, short sleeved and v-necked, on the bed and held up a black straight skirt with a kick pleat at the back. 'What do you think?'

'It's perfectly suitable. All you need is to dress it up a bit. Let me see if I have anything I could lend you.' Helen returned a few minutes later and handed Vina a purple-stone pendant on a silver chain and a silk scarf in a floral design of pink and lilac shades.

Vina chose the scarf. 'This will be ideal,' she said, draping it round her neck to model it. 'Thanks so much, Helen.'

'You're welcome. Now I must go as I need to do some

ironing before bed. Have a super time tomorrow night and I'll hear about it later.'

* * *

Vina took care dressing the following afternoon. She dabbed some perfume behind her ears and splashed it on the inside of her wrists. She'd bought it at the airport on her way over; called 'Suddenly', it reminded her of the Chanel No 5 she used to wear.

Once in town, she found her way to Philip's office easily. 'Sorry for the wait, Vina,' Philip apologised as he came into the reception area, pulling on his jacket. 'My last client took longer than I'd anticipated.'

'Your secretary gave me a magazine and made me a cup of coffee while I waited,' she smiled, pleased to see he was dressed in a casual daytime suit.

'Hope you like Italian food? I've booked a table at a restaurant near the Concert Hall,' he said as they headed out.

They had a leisurely meal, with no awkward silences, and they got through a bottle of Merlot between them. Since Philip was driving later, she noticed he topped her glass up more often than his own.

Afterwards they met up with Philip's friends in the foyer. The two wives, Carol and Marilyn, made Vina most welcome in their company and the three women chatted in the bar at the interval until the men brought over their drinks.

She liked Carol's husband, David, but found Robin too domineering, his brusque manner almost verging on rudeness. 'Glad to see old Phil socialising again,' he said to her, 'he's immersed himself for far too long in his stuffy books.'

Seeing Philip blush, Vina decided not to reply and instead asked Marilyn a question about the Conductor.

Philip ran Vina back to Muirbank after the performance. 'I won't be able to see you for about the next ten days,' he told her when they arrived at the guesthouse. 'I'm going to be in Court for the rest of this week and next week I'll be attending the Conservative Party conference in Blackpool but I'll ring you when I get back.' Getting out of his black two-seater Volvo to open the door for her, he kissed her fleetingly when she stood beside him. He waited as she hurried up the path, the crunching of her feet on the chips magnified in the quietness.

Chapter Thirty-Seven

Molly viewed the glorious autumn colours through the train window and her spirits soared. Autumn was her favourite season and she feasted her eyes on the array of yellow, green, red and brown laid out like a mosaic in front of her.

Her friendship with Beth Cairns, as she was prior to her marriage, went back a long way. Best friends at school in Dundee, they both completed their Degree at Glasgow University. Afterwards Beth stayed in Glasgow and married Greg while Molly returned to her native Dundee and took up a post in the English Department at Harris Academy. She left when Luke was born but returned once he was at school.

As the train sped on, its wheels clickety-clacking along the track, Molly thought back over her married life. During the twenty-six years she and Ted had been together, they'd been living apart in the same house for almost half of that time and had play acted their way through their Silver Wedding eighteen months ago. She'd only stayed under the same roof as Ted for her son's sake but now that Luke had moved out of the family house, their sham marriage was unnecessary. She looked forward to the day her Decree Nisi came through.

Her thoughts moved on to Beth and Greg. There was no chance of Greg Urquhart cheating on his wife. Molly was ashamed of her previous feelings that he was dull and boring on being introduced to him for the first time. Greg had proved to be a caring and supportive husband to Beth, the very opposite of how her flamboyant, exciting Ted had turned out. Beth had retired early from teaching when Greg was promoted to Police Superintendent. With no children to provide for there was no need for her to continue in full-time employment.

It was typical of Beth's caring nature that since then she'd devoted her free time to unpaid charity work.

Looking at her watch, Molly saw that the train was due to arrive in Glasgow shortly. She got her case down from the luggage rack and put on her coat.

* * *

'The train should be here any minute now,' Greg said to Beth, as they stood outside Platform 4 at Queen Street railway station.

He had scarcely uttered the words when the Dundee train came into sight. Before it came to a halt, Beth shot off, past the two ticket collectors at the entrance, and raced up the platform. She opened her arms when Molly stepped down from the train and the two women went into a tight embrace.

Greg watched them with a smile. He knew how much Beth valued her friendship with Molly and how sad she'd been to hear about the split with Ted. Greg had never liked Ted Bishop, finding him arrogant and condescending, but for the sake of both Beth and Molly, he had remained polite in Ted's company.

Molly showed her ticket as the two women came through the barrier and walked towards him, arm in arm. 'Hello, Molly, you look well,' Greg said, taking her case.

'Older and fatter than last time we met, but otherwise the same,' she smiled, and he kissed her on the cheek. 'Retirement's agreeing with you Greg,' she added, noting how relaxed he looked since giving up his work with Strathclyde Police two months ago.

'Yes, definitely to be recommended. Now, let's get back to the car. They've closed the short-stay car park in the station so we had to park in the multi-storey round the corner.'

From the moment Greg turned the key in the ignition, the two women chatted non-stop on the journey to the Urquhart's house in Highfield. When Beth and Greg first went to live there in the early days of their marriage, it was only a village but since then Highfield had grown into a thriving town, with good local shopping and leisure amenities.

The conversation was still in full flow when Greg drove up the driveway of No 2 Laburnum Wynd and switched off the engine. Beth ushered her friend in the side door, leaving Greg to bring in the luggage. 'Tea or coffee before unpacking?'

'Tea would be great thanks. I've stopped drinking so much coffee, seem to have gone off it. You'll remember I used to drink gallons of the stuff.'

'I take it you're talking about brandy,' Greg teased her, on his way to the spare bedroom with her case.

Molly gave him a playful shove as he walked past. 'Haven't had a drop for at least four days. Mind you,' she winked at Beth, 'I'm not saying I'll refuse it when I'm on a weekend break.'

Beth carried a tray with three coffee mugs into the sitting room. 'I've brought one for Greg but he might want to go into his workshop.'

'Is he still as interested in his carvings?'

'I'd say even more so since he retired. He's currently working on a garden bench. Making quite a good job of it too.'

'He should go into business.'

'He's sold quite a few things but he doesn't really want to do it in a professional way, prefers to keep it as a hobby.'

'And how is Luke doing?' Beth was asking when Greg came in. Her voice held the usual wistful note, thinking of the children she and Greg had been denied.

'Sorry to interrupt, ladies, but I'll take my coffee and leave you to your catch up session.' Greg was smiling as he lifted his mug, sure that they'd soon be back in primary school together, if they weren't there already.

* * *

Molly smiled at Beth across the table in the café at the House of Eden the following afternoon. 'Like the old days, though we couldn't afford this place as students.'

'I liked some of the cafés we frequented in the West End, the ones off Byres Road. Two fruit scones with jam and cream and two lattés please,' Beth said to the waitress who came to take their order.

Molly leant back in her chair with her clasped hands resting on the table. 'The shops here are so much better than what we have in Dundee. I heard that the House of Eden was opening there soon, but I don't know if there's any truth in it.'

'It is a bit pricey but fine if you watch out for their sales. I've picked up quite a few bargains in here.'

'I might get some myself while I'm here.'

Beth smiled at her friend. 'It's good to see you looking more relaxed Molly, you were pretty tense when you first arrived.' She sat back as their coffee arrived.

Half an hour later Beth pushed back her chair and scrunched up her paper serviette. 'That was heavenly. Now what about a wander round the Princes Square Mall before we head back for the 4 o'clock train?'

* * *

'Would you like to come with me to my friend's art exhibition this afternoon?' Beth asked Molly the following day when the two women were enjoying a late breakfast.

Greg, a regular Sunday morning golfer, had eaten early and would already be halfway round the course by this time.

'Didn't know you were acquainted with any artists.'

'My friend Fiona is a member of an art group in Highfield and they are exhibiting their work at Chatelherault this weekend.'

'Is it near here?'

'It's only a short bus journey away and we can have a snack and a glass of wine – or two – in the café there. We could probably sit outside on such a lovely day.'

'Sounds really civilised.'

'Yep, I think you'd like it there. It was built as a hunting lodge for James, 5th Duke of Hamilton. But back to the paintings. I bought one of Fiona's paintings last year; a picture of a pohutokawa, a gorgeous New Zealand flowering bush. It's hanging in the study if you want a look at it.'

'I'll see it before we go out. What about Greg?'

'He'll be fine. I'll text him where we've gone and I'll leave out something he can pop into the microwave when he gets home. If we leave your luggage in the hallway, he'll come and collect us from the exhibition and run us to the station for your train home. You're sure I can't persuade you to stay another couple of days?'

'No Beth, I've really enjoyed my time with you both but I've loads of chores I need to do before I go back to work.'

'Okay, but we must arrange to meet again soon for lunch, either in Glasgow or Dundee. Do you want the first shower?'

'Thanks.' Molly pushed back her chair and got to her feet. 'I'll call you when the bathroom is free.'

* * *

After Sunday breakfast, Vina was showering when her mobile rang. She raced out, wrapped in her bathrobe, and grabbed the phone. 'Hello,' she said breathlessly.

'Did I phone at an awkward time? Do you want me to phone back later?'

Vina had missed Philip greatly since the night at the Concert Hall and was delighted to hear his voice again. 'No, I was going to ring you today anyway to hear how you got on at the conference and to let you know how my search was going.'

'I'm keen to hear how far you've got. When I got back last night, there was a note from a friend of mine inviting me to attend his art exhibition at Chatelherault. If you're free this afternoon, I wondered if you'd like to come with me.'

'I told Helen that I would go to the cinema with her this evening but as long as I'm back at the guest house by five o'clock that would be fine.'

It was a pity the two outings had clashed but Helen had been a good friend to Vina during her stay and she wasn't going to let her down at the last minute.

'No problem, Chatelherault is on the M74, dual carriageway. I'll make sure you're back in time for Helen.'

'So what about Frances Gellatly?' Philip asked when they were on their way to Chatelherault. 'Has she uncovered any new information?'

'I was in Edinburgh a few days ago and Frances gave me a copy of her findings so far. My original birth certificate doesn't name my father so it may be impossible to track him down. Jean worked as a grocery assistant in Glenburgh. She married a Frank Morrow but there's no record of a divorce so I don't know whether he's my father or not. It looks more and more like I was illegitimate.'

Hearing the sadness in her voice, Philip glanced round at her for a second before turning back to the road ahead. 'You know, Vina, I think your story must have been fairly common in wartime. Maybe they married later. Don't forget there was a war on at the time so perhaps Jean was waiting for him to return and then they planned to marry.'

'That didn't happen because Frances has discovered that Jean died a few weeks after the war. She has requested a copy of the death certificate.'

'Have you been to Glenburgh?' he asked softly.

'Not yet, haven't had the courage so far but I hope to go there tomorrow.'

Her sadness cut through Philip and he laid a hand on her knee, still looking straight ahead. 'Would you like me to come to Glenburgh with you?'

She couldn't help comparing him with Kev. Philip was such a caring and sensitive man, so different from Kev's controlling behaviour. 'But what about work?'

'I've a couple of clients to see first thing in the morning and I'm in court at three o'clock but I could spare a couple of hours in the middle of the day.'

'That's great, thanks. I feel you're part of my search by now.'

She fell silent as Philip drove into the Chatelherault estate and parked the car at the side of the house where it was shaded from the sun.

'Hello there, Phil,' a voice said as they were admiring one of the pictures, 'glad to see you made it.'

Philip turned to the man and smiled. 'Have been looking out for one of your paintings, Josh. This is Vina West,' he said.

The man smiled at Vina and took her hand. 'Josh Begley at your service, ma'am. Phil and I go back a long way.'

He turned back to Philip. 'My offerings are Nos 28 and 52. I think both of them are round the corner in the other section. Are you interested in art, Vina?'

'I don't know as much as you obviously do, nor Philip, but I do like paintings, especially the ones I can understand,' she laughed.

Josh nodded. 'Yeah, some can be a bit obscure but most of the folks in the art group tend to do traditional scenes or still life.'

'Josh, a moment,' another group member called and he excused himself and left them to continue their viewing.

'Will we grab a table outside for a snack and a drink?' Philip suggested, once they'd done a couple of rounds of the exhibition. They were served their wine first, before ordering sandwiches and coffee.

Vina draped her lime green jacket round the back of her seat. 'This is lovely,' she sighed, sipping her glass of Chardonnay.

'Weather as good as home?'

'Almost but not quite. More like one of our better days in winter.'

He laughed. 'I know, your winter days are almost equivalent to a t-shirt and shorts day over here. Still, we just enjoy it when we get it.'

* * *

'The pictures look really professional,' Molly said, as they made their way towards the café. 'I like your friend's painting of the wildflowers. At least I can understand most of these paintings, I hate these modern things.'

Beth nodded. 'Pity Fiona's manning the ticket desk this afternoon or she could have had a coffee with us. Will we try and find a table outside?'

'I don't see any spaces.' Just as Molly finished speaking they noticed a couple at one of the tables collecting up their belongings as though about to move.

'We're just going,' the man said, aware of the two women hovering, ready to pounce when the seat became vacant.

'Oh dear,' Molly laughed, 'did we make it so obvious?'

His companion got up, her greenish/grey eyes sparkling. Her green jacket complimented them and her dark hair was sleek and shiny. 'No worries, we need to go anyway.

I can recommend the latté,' she added.

She got to her feet, pushing the strap of her bag up on to her shoulder. 'And the wine's not bad either,' was her parting shot.

Molly and Beth sat down and Molly watched the couple move away. An attractive pair, she thought, and they looked well suited; he with his handsome looks and strong physique and she couldn't help but admire the woman's terrific figure and the way she carried her clothes. She watched them until they went through the exit to the car park before turning her attention to the menu.

Greg picked them up at Chatelherault. He had Molly's case in the boot and they drove straight to the station to catch Molly's train home.

The train was held up near Perth for an hour and it was almost eight o'clock when it finally drew into Dundee station. By the time she got home, Molly felt really jaded. The phone was ringing as she got in.

'So you're home at last,' Beth said as she lifted the receiver. 'I was sure you'd be back ages ago.'

'I should've been but we were held up. Thanks for everything Beth.'

'Greg and I were delighted to have you and you must come back again soon. I'll make this a quick call, as I know you'll be needing something to eat.'

After she hung up, Molly's thoughts went back to today's art show and the couple from the café. The woman had the sort of face you didn't forget. Were they a married couple or just friends?

Molly had sensed an air of romance between them, like two teenagers in the first flush of love. And yet neither of them could be described as young, probably somewhere in the sixties.

Molly laughed out loud. Here she was deliberating about the relationship of a couple she'd seen for all of two minutes.

I'm turning into a right agony aunt, she thought, as the opening scene of a mystery drama flashed up on to the screen.

* * *

'So how was your date with Philip?' Helen asked Vina, as the two women waited in the queue to buy their cinema tickets that evening.

'We had a lovely time and his friend Josh is an excellent artist.'

'Did you buy anything?'

'No, Philip says he has no more space on the walls at home and I couldn't transport a painting very easily.'

When they reached the head of the queue, Helen handed a twenty-pound note to the girl behind the counter. 'Two tickets for Cinema 8 please.'

'Think this is a weepy, so I hope you've remembered your tissues,' she laughed, once she'd been given the tickets and Vina handed over the money for hers.

'So, what was Philip's conference about?' Helen asked as they were making their way upstairs to Cinema 8.

'It was the Conservative Party conference in Blackpool. Philip's a member of the party and he goes to their conference every October.'

'I vote Lib-Dem myself, but I won't hold his political persuasions against him,' Helen laughed.

'I don't know anything about British politics. I've seen your Prime Minister, David Cameron, on TV. Is he a Lib-Dem?'

'No, he's a Conservative but they formed a coalition with the Lib-Dem party at the last election as they didn't get an outright majority.'

'How's that working?'

Helen shrugged. 'So-so, a lot of differences but I guess time alone will tell.'

Before they went through the door into Cinema 8, she looked at the tickets. 'We're in Row J, should be in the middle somewhere.' They found their seats just as the lights dimmed and the performance started.

Home again, Vina made a cup of coffee in her bedroom and sat thinking back to the art show. As always she'd felt very comfortable with Philip.

She didn't feel sleepy yet so decided to write to Sue. She'd sent a few texts up to now but thought that her siblings would appreciate a letter.

Sunday 14th October 2012

Dear Sue and Andy

I've settled well in Muirbank and have formed quite a close bond with one of the other guests staying here, Helen Barclay. Helen comes from the Orkney Island but was sent to work in Glasgow by her employers, Bank of Scotland. In her mid 50s, Helen is bright and bubbly and has been helpful in directing me around this vast city. It's a shock to find myself in such a large city after spending my life in a small town like Penguin. But the Glasgow people are a friendly bunch and have welcomed me with open arms.

There's been a sad development in my search. I've been twice now to Edinburgh to meet with my contact at Find Your Family. Frances, who is working with me, has discovered that my biological mother, Jean, died when I was only a few months old. I was devastated to hear this; obviously after 67 years I had to keep the possibility of her death in mind. As Jean seems to have been a lone parent, this probably explains why I was put up for adoption.

Frances is now trying to track down my biological father. He's a shadowy figure right now and I'm waiting to hear if he's dead or alive and if the latter is the case then I hope he is still living in the U.K. I pray that he is alive and will want to meet me and hopefully tell me about my mother Jean.

You were asking about Philip Dawson, Sue. He's a lawyer in Glasgow and has been really kind to me, showing me many places of interest in the city. But don't start marrying us off yet Sis, we're just good friends! Philip is taking me to Glenburgh tomorrow and I hope to visit the address where I was born and try and find out more about Jean.

You and Andy have both asked me when I'll come home. I really can't answer that as it depends on how long my search takes. I've waited almost sixty years to come and look for my roots and I need to get some answers. Will text when I have more news.

Love from Vina xx

Chapter Thirty-Eight

Vina arrived at Philip's office half an hour early the following day, thinking that if one of his clients failed to turn up, he might be keen to set off sharp. The October day was chilly and she wore a mohair polo-necked jumper for extra warmth. Its cream colour was a good match for her beige denim trousers and her shoes and bag to complete the outfit were rust-coloured.

Philip's secretary recognised her and once again offered her a coffee while she waited. 'No thanks, I had coffee before I left home,' Vina said, as she took a seat in the waiting room. This wasn't strictly true since she'd breakfasted over two hours ago but too much coffee could have a detrimental effect on her bladder and the last thing she wanted was to waste Philip's precious time in searching out a public loo.

'Hello, Vina, hope you haven't been waiting too long?'

She looked up from the Scottish Field magazine she'd been browsing through to see Philip standing beside her chair.

She put the magazine down on the table at her side and smiled at him. 'I've been quite comfortable here. I thought I'd be early as I know your time is limited.'

'Will we grab something to eat en route?' he suggested.

'Good idea,' she nodded, and let him escort her out through the front door.

* * *

'So this is Glenburgh,' Vina murmured, when Philip was driving along High Street. They were passing what she assumed was the Town Hall, with a large clock on its tower and the Union Jack on the flagpole. Thanks to the time of day, the traffic had been fairly light and Philip had got them here in record time.

'I've got goose pimples at the thought of being in the town where I was born.'

'I can only hazard a guess at what you're feeling right

now. Look, there's a sign for a car park down this street on the left, we can walk back to High Street.' She saw the name Castle Street as they turned left and Philip got a space immediately as another car was moving away.

Back on High Street they walked past the Black Bear pub, an old building that looked as though it had been there forever. The smoke-coloured windows kept the gaze of passers-by off the punters inside trying to enjoy a quiet pint. A strong aroma of beer came up through a large grating outside the front door, probably a short cut down to the cellar where the barrels were kept. A board outside the pub offered a two-course lunch for £4.99.

They found No 14 Queen Street, the address on Vina's birth certificate. An elderly resident remembered a Jean Morrow who'd lived in the tenement during the war. This old man recalled that Jean and her mother had previously lived at 80 High Street. He hinted at some scandal that had occurred at the time but either couldn't exactly remember the details or didn't want to disclose them to Vina.

They thanked him and went to the High Street address. The tenement building looked newer than the one in Queen Street, either that or it had been refurbished and the stonework cleaned up. It was a sturdy looking building, with a baker's shop on the one side of the close and a newsagent's on the other.

Vina's tension was palpable by this time and Philip put his arm around her waist as they entered the green and cream tiled close.

The first resident they spoke to, Mrs Ross, couldn't help them. 'I've only lived here about four years but I think you should ask Mrs Eaglesham on the top floor. She's pretty deaf so you might need to ring her doorbell a few times.'

'You don't think she'll be annoyed at us disturbing her?' Philip queried.

'I'll come with you, she might be happier to speak to strangers if I'm there too.' The woman pulled her door closed and put her key into her cardigan pocket.

Mrs Eaglesham eventually answered her doorbell and

smiled at her downstairs neighbour, but gave Vina and Philip a suspicious look.

'Peggy,' Mrs Ross spoke directly into the old lady's ear, 'this lady is looking for information about a Jean Morrow who lived at No 80 during the war. Have you heard of her?'

The old lady folded her arms and stared at Vina, who played with her fingers, praying that Mrs Eaglesham hadn't lost her memory as well as her hearing.

'Does the name Jean Morrow mean anything to you?' Vina asked, repeating the question when the old lady appeared not to hear.

Peggy heard her second attempt. 'No, I don't think so. The people who were in this house before us were called McQueen. And there was no Morrow at the other flats.'

'Do you know what happened to the McQueens?'

Peggy shook her head.

'Would anyone else in this building perhaps remember Jean Morrow?'

'I don't think so, I'm the longest here.' Peggy saw Vina's crestfallen look. 'But wait a minute, the Blacks who lived across the landing from us when we first moved here knew the McQueens.'

'And do you know where the Blacks live now?' Philip asked.

'I can't remember, it's so long ago. I'm sure Mr and Mrs Black are dead but their daughter, Betty, might know about this Morrow person,' Peggy shrugged.

'You've been a great help,' Vina said, speaking as clearly as she could, 'and at least I have another name to seek out now.'

Back out on the street, Philip looked at his watch. 'Why don't we buy something for lunch in this bakery here? I've got some bottled water in the car and we could maybe find somewhere to sit and eat.'

Vina, preoccupied with what she'd just heard, followed him into the shop.

The ginger-haired baker stood behind the counter in his pristine white coat. 'What can I get you folks?' he greeted them.

'What kind of fillings do you have for your rolls?' Philip enquired.

'Ham, turkey, cheese, tuna,' the baker rhymed off all the many fillings, half of which Philip forgot by the time he got to the end of the list.

'Will ham be alright for you?' he turned to Vina, who nodded.

'One or two? … rolls?' he prompted.

'One's fine,' she said.

'Two ham rolls, please.'

'Not from around here, then?' the baker smiled, as he made up their rolls.

'No. Is there anywhere we could sit to eat, like a park?'

'The park's in Stonefield Road, just round the corner. You could walk there in a few minutes.' The baker put the rolls into a paper bag and handed them to Philip. 'That'll be £2.50 please.'

Philip handed over a £5 note and when the baker returned with his change, Vina suddenly spoke. 'Has this shop been here a long time?'

'Maxwell's has been trading for over a hundred years. My father and grandfather and even my great-grandfather have baked on these premises.'

'I was born in Glenburgh in 1944. I … I was adopted,' she said hesitantly. 'I was brought up in Australia, but I'm trying to find my original family. My mother's name was Jean Morrow and she used to live in this building.'

'A bit before my time but my grandfather might remember her.'

'Is there any way you could find out for me?'

The baker hesitated but saw Vina's desperate look. 'I'm about to close for lunch but why don't the two of you come into the back shop and have your rolls there. I'll put the kettle on and while you're eating I'll give my mother a ring. My grandfather lives with them so she can check if he remembers a Jean Morrow.'

'Are you sure?' Philip said. 'It's very kind of you but we don't want to cause you any inconvenience.'

'It's no trouble,' the baker assured him, locking the front door, before he showed them into the back shop.

'Sit down and make yourselves comfortable,' he said, directing them to a bench seat with some bakers' overalls hanging up behind them. 'I'm Colin Maxwell by the way, my great-grandfather, Nathaniel, started the business in 1908.'

After he'd made a cup of tea for the three of them, Colin took his mug with him over to the telephone attached to the wall just inside the back shop. 'Mum,' he said, when his call was answered, 'could you ask Grandad if he remembers a Jean Morrow who lived at No 80 during the war?' He listened to her response and shook his head. 'No, it's for a lady and gent who are in the shop just now. The lady comes from Australia but she used to live here and her mother was Jean Morrow.' He waited while his grandfather was consulted.

'Hello, good, and he's quite definite about that? That's great, have you got the address? Okay, fire away,' he said, taking the pen out of his white coat pocket and jotting something down on the back of a paper bag. 'Thanks, Mum. See you tonight when I call round with your bread. Bye.'

'Sounds promising,' Philip said when Colin had hung up.

'Grandad does remember the Morrow girl but he thinks her name was Nancy, not Jean. Nancy's mother Agnes died but he doesn't know where Nancy went. He thinks their old neighbour, Betty Black, might be able to help you.'

'But I was Nancy,' Vina told him, 'your grandfather must be mistaken, my mother was called Jean.'

Colin shrugged. 'The Blacks moved to a housing scheme called Westerhill back in the fifties. My mother sometimes meets Betty in the High Street and Betty has never mentioned moving away from Westerhill. This is her address,' Colin said, handing Vina the details he had written down.

'How far away is Westerhill?' Philip interjected.

'Not too far. Are you in a car?'

Philip nodded.

'Then drive up Stonefield Road, take the third turning on the right and pass the cemetery. At the top of the hill go under the railway-bridge and Westerhill is on your left. Once you are in the estate, anyone will direct you to Booth Drive. Betty lives at No 22.'

Philip shook Colin's hand. 'Thanks for your help and also for letting us eat our lunch on your premises.'

'You're welcome, mate. Good luck,' Colin called to Vina as they left the shop.

'I need to get back to work Vina,' Philip said when they got into his car, 'but if I drop you at 22 Booth Drive, will you be alright seeing Betty on your own?'

'Sure,' she smiled, 'I feel confident I'm going to get the information I need.'

'How will you get home?'

'I'll take a cab to the High Street and board a bus or train back to the city centre. Don't worry, I'll be okay.'

'Good. Can you meet me for lunch on Thursday?'

'Yes, will I come to the chambers about midday?'

'Great.' He dropped Vina outside Betty Black's gate in Booth Drive. He could sense her excitement as he drove away and hoped that she wouldn't be disappointed.

* * *

Vina stood on the top step of No 22 and rang the doorbell, her insides shaking.

When she got no reply, she rang again and waited. In her desire to meet Betty Black, she'd closed her mind to the thought that the woman could be out but, after ringing a third time, it was obvious that the house was empty.

There was nothing else for it but to leave a note. Vina sat down on the garden wall and took out her pen. The curtain in the next door house twitched, the neighbour obviously wondering what she was up to. She gave only scant details, simply her name, what her previous name was, and that she was trying to get information on Jean Morrow and believed Betty could help. She wrote down both her mobile number and the phone number at the guesthouse in the hope that Betty Black would contact her.

All her earlier excitement vanished and she felt despondent as she left Booth Drive. She got as far as the cemetery without seeing a taxi and boarded a bus that took her back to the High Street.

Once there, a passer-by directed her to the correct bus stop for transport into the city centre. The bus arrived a few minutes after two o'clock and, once seated, Vina decided that it wasn't too late in the day to text Sue and Andy. Probably around 11 pm in Tassie and neither of them went to bed much before midnight. They'd be eager to hear how Vina's search was going. How I'd love to hear their voices, she thought, but knew it would cost an arm and a leg to phone from a mobile so she resisted the temptation.

She kept the message brief, using text language.

Hi S and A, hope u r both well. Bn 2 G'Burgh, 0 yet abt Jean but left note 4 an old naybur. Speak soon. xx

Back at Harwood Drive, she mooned about in her room, unable to settle to anything. Dinner over, Gwen was relating a tale of something that had happened in the store that day, when Monica popped her head round the sitting room door.

'Someone asking to speak to you on the guest phone, Vina?' she said.

Vina was surprised to hear from Frances Gellatly so late at night, then remembered that on Mondays Frances started at two o'clock and worked on later.

'Have you made any contact yet?' Frances asked.

'I went to Glenburgh today. No one at 14 Queen Street could help but I was told to go to 80 High Street, Jean's earlier address. Got the address of a Betty Black, an old neighbour of Jean's but she was out. I left a note asking her to contact me.'

'You've done well considering you are just at the start of your search. I don't have a lot to report either but have a few feelers out. Meantime, don't forget to phone if you want to chat. Remember that I am here to help you in any way I can.'

'Thanks. I'll let you know if I hear from Betty Black, the neighbour.'

Chapter Thirty-Nine

Molly glanced at the clock and went upstairs to dress. Her plan was to call in and see her dad this morning and go into school in the afternoon. She was still on holiday but had a huge backlog to deal with. She fixed her hair, applied her lipstick and stood back to check her appearance in the mirror.

'Your dad's brighter today, quite lucid too,' his key worker, Paul, told Molly when he opened the door to her.

'Hello Dad,' she smiled when she saw him and was rewarded by a look of recognition. Her elation was short-lived though when a moment later he asked who she was. At least he did respond though, something that had been missing recently.

'I thought we could go for a run in the car Dad and perhaps find a teashop.'

He slowly got to his feet. Molly took this as agreement and helped him put on his coat and hat before he changed his mind.

She drove along the coast to Arbroath, her dad staring out through the front windscreen blissfully unaware of passing the bungalow that had once been his home. When he'd first gone into Hollytrees, Molly had avoided driving past the bungalow but by now she realised that his previous life was all but erased from his memory.

She parked down by Arbroath harbour and he became more animated, his love of the sea evident in his expression. 'I wonder how many times you've walked around this harbour, Dad,' she smiled at him as they got out the car and she put her arm through his, 'dozens of times, no more like hundreds, maybe?'

He made no response but stared at the small number of craft bobbing about on their moorings, the boat nearest them called 'Seagull'.

Molly led him to a bench overlooking the harbour where they sat down. 'Do you remember the smokies we used to buy over there?' She turned slightly and pointed towards the Harbour fish shop behind them, its bright blue painted door standing out against the white stone walls. The smell of cooked fish wafted over and made her feel hungry. 'Would you like a fish supper, Dad?' she asked and he gave a slight nod of his head. 'You sit here then and I'll go and get them.'

The shop door was wide open and while she waited for their freshly caught haddock and chips, she kept an eye on him in case he got up and wandered away. They both tucked in, enjoying their meal out of the newspaper. 'This is the only way to eat fish and chips isn't it, Dad?' She gathered up the paper when they were finished and stuffed it into the nearby litter bin. 'What about a stroll around the harbour before we get back into the car, Dad?'

Although Adam said nothing he got to his feet and ambled along happily at her side as they strolled round to the opposite side of the harbour and back. Molly looked up longingly at the cliff walk ahead of them, memories flooding back of the happy times she'd enjoyed being up there with her parents. But she kept her thoughts to herself, knowing that they would mean nothing to Dad.

'That was nice, wasn't it, Dad?' she said as she started up the car engine.

Her father sighed and looked round at her. 'Are you Jean?'

'No, Dad, I'm Molly, your daughter.'

'Do you know Jean?'

'No,' she said again. 'I don't know Jean. Who is Jean, Dad?'

But he'd lapsed into his own world once more.

After returning him to Hollytrees, she felt too exhausted to go into the school and decided to leave it until the following day.

Chapter Forty

By Thursday morning, with no word from either Frances or Betty Black, Vina was becoming despondent. Then Philip phoned to cancel their lunch as an urgent meeting had been convened.

'I'm so sorry, Vina.'

'Your work has to come first,' she tried to hide her disappointment.

'How's your search going?'

'Very slowly I'm afraid. I'll tell you more when I see you.'

'We could meet on Saturday or Sunday, I'll phone you tomorrow.'

A few minutes after her conversation with Philip, her mobile rang again. A woman's voice said, 'Could I speak to Vina West, please?'

'This is Vina.'

'It's Betty Black, I've just come home from holiday and got your message. I can't tell you how pleased I was to get it. Can you come and see me tomorrow?'

Vina felt her heart pound. 'Of course I can, I'm really keen to meet you.'

'Me too. Would eleven o'clock be suitable?'

'Excellent. Thanks for contacting me.'

'Till tomorrow then.'

Vina could hardly contain herself overnight and ended up arriving at the house in Booth Drive twenty minutes early. She was going to wait outside until eleven o'clock but a small, slim woman opened the door and called to her.

'Vina? Come away in, it's wonderful to meet you.' Betty beamed and led the way into the sitting room.

The room had a bay window, with décor in soft beige. A magnificent white marble-effect fireplace was the main focal point.

'I was over the moon when you rang me last night.'

'As I was to get your note,' Betty said, taking Vina's hands in hers. 'But I'm forgetting my manners. Take your coat off and make yourself at home. I can't believe you're really here, you were a year old the last time I saw you.'

She went into the hallway to hang up Vina's coat. 'Tea or coffee?' she asked, when she came back into the sitting room.

'Tea would be lovely, thanks.'

When Betty returned with the tray, Vina was looking at a framed photograph that sat on the sideboard.

'Do you recognise anyone?'

'The tall girl with the spotted dress looks like me when I was a teenager.'

'Probably because that's Jean, your mother. I'm the younger girl but with my white hair I don't look like that girl with the long blonde plaits anymore. The baby I'm holding is you.' She held out a plate of biscuits to Vina, then sat down facing her guest. 'I was delighted to hear from you. I always hoped you'd come back to trace your family. I used to babysit you when your grandmother went out.'

Vina's eyes were moist as she looked over at Betty. 'I've been told by my counsellor at the adoption agency that Jean is dead. I'm so disappointed, I've come so far to meet her and my father,' she finished with a catch in her voice.

'I can imagine how disappointing it must be for you. Your grandmother, Mrs McQueen, looked after you when Jean died. We were all devastated when your grandmother died six months after Jean.'

'Was that the reason I was put up for adoption?'

'Yes. My parents would have taken you but they were considered to be too old and I was only 13 at the time and still at school. I couldn't stop crying when the authorities took you away. Were your adoptive parents good to you?'

'They were wonderful. We left Glasgow when I was four as Dad got a job in Tasmania. I've lived there ever since.'

'Were there other children?'

'My twin siblings were about a year old when we left Scotland.' She took a picture from her purse and passed it to

Betty. 'That's my parents with the three of us.'

'How nice that you had company. I was an only child and it's a lonely life. I think that made it all the more difficult when you were taken away as I'd always looked on you like a wee sister. Do you have any nieces or nephews?'

'My brother Andy isn't married but Sue, his twin, has a daughter with two children, a boy and a girl.' Her earlier sadness was replaced by a joyful laugh. 'I can't help wondering as I look at your pale gold carpet how long it would stay that colour in Sue's house with the grandkids dragging in skateboards and bikes.'

'Yes, the carpet's a nightmare to keep clean. And you, Vina, are you married with a family of your own?'

A shadow passed over Vina's face and she shook her head. 'No, I was married but unfortunately it didn't work out. We didn't have any children which was perhaps a blessing.' She didn't elaborate further.

'I see,' Betty said and changed the subject back to Vina's biological parents. 'Now, where will we start?'

'I've got loads of questions but they can keep. I'd like to hear about Jean and I promise I'll try not to interrupt every five minutes.'

Betty leaned back in her chair and started to speak.

'Jean's father died when she was in primary school. She was close to her mother but found her over-protective at times. Understandable, I suppose, with Jean being her only child. When Jean was 17 she married Frank Morrow, a local ruffian from a thoroughly bad family. Mrs McQueen tried to talk Jean out of marrying him.'

Vina sat up straighter, her hands clenched.

'Jean's marriage was unhappy. Frank abused her physically, and it was a relief to her when he joined the Army and was sent overseas. She didn't shed any tears when word came that he'd been killed in Italy.'

'Was he my father?' Vina posed the question hesitantly.

'No, your father was a sailor, Bill Prior. Jean met him at a dance. It was love at first sight and Jean looked radiant during the four weeks of their courtship.'

Betty fell silent and stared out of the window for a few moments. 'After Bill returned to his ship, she received three letters from him and then he stopped writing. By the time the news leaked out that the ship Bill was on had been sunk, Jean had discovered she was pregnant.'

Vina felt nauseous. 'He's dead, and Jean didn't know till she read it in the papers?' she asked, her eyes wide.

'The authorities would have contacted Bill's parents as his next of kin but his parents had never met Jean and wouldn't have known her address. Eventually Jean had to confess to her mother that she and Bill had spent their last night together in a hotel in Glasgow and that she was carrying his child.'

'I bet that didn't go down too well,' Vina sniffed.

'It certainly didn't but, despite her initial anger, your grandmother stuck by Jean.' Betty stared at the fireplace for a moment, lost in memories. Vina didn't interrupt, not wanting to push her too much.

'Poor Jean, it was only after your birth that she regained some happiness. You were the only part of Bill she had left. Your grandmother looked after you while Jean went to her work in Hamilton's grocery store.'

Betty stopped again, a shadow crossing her face. 'Then just after V.E. day Jean received the bombshell that Frank had survived the war and would be returning home within the next couple of weeks.'

Vina clasped her hands even tighter, the knuckles turning white.

Betty twisted her cup around in her hands. 'She was terrified of him. It was a valid fear too, going by his previous treatment of her.' Moving over to the settee, she sat beside Vina and put her frail arm round the younger woman's shoulder.

'This is the most difficult part for me to tell you, Vina. Your mother had suffered so much physical abuse at his hands in the past that she was scared rigid at the thought of him discovering she'd been unfaithful and given birth to you. She was so scared that she … oh Vina, there's no easy way to tell you, she threw herself under a tramcar.'

Vina winced audibly, as she tried to take in what Betty had just told her.

'I'm so sorry, Vina, to have to tell you such a horrible story. I've never been able to come to terms with it myself so I can't even try to imagine what it must be like for you to hear it.' She cupped Vina's chin in her hand and looked gently into her eyes. 'Jean adored you, my dear, and it was her fear of Frank that drove her to such a terrible act. I think she knew that her mother would take over her role and would not let Frank harm you in any way. Vina, are you sure you want me to go on?'

Wiping away her tears, Vina nodded. 'I've waited for over sixty years to hear about Jean's life and I want you to tell me everything you remember.'

'One lovely memory is your first birthday party.' Betty smiled at the thought.

'It was a very happy day. Mrs McQueen saved up coupons to buy the ingredients for your cake and invited all the neighbours. She made you a pink and white gingham dress.'

Vina used her hankie to wipe away her tears. 'I have that dress, my adoptive Mum kept it for me. How did my grandmother die?'

'She died of a haemorrhage. My mother heard you crying the morning after your party and when she went in she found Agnes lying on the kitchen floor in a pool of blood. She'd been suffering from blood loss for some time but was scared to go and see a doctor in case they put her in hospital and you were taken away from her. She loved you so much that she couldn't bear to be parted from you.'

Betty paused and put her hand over Vina's. 'Look, we're both quivering wrecks with all this. Let me make us some lunch, you need time to recover.'

Vina nodded. 'Can I use your toilet please, Betty?'

'Certainly, the top of the stairs, first door you come to.'

After lunch, Betty gave Vina a tin box. 'This belongs to you, love. My mother found it in the house that morning and I've kept it, hoping that one day you would come to claim it.'

Vina took a deep breath and opened the box. She pulled out a green silk scarf and spread it over her knees.

'Bill bought that scarf for Jean. She wore it constantly.'

Vina held the soft fabric against her cheek, savouring its silky feel. 'There's a very faint smell of scent,' she said, her voice husky.

'It was Jean's favourite perfume, Evening in Paris. She kept the little royal blue coloured bottle on her dressing table and sometimes let me dab some on to my wrists.'

'Thank you, Betty, it's wonderful to have something of Jean's.'

'These are her diaries,' Betty said when Vina took two black leather books out of the box. 'One for 1944 while the other runs up until her death in May 1945. You'll be able to read them later when you're alone. That's a photograph of Bill, the only picture Jean had of him.'

Vina held the picture in her shaky hand. 'He's so handsome, I can well understand Jean falling for him.' She looked down at the bottom of the photograph. 'All my love, darling, Bill' she read out and the tears welled up again.

'You'll see that Jean wrote the address of his shipping company on the back.'

Vina laid the picture on top of some faded letters and attached the elastic band once more.

'I'm glad the picture's with its rightful owner.' Betty got up and walked over to the sideboard. 'I want you to have this one too.' She held out the photograph Vina had looked at earlier. 'I insist,' she said, 'and I've got others I'll look out for you.'

'Do you know where my mother and grandmother are buried?'

'Beside Mr McQueen in the local cemetery. Would you like to see the grave?'

Vina's voice was barely a whisper. 'Yes please.'

'I'll be pleased to take you but not today with the light fading.'

'Gosh, I didn't realise how late it was.' Vina looked towards the window and saw that the streetlights had come on although it wasn't yet five o'clock.

'The darkness comes down early at this time of year but I'll take you another day. Now, you go and wash your face, and I'll come with you as far as the bus stop to make sure you get the right one home.'

* * *

Vina could hardly contain herself on the journey back to Muirbank.

After dinner the other boarders all went out and she had the sitting room to herself. As the evenings were becoming decidedly chilly, she was glad of the lovely log fire Monica had lit, much cosier than the gas and electric ones people used nowadays. It made her think of her times spent in front of Sue's log fire back home.

She lifted Jean's box on to her knees, noticing for the first time that it had once contained Huntley & Palmer's biscuits. She wondered if Jean had brought the box home from Hamilton's. Every day had been recorded in Jean's neat handwriting and the first entry of interest was on Friday 7th January 1944.

Went to the Locarno with Brenda. Wore my green dress, my hair just right. Met a gorgeous chap, Bill Prior, a sailor on leave from the Merchant Navy. He's tall, even with my high heels he towered above me. I hate dancing with anyone short.

Bill is good fun and a super dancer. I really fell for him, was terrified he didn't feel the same so it was a relief when he saw me to the bus and asked to see me again. Roll on tomorrow night.

Vina felt close to both her parents. She devoured the written words and was there with them during their dates. Her excitement mounted as she read the entry dated Monday 31st

January.

Met Bill again tonight. I told Mum that I was going dancing with Brenda but I don't think she believes me any longer. We had an almighty row and she tried to stop me from leaving but I stormed out.

I was glad I'd gone when Bill told me that he'd to report back to his ship in Portsmouth next morning. We spent the night together in a hotel in Bath Street. I knew that Mum would be furious if she found out but goodness knows when we will be together again. With this war, there is no certainty about anything anymore and anyway, we both know ours is true love.

Bill's lovemaking was tender and gentle, so different from Frank's. I've never known such joy and can't wait for him to come home on his next leave. I promised to wait for him, which won't be difficult as I could never look at another man now.

Vina welled up, guessing this must have been the night she'd been conceived as Jean had never seen Bill again. Leafing through the pages, they revealed how desperately Jean missed Bill. She'd recorded her joy at receiving his letters, little guessing that they were soon to stop abruptly.

Vina looked at Bill's picture again and her fingers shook as she opened up one of his letters. She knew she was justified in reading it, but it felt like she was somehow intruding all the same.

14ᵗʰ February, 1944.

My Darling Jean,

Happy Valentine's Day and how I wish I could say these words to you in person. Just imagine I'm doing so until I get back. Meantime I.O.U. red roses!

I'll never forget our last night together. I love you Jean and can't get back home quickly enough to marry you. In

Rabbie's words, you are 'my bonny Jean'. If only this damned war would end but it will do one day and we will be together until we are old and grey and beyond into eternity.

Vina smiled at the poetry in her father's last two lines and wondered if the same thought had struck Jean as she read his love letter all those years ago.

My journey down to Portsmouth was smooth although we've been busy since we arrived here getting the vessel ready. Yesterday I managed a bit of a pub-crawl with some mates. We were all able to walk back to the ship – just!
I hope to get a letter from you soon, darling.
All my love, Bill. xxxx

Vina read the entire letter through a screen of tears. Then she returned to the diary. She missed some pages meantime and leafed over, stopping at 17th April. She gasped as she read the entry.

I told Mum tonight about my pregnancy. I had to as the abortion didn't work and I'm beginning to show now. She went beserk and I thought she would throw me out of the house but she calmed down after a while and called the doctor in.

Everything is going well and the baby is the correct size it should be at this stage of pregnancy. I tried to get rid of it out of fear but I'm glad it didn't work. I really want Bill's baby. If only he hadn't died. I'm not even sure if he got my letter telling him I was pregnant. But in some ways I prefer that he died than have to accept that he'd stopped loving me.

Why did you let him die, God? I asked you to keep him safe, I prayed like I've never prayed before but you didn't listen. Where are you, God, if you do exist?

If you are there, please don't let him have suffered, let his end have been quick. What will I do without him? I know Mum will not let either the baby or me starve but I can't live without Bill. And he'll never know his baby. Oh God how will I go on?

The ink was smudged at this part from Jean's tears. Vina was forced to put the diary away, unable to face reading more of her mother's desperate words. Jean must have been going through such torture at that moment and to think that she, Vina, might not even be here had the abortion worked.

Chapter Forty-One

It wasn't until Friday morning that Molly got a chance to look out some old family photographs, hoping that this woman Jean was in them.

She'd decided to bring her dad to Farquhar Drive during the school holidays, sure that it would be good for him to get away from Hollytrees for a couple of hours and Paul, his care worker, had offered to bring him today. She was so glad Paul had been chosen for this role since, out of all the staff, he could get the most response from Dad.

'Hello Dad,' she ran outside and greeted him as Paul stopped the car outside the front gate. Paul helped him out of the car but Adam shrugged his hand aside and went ahead on his own. He still walked in a fairly erect manner, no doubt a throwback to his wartime training. They led him through to the kitchen from where, when he was seated at the table, he had a good view of the River Tay. 'You always liked the view from here, didn't you Dad?' Adam failed to reply but continued to stare at the view.

'Enjoy your time with Molly,' Paul patted Adam's shoulder.

'He'll be back for his dinner,' Molly said as she saw him out.

'Are you hungry, Dad? Will we have lunch in here and you can watch the traffic on the bridge while you're eating?' Molly prattled on as she served lunch but got no response. Later, when she laid his dessert in front of him, he caught hold of her arm. 'Who are you? Is this your house?'

'Yes, Dad,' she sighed, 'and you've been here often. Don't you remember?' she pleaded, wishing there was some way to remove all the fuzz that was entangling his brain and let him think straight again.

When a tear escaped out of the corner of his eye and ran down the tramline etched on his cheek, guilt washed over her. 'It doesn't matter whether you remember or not, Dad,' she soothed him, stroking the back of his hand, 'who cares anyway, the main thing is you're here now and it's good to spend time together.'

The door opened and Luke appeared in the kitchen.

'Great you could make it, darling,' she smiled up at her son. She'd told him that Grandad was coming today on the chance that he could pop in. 'Help yourself to a sandwich and I'll make a coffee,' she said, switching on the kettle.

'I had a gap between tutorials. Hi Grandad, how are you?' Luke smiled at the old man, who ignored him and continued to stare at the view.

Molly wrinkled her nose at Luke. 'We're not very communicative today.'

She placed the box of photographs on the middle of the table and laid some out in front of her dad. 'Anybody there you recognise, Dad?' she asked, while she poured Luke's coffee.

The old man stared down at the faces in the pictures with no sign of recognition.

'Is he still talking about Jean?' Luke asked, taking his coffee mug from Molly.

She nodded and continued to put pictures down on the table, moving one lot away as she brought out the next. They both studied Adam's face closely but he remained unmoved until she put the crumpled picture she'd found earlier on the table in front of him. The young, pretty girl in the picture had long dark hair and wore a dance dress.

Adam's eyes became alert.

'Is this Jean, Dad? Is this her?'

He looked perplexed for a moment and then tears started to fall again.

Molly leaned over and wiped them away with her hankie. 'I don't know Jean, Dad. Was she someone you knew when you were young? A friend of Mum's maybe?'

Luke put his hand over his Grandad's. 'Who is she? If you tell us, we could ask her to visit you?' But the old man was now becoming agitated and he pulled his hand away angrily. He muttered something that didn't make any sense and threw his arms out, scattering the pictures all over the floor and knocking the mug out of Luke's hand. A puddle of coffee landed on the table top and formed a stream that dripped over the side of the table and landed on top of the photographs.

'Don't push him any more, darling,' Molly cautioned her son, grabbing a cloth to wipe the table and mop up the coffee from the photographs. 'He has no memory of who she is, even though he continually asks about her.'

Once things had settled down again, Luke changed the subject. 'How was your weekend with Aunt Beth and Uncle Greg?'

'I had a great time and Beth is coming up here for the day tomorrow. We're going to have lunch in The Park Hotel, the refurbished one beside D C Thomson's.' She noticed her dad wringing his hands together and tapping his feet on the floor. 'I think Grandad's been here long enough. I best take him back now.'

'Will you manage him on your own Mum or will I skip the next lecture and come with you?'

'No love, I'll manage him.'

Luke said farewell to his Grandad, then hugged Molly. 'By the way, I had a drink with Dad the other night,' he announced as they walked towards the door.

'Good.' Molly encouraged him to keep in touch with his father.

'I think Dad's missing you Mum, and I know he's split up with his secretary. He's on his own in the flat now.'

'I doubt if that situation will continue for long, knowing your dad.'

Molly kept her voice calm, even though she was livid that Ted was using their son's emotions to try and get back with her. He'd hurt her too often to be forgiven as easily as that. Luke of course knew nothing about the rape and she intended to keep it that way.

* * *

'We're only going for two nights remember, you've enough luggage for a fortnight,' Ted grumbled as he stowed his latest conquest's case into the spacious boot on Friday afternoon. He reckoned they'd be in Manchester in plenty of time for the dinner before the Conference started on Saturday morning.

'Well you want me to look good and do you proud, don't you?' Claire smiled.

Ted grinned. 'I certainly don't have any complaints on that front.'

He'd met Claire in a bar a couple of weeks ago and his chat-up lines had succeeded. She was a good ten years his junior and worked as a receptionist in a local hotel. Although her conversation wasn't the most stimulating, he enjoyed the sex with her and so their first date had been repeated on a few occasions.

He'd only invited her to accompany him to Manchester at the last minute. He'd planned to go to the Conference alone but discovered from other colleagues that their wives were going too. He knew Molly wouldn't go with him so he plumped for Claire rather than stand out on his own in the evening. He was sure that the wives would find Claire unsuitable company; a number of them were quite snobbish bitches. Well, hey ho, if she found herself out on a limb, Claire would be able to find something to amuse her during the day while he was at the Conference. He could give her some cash to go on a shopping spree.

He whistled as he got into the driver's seat and switched on the ignition.

Even if the Conference proved boring, two nights of passion with a pretty blonde would make it all worthwhile.

* * *

Just before midnight the bedside phone rang. Molly wakened with a start, rubbing her eyes as she said 'hello'.

'Mum, it's me,' Luke's anxious tone brought her to full alertness. 'Mum, it's Dad, there's been an accident and we need to go to him.'

'What's happened?'

'Dad's been in a car crash,' Luke said. 'He's alive but the police came to the flat to tell me as they didn't want to scare you in the middle of the night. We need to leave immediately.'

Still with the phone at her ear, she padded towards the wardrobe for some clothes. 'Damn,' she yelled when she stubbed her toe against the chest of drawers. 'Who phoned you? Where is Dad?'

'He's in the neurology ward of a Manchester hospital. He told me in the pub the other night that he was going to a Conference there. The woman passenger in Dad's car died at the scene and the police want us to try and help identify her.'

'His passenger?' She tightened her grip on the phone as she spoke. One of his bits on the side no doubt, she thought bitterly.

'Mum, they've asked us to get there straight away. They don't know if he's going to make it.' Luke's voice faded and she heard a sob on the other end of the line.

'I'll be ready in ten minutes,' she shouted through the receiver but the line had already gone dead.

* * *

Few words passed between them on the drive south, both too stunned to speak.

Luke kept up a steady speed of 70 mph, the only other traffic being articulated vehicles.

Molly had no idea whether Ted would be able to speak to them or indeed if he would still be alive when they reached the hospital. She summoned up what worn and tarnished faith she still had in a supreme being and made a silent vow that if Ted lived she would try to stay on better terms with him. She couldn't promise to take him back; that was a step too far after all that had happened.

They drove into the hospital grounds at about twenty past three in the morning. A member of the nursing staff ushered them into Ted's room. He lay in a coma, attached to a myriad of machines, while a nurse wrote up his treatment chart.

'I'm Nurse Bertram,' she said, when Molly and Luke came into the room. Her hair was drawn up under her cap and her badge identified her as a Staff Nurse. She placed a chair at either side of the bed. 'I'll bring you and your son a cup of tea

Mrs Bishop and please keep speaking to your husband. If patients hear familiar voices it sometimes brings them back to consciousness much sooner.'

Molly looked up at the nurse. 'How badly injured is he?'

'He needed an urgent repair to his spleen and he's fractured both legs and one arm. The neurologist on duty doesn't think he has any serious head injuries but we can't say definitely just yet. I'll ask Dr Sharp, the neurologist, to have a word with you later,' she said, closing the door quietly behind her.

Luke's ashen face peered down at Ted. 'Dad, it's me, Mum's here too.'

'How did the crash happen, Luke?' she whispered. 'Did they tell you?'

'All the police would say was that Dad had been involved in an accident on the M6, close to the Manchester turnoff, sometime around late afternoon. They said his condition was giving cause for concern but I got no further details.'

'Was any other car involved?'

'Yes, they said it was a two car collision, but that's as much as they said.'

Ted's arm on Luke's side of the bed was under the duvet, the plaster visible near his shoulder area. Molly lifted the bedclothes and his legs were encased in plaster from ankle almost to hip.

Nurse Bertram returned with some tea and toast. She tapped Ted's IV fluids bag and Molly watched the fluid dripping down like teardrops. The catheter bag hanging from the bed was half full and a machine near Luke was monitoring Ted's heart function, bleeping constantly as it did so.

'Ted,' she said, 'they've fixed your spleen and attended to your fractures and you'll soon be good as new again.' Even though she was unsure if he could hear what she was saying, she knew he wouldn't be satisfied with less than the full story.

She stared at this man she'd lived with for most of her

adult life, the father of her only child, and all the past hurt and bitterness drained away. 'Please let him live and lead a normal life again,' she prayed to the God that she'd drifted away from.

Luke brushed his fingers through Ted's hair. 'Dad, we'll be here until you're better so don't worry, you won't be on your own.'

'I think on Monday you should get back for college. We'd better drink this tea while it's hot,' Molly murmured, getting up and slipping her hand away from Ted's.

'Mum, his hand moved.'

Molly sat down again and took Ted's hand for a moment. When she let go, his hand moved across the bedclothes searching for hers. 'He must be aware we're here,' she whispered, looking at her son through a veil of tears.

A white-coated figure entered the room, a tall thin man wearing glasses and balding at the temples. 'Hello, I'm Dr Sharp.'

'How's he doing, doctor?'

'We've done all we can for the moment, Mrs Bishop. Your husband's spleen has been repaired and now we must wait and hope he regains consciousness in the next few days.'

'I think he knows we're here. When I moved my hand he tried to find it again and his eyelashes fluttered when my son spoke to him.'

'That's promising, the fractures should heal as your husband is a fit man.'

'Yes, he certainly is, plays tennis, squash and rugby.'

'The main worry of course is whether he has sustained any major head trauma and that's something we won't be able to rule out for a few days yet. However, you and your son being here will help his recovery greatly, especially if you continue to talk to him and he hears familiar voices. Even hearing some favourite music can help.'

'I might have something on my mobile phone,' Luke suggested, 'although maybe not to Dad's taste.'

'Do you know what happened doctor? In the crash I mean. He's usually a very careful driver.'

'I'm afraid my information is pretty sketchy. I only

know two cars were involved. The driver of the other car escaped serious injury but your husband's car came off worse and his passenger was killed outright. We were hoping you could help us identify the dead woman.'

Molly shook her head. 'I'm afraid not, she must have been a colleague he was giving a lift to the Conference. Doctor, my son needs to return to Dundee on Monday for college but I'll stay for as long as it takes.' Molly knew that, under the circumstances, her Head of Department would use a supply teacher in her absence.

'I think the police personnel who attended the scene will have a word with you and your son tomorrow, Mrs Bishop, and they'll be able to give you some information about what happened.'

Dr Sharp's pager bleeped and, since meantime they had no further questions for him, he excused himself and left the room.

Chapter Forty-Two

November 2012

On Monday morning Vina's letter to Bill's shipping company was returned to her marked 'unable to be delivered'. She phoned Frances straight away and left a message on the answering machine that she had drawn a blank with the shipping company and would like to come through to Edinburgh to discuss where they go from here.

She'd already been in the UK for over five weeks and was disappointed by how slowly her search was progressing. She hung about her bedroom for a while but with no response from Frances and keen to feel she was making some progress, she keyed in Betty Black's number on her mobile. Betty replied after a few minutes and the two women arranged to visit Glenburgh cemetery that afternoon.

Vina got off the bus in Glenburgh High Street and bought a small posy of flowers. She walked the rest of the way to Booth Drive. Betty was waiting for her when she got to the house and they walked to the cemetery together. The ornate gate creaked open to admit them. It was a large cemetery and some of the gravestones had been vandalised while others looked more like they'd crumbled and fallen over due to weathering. Betty led the way up the centre path, where the ground levelled out. She stopped about five graves in from the centre path. The McQueen grave was in a quiet spot at the rear of the cemetery, shaded by a small plantation of larch trees.

Betty walked further along the path to allow the younger woman time to mourn her dead relatives. Vina read the rather worn inscription on the stone.

> In loving memory of
> Alexander McQueen
> Born 10th October 1900
> Died 7th April 1934
> Aged 33 years

His Beloved Daughter
Jean Ann Morrow (nee McQueen)
Born 4th June 1924
Died 30th May 1945
Aged 20 years

His Loving Wife
Agnes Mary McQueen
Born 13th February 1902
Died 24th November 1945
Aged 43 years

Vina stared at the date of her grandmother's death, her own first birthday, and appreciated even more what that lady had done for her. She'd sacrificed her own life rather than have Vina put into care. 'Thank you,' she whispered and laid the posy against the headstone. Sadness ripped through her but she was grateful to have some closure, at least on her mother's side.

She was taking a photograph of the grave when Betty silently appeared at her side once more. 'If I leave money, Betty, would you arrange to have the stone cleaned up and the words on the inscription made clearer?'

'Of course,' Betty said, 'but you might have time to do that before you return to Tasmania.' Vina nodded and Betty led the way downhill again, out of the shadows of the cemetery and into the light of the present day once more. Back at Booth Drive, Betty made afternoon tea before Vina headed back to the guesthouse.

* * *

Back at Muirbank, Frances telephoned. 'Hello Vina, I got the message you left for me. I've tried to contact the shipping company myself and have discovered that it no longer exists.'

'That explains my letter being returned then.'

'The good news is that I got in touch with a Navy contact of ours to see if he could help. Bill's full name is William Adam Prior. I don't know how he managed it but my contact has discovered that Bill didn't go down with his ship after all.' Frances could hear Vina's sharp intake of breath. 'He hadn't been on board that day and served later on another ship. He was eventually captured by the Germans and imprisoned until the end of the war. I don't know why he didn't get in touch with Jean. Perhaps he somehow heard about her death.'

'And according to the neighbours in Glenburgh the McQueens moved to another flat during the war.'

'Yes, that could explain it. Anyway my contact has come up with an address for Bill when he left the Navy at the end of the war. I'm not supposed to give clients information on the phone but to save you another trip to Edinburgh I'm going to break the rules. The address I've been given is 5 Fairley Street, Riverdale. Do you know where that is?'

'I don't but I'll find it,' Vina wrote down the address as she was speaking. 'That's welcome news Frances, especially as I've just been to visit Jean's grave this afternoon. I'll get directions to Riverdale tomorrow and let you know how I get on.'

Early the next morning, she set off for Riverdale.

The town was situated in the shipyard area of Glasgow. Most of the yards were closed nowadays due to the lack of orders for the famous liners previously built on the Clyde.

By the time she arrived in Riverdale the grey, dismal start had lifted and a watery sun was beginning to break through the clouds.

It was a rundown place although the town centre appeared to be in the process of modernisation. Trying to contain the excitement throbbing inside her, she asked directions from a passer-by.

She was told that Fairley Street had changed its name to Laurel Walk and was advised to board a No 2 single-decker in the town centre. Her stomach churned as she made her way to the bus stop. At last she would see the house where her father, and Jean's lover, had lived. Better still, he might even live there yet.

At Laurel Walk, Vina found a vacant space where No 5 must once have stood and the terraced houses that remained started at No 7. Disappointment seared through her as she rang the doorbell of the end terrace house.

The woman who opened the door was holding a young baby in her arms. The radio blared from one of the rooms inside the house and the woman had to shout to be heard. 'Kin ah help ye?' she asked, in a strong Glaswegian accent.

She pulled the door closed slightly behind her, helping to take away some of the din and allowing Vina to speak in her normal voice. 'I'm sorry to disturb you but I wondered if you could tell me anything about a relative of mine who used to live at No 5 Fairley Street before it changed its name to Laurel Walk. I know he lived there during the war.'

The woman shook her head while the baby played with the pendant around her neck. 'Ah'm sorry hen, ah've only lived here fur a year but the tenements that wir here hiv'nae been replaced since they fell doon in the bombin' durin' the war.'

Seeing the desolation on Vina's face, she said, 'Ah think the Coonicl Offices in the Toon Centre might be able to help ye.'

Vina was lucky enough to find a helpful Council employee, who did a search for her.

'Our records show that the Prior family left Riverdale in 1946 and moved north to Dundee to live.' Jotting down a telephone number on a piece of paper, she handed it to Vina. 'It would be worth giving the Council Offices in Dundee a ring although I don't know if they'll give out such confidential information. Good luck,' she smiled.

Chapter Forty-Three

Frances phoned a couple of days after Vina's visit to Riverdale, having agreed to contact the Council in Dundee on Vina's behalf. 'Hi Vina, I've got some information on Bill. I think my findings will be of help to you.'

'That's fantastic news, Frances. I need something positive after finding that the tenement in Fairley Street is no longer there.'

'Don't get disheartened, Vina, your search is going well. Now, rather than you coming to Edinburgh, what do you say to me posting my information first class?'

'That would be great, Frances, and I'll let you know when it arrives.'

* * *

Vina came downstairs next morning as Helen was leaving for work.

'Morning, Vina,' her friend smiled at her, 'there's a letter for you in the mail tray,' she said as she dived out of the front door.

Vina's heart leapt when she saw the Edinburgh postmark. She wolfed down her breakfast, eager to get upstairs again and check the contents.

Wednesday 14 November, 2012.

Dear Vina

As promised, I am sending you some further information about your biological father, William Adam Prior. My enquiries have revealed that William moved to Dundee with his family after the war. His father found work in the jute mills there and William took up employment as an electrician. He married a Margaret Donnolly in Dundee in 1947 but I have no details of any children they might have had. He started up his own business the same year and seems to have done well for himself.

The paper shook in Vina's hand but, with great difficulty, she remained calm enough to read the rest of the letter.

The address on William's marriage certificate is C/O Donnolly, 24 Forrest Drive so one assumes that he was a lodger in Margaret's parents' house before the wedding.

His present whereabouts are still a bit vague but my contact in Dundee has provided me with the following address to try.

20 Fox Street
Dundee
Angus

Knowing how quickly your time in UK is passing, I expect you will try and make contact with your father via this address in the next few days and I await the outcome with interest.

Yours sincerely
Frances Gellatly

Vina stared at the letter for some time after she'd finished reading. Why had Bill stopped writing to Jean and did he try to find her after the war? So he had a wife in Dundee and maybe even children, who would be her half-siblings.

Vina couldn't stop now. She had to get the full story, however good or bad. Nothing but the truth would satisfy her.

She phoned Frances to say that she'd received the letter and would be taking the train to Dundee the next day.

Chapter Forty-Four

The woman who sat beside Vina on the Dundee train on Friday morning was a chatterbox. She hardly stopped for breath for well over an hour and each time Vina made an attempt to read more of Jean's diary she was interrupted by her fellow passenger launching into some other boring tale.

Her fellow passenger finally got off the train in Perth and Vina opened the diary at an entry for 27th March.

Brenda took me to see Mrs Brown tonight. The close was very dirty with the paint peeling off the walls but Mrs Brown herself appeared quite clean and tidy. She did what she had to do and I hated myself for going down this path but felt powerless to do anything else. To tell Mum about my pregnancy was unthinkable, yet this action tonight was like stabbing Bill through the heart. I was killing his child.

Even though she'd already read this section of Jean's diary it still made Vina draw breath sharply. Jean must have been desperate when she wrote these words, desperate enough to kill the child she was carrying despite her love for Bill. She moved on to the entry for 10th April and thought about how different things had been in the forties; nowadays there were more single mothers than married ones.

Mrs Brown's attempt to abort the baby has failed and I am still pregnant. Part of me is glad that she failed as I so want to have Bill's baby but the other half of me is terrified at the thought of telling Mum. But I must tell her and have decided to do so in the next few days. Dear Diary, if I am still alive afterwards, I will continue my recordings.

Survive she did as the later entry for 17th April had already told Vina. Thereafter entries were routine, work in the daytime and listening to the radio at night.

Vina leafed over to Friday 24th November, the day of her birth.

Dear Diary, I'm a mother, I have a gorgeous little

baby girl, seven and a half pounds and absolutely perfect. She was born at eight minutes past eleven this morning, and I think she looks just like Bill but Mum says you can't see a resemblance to anyone in such a young baby.

The delivery was short and sharp but I forgot the pain the minute they laid little Nancy in my arms. She is so warm and cuddly and I feel very protective of her. She is sleeping at the moment and I am writing this in bed as the midwife says I must rest for the remainder of the day. Nancy is my link with Bill and I will do everything in my power to give her a happy life.

Mum was out shopping and Nancy was already born by the time she arrived home. She's thrilled to be a grandma and also that I have called the baby Nancy. I wanted to call her after Mum but Agnes sounds too much like an adult's name.

Vina closed the diary at this happy entry.

* * *

Never good at reading maps, Vina asked for directions when she arrived in Dundee late morning. The station porter she approached told her that Fox Street wasn't far away and gave her elaborate directions, spoken quickly in a broad Dundonian accent. Vina thanked the man politely and followed her nose instead.

Soon she found herself on Nethergate, a busy shopping street. She skirted round a woman dragging a fractious toddler behind her and stood in a shop doorway to consult the Dundee street map Monica had loaned her. Her instinct sent her off to the left and she reached Blackness Road pretty quickly.

With directions from passers-by, she made a few twists and turns to get to Fox Street. In all it had taken her less than fifteen minutes.

On the way she was high with anticipation, certain that she was going to find Bill soon. As she turned into Fox Street, she was already rehearsing what she'd say when she came face to face with him. She could say, 'Hello, Bill, you don't know me but I'm your daughter.' Or perhaps, 'Hi, Bill, I guess it's a bit of a shock me turning up like this.'

She started to count down the house numbers until she reached No 20. It was a solid stone dwelling house and proved that Bill had done well for himself. But when she saw the sign outside the front entrance, her heart sank. The lovely home had been turned into the offices of an insurance company. She went into the entrance hall, her heels ringing on the floor tiles as she crossed over to the front desk.

'Can I help you?' the young receptionist, her name badge identifying her as Hazel, asked with a smile.

'I'm trying to find a relative of mine called William Prior. I believe he owned this house previously and I wondered if anyone on your staff would be able to provide me with Mr Prior's current address.'

'I've worked here for three years and I think the office has been here for many years before that. But if you could have a seat I'll check with Mrs Martin, the General Manager's secretary. If anyone can help you, it'll be her.'

Vina took a seat in the foyer and shortly afterwards Hazel returned, her expression telling Vina that it wasn't good news.

'I'm sorry but Mrs Martin doesn't know anything about your relative. She's worked here for almost twenty years and says the building had ceased being used as a private house long before that. I'm so sorry we aren't able to help you.'

'That's okay, it was kind of you to check for me.' Vina got to her feet, aware of Hazel's eyes on her as she made her way out of the building again.

Once outside, she wandered about, unsure what to do next. She stumbled across a café called 'The Lunch Box' and decided to go in there and gather her thoughts. Before she had time to order, Frances rang her. 'Did you go to Dundee?'

'Yes, I'm here but I've drawn a blank. The address in Fox Street belongs to an insurance company and the staff know nothing about the previous owner.'

'I have another address in Broughty Ferry, along the coast from Dundee.'

'That's great news.'

Detecting some weariness in Vina's voice, Frances tried to keep upbeat. 'Right, forget our rules, the new address is 15 Shore Road, Broughty Ferry. I'm told it's just facing the lifeboat station. You can get a bus to Broughty Ferry though you might need to stay overnight if there is no late evening transport back to Glasgow.'

'Think I'd be as well to go to the second address while I'm here, Frances. If I stay overnight, I could continue my search tomorrow if need be. Could you recommend any decent hotels here?'

'Our staff members always use The Park Hotel when they are in Dundee. It's near the offices of D C Thomson, the publishers of The People's Friend and other magazines. Anyone in Dundee could direct you to The Park.'

'Thanks, now could you repeat the address again?' Vina asked and scribbled it down on a paper hankie.

Vina hurried out of 'The Lunch Box' before she'd ordered anything. She obtained a single room, breakfast optional, at the hotel. Afterwards she went to a nearby pharmacy and bought toiletries for her overnight stay, then she found a store where she purchased some underclothes and nightwear.

The limited stop bus soon dropped her in Broughty Ferry, where disappointment once more awaited her as Mr and Mrs Thom, the middle-aged couple at No 15, didn't know the previous owner's whereabouts.

'He was an elderly man and I think he might have gone to stay with a relative,' Mr Thom said, 'although I couldn't be certain about that. It's a pity the people at No 9 are visiting their daughter in Arbroath today as they were friendly with Mr Prior and might know where he is now.'

'If you leave us your phone number, we could ask them and get back to you?' his wife, who'd followed him to the door, suggested.

'I'm staying at The Park Hotel in Dundee tonight but your neighbours might not want to give out such information without speaking to me first. Perhaps it would be better if I come back here tomorrow. I will be checking out of the hotel after breakfast.'

'An excellent idea,' Mr Thom nodded, 'but leave it until afternoon, just to make sure the Spencers are home and to give us time to speak to them about you.'

Vina felt much more relaxed on her journey back to Dundee and sent another text to Sue and Andy.

Hi S and A, still no breakthru but got lead on W.P. Luv to u all. xx

Realising that she would be missed in the guesthouse, she sent a second text, this time to Helen.

Have dcided 2 stay in Dundee hotel 2nite. Cd u pl let Monica no? Back 2moro sumtime. x

She decided to tell Helen about her search when she got back. Helen had been a good friend over the past few weeks and she deserved to know the true reason for Vina's visit. Vina lay back in her seat and was soon cat napping.

Back at the hotel again, Vina rang Frances to update her on the situation. After dinner, she returned to her room, deciding on a hot bath and an early bed.

Vina's sleep was disturbed that night. She tossed and turned on the hotel bed, dreaming of Bill Prior. In her dream he seemed to recognise her immediately. While they were chatting, the lady who'd been in her dreams recently appeared out of nowhere. The woman was smiling happily although Vina couldn't see her face properly. Who was she? Could she be the ghost of Jean? Vina wakened with that thought still in her mind. She skipped breakfast and went down to the restaurant the minute the lunches started. She was served quickly and galloped through her food, keen to be off.

The Spencers at No 9 invited Vina in when she arrived on their doorstep. 'Adam Prior was a good friend of ours,' Mr Spencer told her. 'He took the death of his wife, Margaret, hard but we managed to persuade him to attend the occasional social evening with us in our bowling club.'

'I think of him as Bill, but I know he is William Adam.'

Mrs Spencer nodded. 'That's right and he uses his

middle name. Being a Navy man, he was heavily involved in his group for old sailors, but he was never the same after Margaret's death.'

'And do you know where he lives now?'

'Sadly he suffers from dementia and his daughter had to arrange for him to go into Hollytrees nursing home.'

Vina's heart was pounding. She was about to find Bill and a half-sister.

'What's she called? His daughter, I mean.'

'Molly, so attentive to her dad.' Mrs Spencer shook her head. 'It broke her heart to put him into care but she had to, he doesn't know the time of day, poor soul.'

Vina's elation evaporated when she heard this. Bill was not going to be able to tell her anything about her early life if he couldn't even remember his own. But she couldn't leave it here; she had to see him. 'How do I get to Hollytrees?'

'Are you travelling by car?'

'No, I came by bus.'

'I put my car in for its MOT when I got home today, or else I'd have driven you there,' Mr Spencer said, 'but the nursing home's only a stone's throw away so you can walk to it.'

Stomach churning and throat dry, Vina soon reached Hollytrees. It was a lovely old building, in some ways reminiscent of Bill's home at Fox Street. She wondered if Molly had chosen Hollytrees because of that. 'Molly,' she said her half-sister's name aloud as she crunched her way up the stony drive. Molly would be Bill's legitimate daughter while she, Vina, was his bastard. But there must be some rational explanation. From the way the Spencers had spoken about Bill, he couldn't be an uncaring man.

She asked to see Adam Prior and was invited to sign her name in a book on the hall table. 'It's for security reasons,' the staff member who'd let her in explained, 'in case of fire so that we can account for everyone in the building.'

Vina signed her name under the visitors' column and with a little thrill of excitement wrote Adam Prior (Bill) under the column headed Resident.

In his room, her biological father sat in a chair in front of the window. The daylight coming in from behind struck Bill's bald patch. What hair he had was around the back of his head, giving him the appearance of a monk.

He didn't look up when Vina walked towards him. She sat down and, clearing her throat, went straight in. 'Hello Bill, I've been looking for you.'

When he didn't respond, she swallowed hard and went on.

'You see, Bill, I'm your daughter, your daughter Nancy. I'm Jean's daughter. Do you remember Jean?'

Trembling with emotion at finally meeting her biological father, she was desperate for him to speak to her. She raked her fingers through her hair, sobbing quietly over the frail figure sitting beside her. 'Your cruel illness has robbed us both,' she whispered through her tears.

She laid her hand over his, stroking his wafer thin skin. He looked up suddenly and she was struck by how blue his eyes were. She tried to imagine him as a young man, looking handsome in a naval uniform. If only she'd brought Jean's photograph with her.

He stared at her intently and smiled. 'Jean,' he murmured, 'you're back.'

'Sorry Bill, I'm not Jean, I'm her daughter, Nancy. I'm your daughter too. I didn't get to know Jean so can you tell me about her, Bill?' she pleaded, taking both of his hands in hers.

But he'd gone into his other world again and Vina was still sitting there, holding his hands, when a young man came into the room. He drew himself up sharply when he saw Vina. 'I'm sorry, I wasn't expecting anyone to be here. Adam doesn't usually get visitors in the afternoon.'

Vina let go of Bill's hands and stood up. 'I'm Vina West and I believe Adam's my father.' Seeing the look of disbelief on the young man's face, she explained further.

'I was adopted as a baby and reared in Australia. I'm trying to trace my biological parents and it seems that Adam is my father.'

'I'm Paul, Adam's care worker,' the young man told her.

'I've discovered that my mother is dead, Paul, and was hoping that Adam could tell me about her.'

'I'm afraid Adam couldn't tell you anything but I do know his wife was called Margaret.'

'I know about Margaret, but my mother was called Jean Morrow.'

Paul shrugged. 'Probably best to speak to Adam's daughter, Molly.'

'Could you let her know that I am trying to trace my biological parents and I think she is my half-sister?'

Paul took his time replying and when he did, he simply said, 'I will mention it to her next time I see her. She usually visits her dad regularly but at the moment she is in Manchester, where her husband is in hospital following a car accident. I don't know exactly how long she'll be away. Don't think she knows herself yet.'

'I'm sorry to hear about the accident. Unfortunately I have to leave shortly on the train back to Glasgow but I could leave my name and phone number if you would be good enough to pass it on to Molly when you are in contact with her? I don't expect her to call me immediately as she has problems enough at the moment but I'd welcome a chat with her when it can be arranged.'

'Yes, that would be fine,' Paul agreed, noting down Vina's details before showing her out.

Vina's head was swimming on her way back to Glasgow. She went over and over in her mind all that had happened since yesterday and prayed that Molly would contact her soon.

Chapter Forty-Five

Andy put his TV programme on hold when the phone rang.

'Hi, Andy,' his twin greeted him.

'Hi Sue, thought you'd be tucked up in bed by now,' he said, noting that it was after one o'clock. A bit of an insomniac, he usually watched movies late into the night, especially on a Saturday, but his twin sister was usually in bed by midnight.

'Sorry I haven't caught up with you recently but I seem to be running a permanent taxi service for the kids these days.' Sue's daughter, a single parent, was a second steward on the 'Spirit of Tasmania' ferry. The job was well paid but meant her being away from home quite a bit, leaving Sue to look after her kids.

'Yeah, we'll get together soon.' Being close to his twin, he knew she wasn't phoning late at night just for a chat. He didn't have long to wait for the real reason.

'Andy, I'm worried about Vina over there on her own. Reading between the lines of her text messages, I think she's quite depressed. She's come up against a few difficulties in tracing her biological father and although she's made a friend in the guesthouse, I think she's lonely.'

'Not much we can do from over here, Sis. Guess we'll have to hope she strikes lucky soon.'

'I thought I might fly over there next week and spend some time with her. Give her some support. I'll be back before Christmas.'

There was a silence while Andy tried to take this in. 'But how can you do that? What about the kids?' The minute he uttered the words, he knew why Sue had called him.

'I was hoping they could stay with you, Andy.' He was unmarried and lived alone and, worse still, he had plenty of spare bedrooms.

Before he could reply, she continued, her tone cajoling. 'They're both old enough now to allow me to disappear for a couple of weeks, especially if I explain to them that it's to help Aunt Vina.'

'What do you think?' she prodded, when he didn't reply straight away.

He sighed. 'Well, if you think they'd be happy staying here, and Vina would have no objection to you going, then I suppose we could rub along together for two weeks.'

He did love his great-niece and nephew but he was unused to restrictions on his lifestyle and liked to come and go as the notion took him. He knew though that he'd help Sue, even though he was being conned into it.

Chapter Forty-Six

By the following Friday evening, Vina was really depressed, with no word from Molly. It was less than a week since she'd been to Hollytrees. Molly was probably still down in Manchester but the thought of going home without getting any further information was heartbreaking. There was a knock on her bedroom door and Helen peered round it.

'You've a visitor waiting downstairs,' she smiled.

'Thought you might need cheering up so called by to see if you'd like to come to the cinema tonight?' Philip said when she got down to the hallway.

'Oh Philip you're so good to me and I'm such a misery at the moment.'

'You just need a good laugh. Cineworld in town is showing a repeat of 'Bridget Jones' Diary'. My secretary saw it last week and says it's a hoot.'

'I've seen it advertised and it looks good. I missed it first time round.'

'I phoned to check and the film starts at half past seven. We might be a bit late by the time we park but there are usually about fifteen minutes of ads first.'

'Give me a second till I grab my things,' and she scooted upstairs again.

'The film runs for 1 hour, 40 minutes,' Philip said when they were in the car, 'so we'll have time for a coffee afterwards.'

'Reneé what's-her-name was great,' Vina said in Dino's café after the film. They were seated in a booth space, giving them privacy from the other diners.

Neither of them felt in any rush to get home and Philip wanted any excuse to remain a bit longer in Vina's company. He'd sensed a change in their relationship recently and was sure Vina felt it too.

'What was Colin Firth like in that jumper with the reindeer on it?' Vina laughed.

'He did look a bit of a plonker. So what's the latest about Bill?' Philip asked, the first time he'd brought up the subject all evening.

Vina sat back as their coffees were brought to the table. Feeling a bit peckish, they'd also ordered some toast and butter. 'Unfortunately, not a lot,' she said when the waiter turned away. 'I've really come to a dead end until I speak to Molly. Poor Bill doesn't know the time of day.'

'Will you visit him again or wait until you hear from Molly?'

'I don't know,' Vina said, as she buttered her toast. 'If she contacted me I'd be able to decide what happens now. I can't stay here indefinitely.'

That thought had also been on Philip's mind recently. He was dreading her going away as she was the first woman he'd met since his broken engagement all those years ago that he felt comfortable with. 'Maybe you could extend your time over here. I think your type of ticket would allow that,' he reminded her. He stirred another spoonful of brown sugar into his coffee. 'I think you'll hear from Molly soon, after all she must be as keen to meet you as you are her.'

'I thought she would've phoned by this time even though she's down in Manchester.'

'She'll be very worried about her husband though and it might take her a few days to get her head round the idea of having a half-sister. It must have come as a shock to hear about you.'

'Mmm,' Vina nodded, 'that's true. I was so excited about the fact that Bill had a daughter that I hadn't thought of it from her side.' She wiped some froth from the coffee away from her mouth.

She found Philip so calm and easy to talk to and he seemed sensitive to every nuance and twist in her story. She knew he was a very caring person and it worried her sometimes that she was beginning to look on him as more than a friend, aware that she needed to return home soon.

When they drew up at the guesthouse, Philip kissed her goodnight. This was not the kiss of their previous meetings; it was more intense, full of longing and hunger and she found herself returning his desire. Desperate to keep herself from falling in love with him, she pushed him away gently. 'I must go, Philip, I don't like going into the house too late and disturbing the others.'

'Right, what about coming over to mine on Sunday and I'll cook lunch for us both?' When she nodded her thanks, he got out and held the passenger door open for her; then after another brief kiss he watched her until she went into the house.

Chapter Forty-Seven

Vina was glad that Philip had offered to collect her on Sunday with public transport being infrequent that day.

'It sounds as though things are moving, even if at a slower pace than you'd like. I know it's a cliché but Rome wasn't built in a day.' Philip stopped speaking to overtake a typical Sunday driver, going at less than 20 mph on the deserted main road. He continued speaking once they were safely ahead of the slow coach.

'It's a pity about Bill's dementia, but Molly should be able to tell you more when she phones.'

'If she phones. I've heard nothing since I was at Hollytrees last Saturday.'

'She will,' Philip reassured her, indicating to the car behind that he was turning left. 'And with her account, plus what you heard from Betty Black, you'll be able to fit all the pieces together,' he said as they drove along Fern Crescent.

When he turned into the driveway of No 28 Vina had a sharp intake of breath. She couldn't imagine the large town house belonged to him alone but it did.

'I guess it's a bit big for one person,' Philip smiled when he saw her astonishment. 'But I bought it as an investment years ago when we were in a buyers' market.'

Using the remote to open the garage door, he drove in and closed the door behind them. 'We can go into the house from here,' he said, steering her towards a side door in the garage wall.

They went along a small passageway, which led into the large kitchen, a lovely bright one extending out from the back wall of the house.

Before they settled down, Philip gave her a tour. The house was on three levels, basement, ground floor and upper floor. Philip lived on the ground floor level, using the basement as an office and the upper floor mainly as storage space.

Philip led her outside to the back patio, where they sat

at the garden table to enjoy a glass of wine before lunch. The bird table in the centre of the back lawn was full, all the various species chirping madly and nudging their way over to the tastiest nuts. Despite the season, there were still one or two roses in evidence, making Vina yearn for the wattle and jacaranda and all the other native bushes of her homeland.

Philip caught the look on her face. 'Our roses last much later up here in Scotland, I've occasionally had a rose lasting almost until Christmas. Down south their roses bloom earlier than ours but they'll be dead or dying by this time.'

Vina pointed to the barbecue. 'Shades of home,' she smiled.

'Yes, in our climate we can't eat al fresco as often as you do but, saying that, I've used the barbecue a few times this summer. It's covered over now for the winter, a bit too chilly for us to eat outdoors today,' he said, topping up their glasses.

She took a sip of her wine and smiled over at him. 'I've almost finished reading Jean's diaries and I feel as if I know her now, how she ticked and what she was really like. It's been therapeutic.'

'That's good.' Philip waited for her to continue.

'At least I know from her writing that Bill was unaware of her pregnancy, so he didn't desert her after all. I'd have hated to discover that he had.'

'That's excellent news.' Philip got to his feet. 'Please excuse me, Vina, but I want to check on the potatoes and the roast. I don't want to present you with a burnt offering.'

'Can I help?'

'No, just you sit and relax. I enjoy cooking but don't do much when I'm here on my own so it's a pleasant change to have a guest.'

While Philip was in the kitchen, she checked her mobile but there were no messages. Sighing, she switched it off again.

'You can tell me more about your visit to Dundee last weekend since we couldn't discuss it at the cinema on Friday night,' Philip said when they were seated at the dining room table. 'I know about Bill's house in Fox Street becoming an insurance office but you said you went back to his old bungalow in Broughty Ferry the following day.' He filled her glass again but didn't refill his own, having already said he would run her back to the guesthouse later.

'I stayed overnight at The Park Hotel in Dundee and after lunch I took the bus back to Broughty Ferry. The couple at No 9, the Spencers, were very helpful and directed me to Hollytrees Nursing Home where Bill now stays. I think he must have been very handsome in his younger days but he's now a pathetic old man suffering from dementia,' she sighed.

Philip nodded. 'I have a few clients who were astute businessmen in their day but now suffer from Alzheimer's or some other form of dementia. Sometimes I have to visit them to deal with business matters and it's so sad to see them as shadows of their former selves. It's such a cruel illness.'

'Bill's known in Hollytrees as Adam. It's his middle name. I don't think he understood much of what I was saying but he did react to the name Jean and he seemed to think I was Jean.'

'Well it proves you must resemble her and he must have loved her when he responded to the mention of her name.'

'His care worker, Paul, came into the room while I was there.'

'Was he able to help?'

'Not really but I gave him my address and phone number. So now I've reached a bit of an impasse where I can only wait for Molly to get in touch with me.' Although she was trying to remain upbeat, Philip could detect some despondency in her demeanour.

After lunch, Philip suggested they watch a DVD of André Rieu?

'Is he the one who conducts all the Strauss waltzes? That would be lovely,' she said when he nodded, and she settled down while he loaded the DVD.

By the time Philip was driving her back to Muirbank her spirits had lifted once more with the wine, the company and the gorgeous music they'd enjoyed together.

Chapter Forty-Eight

On Tuesday morning Molly was keeping her usual vigil at Ted's bedside.

Luke had returned to Dundee during the week for his tutorials and spent the weekend in Manchester. He'd gone home on Sunday night, leaving Molly at the hospital on her own. There was a supply teacher taking her class while she was away.

Yesterday Beth and Greg joined her at the hospital and they stayed with her last night at the Golden Orb Hotel where she'd been allocated a room indefinitely. She'd enjoyed their company and was grateful for their support.

Ted had remained in the coma throughout this time and Molly felt she was living in a bubble, her world at the moment being her room in the hotel and her days spent in these four walls. What went on in the outside world was of no interest to her and the radio and TV news sounded so trivial with Ted lying here lifeless. Molly prayed that he would regain consciousness soon so that he could be transferred to a Dundee hospital. It would be much easier to visit him there.

Although she knew that things would never be the same between them, she did feel pity for him and hoped he would make it. She found it harder to feel any pity for the young woman passenger, whose parents the police had traced and who'd travelled south to identify their daughter. They had not attempted to see Ted or speak to Molly, for which she was truly thankful.

She brushed her hand down the sleeve of her blue mohair jumper. Luke had brought it, along with a selection of other clothes, when he returned to the hospital at the weekend just past. Until then she'd washed through the only garments she'd brought with her and dried them on the radiator in her room.

She was sure that the Golden Orb had laundry facilities but she didn't have the energy to even think about that meantime.

The heat in the room made Molly drowsy and soon afterwards her head fell on to her chest and she dozed off.

She started to dream. She heard someone say 'water' but she wasn't fully awake yet. The same voice repeated 'water' and in her slumbers she recognised it as the voice of someone she knew. She came to with a start when she heard the word 'water' for a third time.

It was Ted. She got to her feet and sure enough his eyes were open and he was pleading for a drink. 'Ted, you're awake,' she said, and rushed out into the corridor. 'Nurse, Nurse,' she shouted before hurrying back to Ted. She poured some water into a glass and held it to his lips. He had barely enough energy to drink but she put a straw into the glass and encouraged him to try and suck up some water. 'Good, Ted, is that better?' she smiled, smoothing his hair back from his face. 'You've been sleeping for a long time. He's awake,' she said breathlessly when Nurse Bertram came in.

The nurse took Ted's pulse and smiled down at her patient. 'So you're back with us Dr Bishop, I'll get Dr Sharp to come and have a look at you.' She disappeared, her heels clicking their way along the corridor outside Ted's room.

Molly prayed that mentally Ted was intact. Realising that he was trying to say something, she leaned nearer and held her ear to his mouth.

'Sorry,' he said, tears rolling down his cheeks. 'Don't deserve you, Molly,' he breathed, then fell back on the pillow after his exertion.

'Everything's fine, Ted. The past is gone and it's the future that matters. You had an accident Ted, a car ran into you last week on the way to your conference and you've been in hospital in ever since.'

Molly had never seen Ted cry before and she wondered if this was the result of the trauma. He'd always been in control of every situation he found himself in and strode through life with great energy and determination, letting no one get in his way. 'It's wonderful to see you awake at last,' her voice cracked and she had to fight to keep her own tears at bay. 'You gave us all a real scare, you know.'

'Where am I?'

'In Manchester City Hospital. I've been here for over a week and Luke came down at the weekend. Beth and Greg visited you yesterday. None of that matters though, Ted, the important thing is that you are awake again.'

'Have you had any sleep?'

'I've been staying at the Golden Orb Hotel near the hospital. It's very comfortable and the staff have been really kind.'

Ted smiled up at her and she realised how much she'd missed that smile in recent years.

'I was on my way to the Golden Orb Hotel for a conference,' he said, his voice stronger now. 'What happened to the other driver?'

'He was unhurt. The police have interviewed him and think he might be charged with dangerous driving.'

'No, it was an accident. Don't let them press charges.'

Seeing he was becoming agitated, Molly soothed him. 'You can tell the police when they speak to you. Now get some rest.' She was glad he hadn't asked how his passenger had fared; either he had forgotten she was in the car or he didn't want to bring up the subject to Molly. Either way she was spared from thinking up an answer. 'I think he's tired himself out by talking so much,' Molly told Dr Sharp a short time later. Ted eyes were closed but he opened them when the Consultant spoke to him.

Once Dr Sharp had left the room to continue on his rounds, Molly pressed Luke's number on her mobile to give him the good news.

'Dad's awake, darling,' Molly told him. 'Dr Sharp is certain that his brain is fine and thinks Dad will make a full recovery.'

'Thank God,' Luke's worried tones responded, 'is there any word of him getting home, Mum?'

'Not yet but I'll stay here until he's ready to come home. Even then, it won't be home but a transfer to Ninewells. He wants to go home of course but both Dr Sharp and I have explained to him how impossible it would be for him to manage at home.'

'It will seem strange for Dad to be a patient in the hospital where he works. How's his mood? And is he able to speak clearly?'

'His mood seems as you would expect after the trauma he's been through, you know a bit emotional, but we had a normal conversation.'

'I bet he was glad to know you were there.'

'Yes, he was. I've been sitting at the side of the bed reading so that he can get peace to sleep. You know what they say, sleep is the best medicine.'

'It sure is. I'm over the moon Mum at such wonderful news. Will you tell Dad I'll come down to see him nearer the end of the week?'

'I will, darling, and how was college this morning?'

'Okay. We didn't get that boring tutor, the one I told you about. He's off sick and his replacement is much more inspiring, really enjoyed his lecture.'

'That's good, Luke. I'll let you go and get your lunch now and I'll ring you again tomorrow.'

'Thanks, Mum. You try and get some rest now that the worst is over.'

'I will. Bye.' Molly felt almost light-hearted as she hung up, something she hadn't experienced for many months past.

Chapter Forty-Nine

'Vina,' Monica tapped on her bedroom door just after six o'clock on Wednesday morning, 'your sister, Sue, has phoned you.' She knocked again and poked her head round the door, to ensure that Vina was awake.

'Thanks, sorry about the time.' Vina jumped out of bed and banged her head on the cambered ceiling above it.

'That's alright, I was up anyway to get breakfast organised.' Monica's head disappeared again and Vina heard her padding her way downstairs.

Rubbing her head, Vina pulled on a dressing gown and rushed down to the phone in the hallway. Slightly out of breath, she lifted the receiver. 'Hi Sis.'

'Evening, or I guess it'll be morning over there. Have I phoned too early?'

'Not really,' Vina laughed. 'It's only ten past six in the morning.'

'Oops, sorry, difficult to judge the time difference. Anyway, how goes it?'

'Slowly, still waiting to hear from Molly but think she should be home from Manchester soon. Frances from the adoption agency has come to a bit of a standstill too. Everything hinges on Molly being willing to speak to me.'

'And what are you up to today?'

'Philip has taken a few days holiday from work and he's offered to drive me up to Dundee to visit Bill again. I'm going to take the photograph of Jean that Betty gave me and see if it stirs up memories for him.'

'It might do. You and this Philip seem to be getting on well,' Sue wheedled.

'We're just friends, but he has been very supportive of me during my search.' Despite sounding low key, Vina was glad Sue couldn't see her blush.

'Everyone's fine here too, with the usual mad rush of driving the kids around. They all send their love, Andy too.

Says he'll give you a ring in the next few days.'

'Great, but tell him not to worry, I know he's busy. I'll text him soon. Love you,' she finished, yawning.

'Love you too,' Sue responded before she hung up.

* * *

'Do you remember me, Bill?' Vina asked as she sat down on the chair nearest him, with Philip seated on his other side. 'I visited you recently. I'm Jean's daughter and this is my friend Philip.'

'Hello Bill, how are you?' Philip asked. He wasn't looking for a reply and Bill didn't disappoint.

Vina took Bill's thin hand, with the veins on the back standing out blue and puffy. 'Look,' she said to Philip, as she move aside the sleeve of Bill's shirt to reveal a tattoo on his forearm. 'It's the fish tattoo that Jean wrote about in her diary. He got it done because his birthday was in February and Pisces was his birth sign.'

'I was just letting Philip see your tattoo,' she explained to Bill, who continued to stare at her but said nothing.

'Do you not feel cold wearing a short sleeved shirt and no jumper?' Philip asked him.

When no response came, Vina shook her head. 'It's very hot in here, and there isn't much air coming in through the window.'

The old man suddenly spoke. 'Jean,' he said, drawing his fingers down Vina's cheek. Then he sighed and looked down at his feet again.

'I've brought you a picture of Jean,' she said hesitantly and laid the picture on his knee. 'That's Jean,' she pointed to the older woman in the photograph.

Bill stared down at the picture but remained mute.

'The child in the younger girl's arms is me, Nancy. I'm Jean's daughter,' she stopped, 'and yours, you're my father Bill and I'm your older daughter.' Turning to Philip, she murmured, 'I wonder if he understands what I'm saying? I so long to have a proper conversation with him.'

Philip shook his head. 'It's difficult to say how much he is taking in. Maybe you should let him think about it for a while, not give him too much information at once.'

It was only after Vina stood up and went to the window to look out over the grounds that the old man stirred suddenly and held the picture up nearer his rheumy eyes. 'Jean,' he said, smiling at the girl in the picture.

'Do you know Jean?' he asked Vina, when she returned to his side.

'No I don't but I'm Nancy, Jean's daughter, and yours.'

He shook his head and the tears coursed down his face once more, confusion and agitation both evident in his behaviour.

'I think we'd better call it a day, Vina, he's only going to become more upset. Perhaps say more next time you visit. Will you leave the photograph with him?'

'I can do because I had this photograph taken from the original so that I could send it to Sue but I haven't posted it yet. Otherwise I would've been loath to part with it. It's all I have of my mother,' she finished lamely.

Philip took the picture that Bill had dropped on to the floor at his feet and laid it on the top of the bedside locker. 'The more he looks at it, the more he might remember. What about his care worker, perhaps you should have another word with him?'

'The girl who let us in said Paul's on holiday. If only Molly would phone me.'

Philip put his arm round her waist. 'She will,' he said, trying to sound more positive than he felt, 'now, let's go and find somewhere to eat.'

They said their farewells to Bill and left him staring vacantly into space.

Chapter Fifty

On Thursday morning a brighter than usual light coming through the blind wakened Vina. In the accompanying stillness, she opened the vertical blind to betray the snow drizzled over the rooftops. Her gaze dropped to the white dusting on the grass and a sigh escaped from her, her breath painting a picture on the windowpane.

She chuckled softly, her childhood joy at seeing such a scene as strong as ever. Although her memories of living in Scotland were vague, she did recall the winter before her family left Glasgow being a snowy one. At least she thought she remembered it; she did wonder sometimes if it was simply that Mum and Dad had described that winter when they were talking of the family's life in Scotland.

Either way, she saw herself trudging through the deep snow, her wellington boots leaving furrows as she walked. She saw the snow fights with Dad in the garden and a snowball that crumbled and slipped down inside her coat collar. She shivered at the memory.

She headed off after breakfast, glad she'd had the foresight to pack a pair of knee high boots. Although more for dress wear than protection against snow, they were at least better than shoes.

Vina spent the day in the city centre, where she bought gifts for the family back in Penguin. By the time she returned to the guesthouse it was almost four o'clock. The slight covering of snow had melted and it had turned to a dirty grey slush beneath her feet.

Back at Muirbank, she opened her bedroom door to a surprise.

'Hi, Sis, guess who?'

Sue was sitting in the chair in front of the window,

smiling up at her.

'Sue,' Vina screamed with delight and hugged her tightly, laughing and crying in turn.

'When I spoke to you on the phone yesterday morning I was about to leave for the airport. I didn't tell you because I wanted to surprise you. I've come over to spend two weeks with you,' Sue said once she'd disentangled herself from Vina's embrace.

'That's fantastic but how ... who ... when did you get here? And what about the kids?'

'Hey, one question at a time please. My flight landed about 2 p.m. I took a taxi from the airport and here I am. The kids are staying with Andy while I'm away. They'll be fine with him and I'm sure he'll survive them staying, even though I bulldozed him into having them.'

'I bet you did,' Vina grinned. Ever since the twins were born, Sue had been the dominant one, with poor old Andy doing as he was told. 'So where are you staying?'

'I had a chat with your landlady when I arrived and Monica agreed that I could stay here if I slept on a fold-up bed in your room. She's going to bring it up after dinner. Hope you don't mind?'

'Do I have a choice?'

'Not really. Now tell me what's been happening, I want to hear every last detail since you left home.'

'Okay but it isn't very comfortable sitting in the bedroom. Tell you what, let's go along to 'The Coffee Pot', my favourite café just round the corner from here.' Vina's feet no longer felt tired, excitement had put paid to that. 'By the way, my friend Philip is dropping by tonight.'

'Great, I want to meet him. You can begin your story on the way to the café.'

* * *

By the time they returned to the guesthouse it was almost six o'clock. Sue stretched and yawned. 'Think I'll skip dinner tonight, Sis, as I'm feeling a tad jet-lagged. Could I have a nap on your bed while you're downstairs and then I'll be more awake to meet this man of yours later?'

'I wouldn't call Philip this man of mine, we're just friends.'

'So you tell me,' Sue winked, slipping off her shoes before she stretched out on the bed.

Helen greeted Vina when she walked into the dining room. 'I hear Sue has arrived over from Tasmania. It'll be lovely for you to have her company.'

'Yes. She thought she'd spend a couple of weeks with me. Typical of Sue, she just turns up unannounced.'

'Is she staying here then?' Gwen asked.

'Yep, Monica is going to fix us up with a fold-up bed. Sue's having a sleep at the moment. She's tired after the long flight.'

'I'd sleep for a week after travelling such a distance,' Jenni said.

Helen poured some water for Vina. 'Sue can help you with your search.' Vina had told her friends in the guesthouse about the reason for her visit to Scotland and they were all most interested in everything that she'd discovered so far.

* * *

'Philip's here,' Vina said to Sue a couple of hours later, when she'd gone into her room to find her lying awake. 'Do you feel better after your nap?'

Sue threw back the duvet and swung her legs out of the bed. 'Yep,' she said, rubbing her eyes, 'and I'm going to get up now or I won't sleep tonight.'

She got to her feet and crossed the room to the en suite. 'You go back downstairs, Sis, and I'll have a wash and tidy myself up before I join you.'

A short time later Vina broke off from her conversation with Philip when Sue came into the sitting room. Philip got up from the settee and Sue understood immediately Vina's infatuation with him. Distinguished, a couple of inches over 6' she guessed, with warm eyes and a gorgeous smile.

Philip shook her hand, a firm, warm handshake. 'Pleased to meet you Sue, Vina's told me a lot about you and Andy.'

'Oh dear. I hope she gave you the edited version?'

'You've no need to worry on that score,' he laughed.

'And I've been hearing about you too,' she countered, as they all sat down again. 'I believe you're an expert on art and music.'

'I don't know about an expert, but I'm interested in both.' He looked across at Vina. 'We could take Sue to something in the Concert Hall while she's here.'

'That would be good. The acoustics are excellent in the hall, Sue.'

'Vina tells me you're a lawyer, Phil, sorry we Aussies tend to shorten names,' Sue apologised.

'That's no problem, I was always Phil at school. And yes, I work in a law firm in the centre of Glasgow. I was going to retire last year but decided to work on a bit as I really enjoy my work.'

'And his secretary makes a lovely cup of coffee,' Vina put in.

Philip laughed heartily before continuing his conversation with Sue. 'Did you have a problem getting leave from work to come here?'

'I only do casual work part time, I can't earn too much or it affects my pension. So I guess you could call me a lady of leisure.'

'Or as much leisure as you get with two grandkids of 13 and 10 to run after,' Vina added.

'My daughter's ex went off and left her a while back, so she had to take on full-time work again,' Sue explained to Philip. 'To save the cost of a child minder after school, yours truly stepped in.'

'She loves it,' Vina chipped in, 'she's a big kid herself.'

Sue laughed. 'I have to plead guilty to that one. My twin brother, Andy, is in charge in my absence.'

'You'll be able to help Vina complete her search,' Philip smiled.

'Yep, I could maybe come up to Dundee with you, Sis, to visit Bill again?'

'Yes, but I wish Molly would ring. She's the last piece

in the jigsaw.'

'She's maybe not home from Manchester yet. Did you tell Sue about the car accident?'

Vina nodded. 'Right Sue, tell me what's been happening over in Penguin while I've been away.'

For the next half hour the conversation centred round the coastal town, with Philip keen to hear about their lives over there.

Chapter Fifty-One

Luke stood beside his dad's bed in Ninewells Hospital on Friday night. The hospital was opened in 1974 and proved a good replacement for the old Dundee Royal. The Royal closed in 1998 after serving the community for almost two hundred years.

Ninewells wasn't far from the airport and you could hear planes taking off from time to time. With Ted working in the hospital, he was used to the noise and it therefore didn't annoy him.

'Welcome home, Dad. Mum and I had a good run up last night, the motorway wasn't too busy and we had no hold ups.' They'd left Ted in Manchester to come up by ambulance today.

'I wouldn't call it home, being in here,' Ted said. 'I just want to get these plasters off and get back to my own flat.' Dad had moaned that he wanted home but Dr Sharp said it wouldn't be possible, as he'd need specialist care in a ward with the right kind of equipment. Dad was fully aware of this but was making sure he registered his dislike of the idea.

'You know the plasters won't be off for many weeks yet Dad, so you're going to have to content yourself and let others look after you for a while.'

Ted made a face. 'It's all right for you, you're getting to be a hard man, Son.'

Seeing the laughter in Ted's eyes, Luke said, 'I'm remembering what they say, you have to be cruel to be kind.'

'You have to be cruel to be kind,' Ted mimicked.

Luke ignored the jibe. 'Is there anything you want, Dad? Mum said she'd be in to see you tomorrow and would bring whatever is needed.'

'No, I'm fine. You get off and meet your mates, I'm not very good company at the moment.'

'Okay, if you're sure, see you soon, Dad.' Luke turned away, relieved, and walked towards the ward entrance. His relationship with Dad had always been a bit strained and right now it was even harder to think of something interesting to say.

* * *

'How did you find him?' Molly asked, when Luke stopped off at the house on his way from the hospital to meet his pals.

'He's grumbling like mad about getting home but he knows he needs specialist care that he can only get in hospital.'

'Doctors always make the worst patients,' she agreed.

'Did you go to see Grandad today?'

'Yes, I popped in after I'd done the washing. He was looking good, Paul had trimmed his hair and he was wearing that new jumper I bought before I went to Manchester.'

Luke had the feeling there was more to come and he was right. 'A weird thing happened though. Paul was telling me that a woman had called in while I was away and told him she was my half-sister. I'm all up in the air about it; I don't understand it as Dad was never married before he met Mum.'

'Paul didn't mention this to me while you were away. Mind you, I think he was off duty each time I was there. Have you contacted the woman?'

'I haven't got my head round it yet but I need to phone her to find out more.' She chewed her fingernail for a moment. 'I've always dreamed of having a brother or sister, but I'm scared to get too excited in case it turns out to be a hoax.'

'I don't see why, it doesn't make sense for her to lie.'

'I suppose not. I asked Dad about this woman but he didn't seem to understand. We'll need to wait until one of his better days. I think I'll try to ring the woman over the next few days.'

'Good idea,' Luke gave her a hug. 'I better go,' he said, and a few moments later she heard the door close behind him.

Chapter Fifty-Two

December 2012

Sue's eyes opened a crack when Vina came out of the shower next morning. 'You alright, Sis? You look like you haven't slept a wink,' Vina said, moving closer to Sue's fold-up bed.

She got a groan in response. 'I hardly slept at all, just dozed now and again. I've got a thumping headache. Have you any major plans for today, Sis, 'cos I feel really done in,' she said through a yawn, her head going deeper into the pillow.

'Your body clock's all mixed up, love, sleep on a bit longer. Why don't you move into my bed where you'll be more comfortable and I'll tell Monica you won't be down for breakfast?' Before she'd finished speaking, Sue had taken up residence in her comfortable divan bed. Vina smiled and pulled the duvet up over Sue's shoulders, then tiptoed over to the wardrobe to get her clothes. She shivered and dressed quickly in her denims and warm polo-necked sweater. By this time in December the British weather was very cold and she thought longingly of the early summer sunshine they'd be having back home.

After breakfast, she sat downstairs in front of the lovely fire with Jean's diaries on the coffee table beside her chair. She hadn't managed to read any more of the diaries last night so this was an ideal chance while Sue slept off her jet lag.

As ever she came across interesting snippets showing Jean's character. She read again Bill's letters to Jean, not weeping so much as on her first reading but still with a lump in her throat.

Nearing lunchtime she went back upstairs.

'Hi, Sis,' Sue smiled up from her bed, 'thanks for

leaving me in peace. I feel really back to myself again and will last out now until my normal bedtime. Has it been hard-going?' she asked, nodding towards the box, lying open on Vina's bedside table.

'Yep, but I'm glad you've wakened as I can't read any more at the moment. Are you hungry?'

'A bit, but not ravenous. By the way, I've got something for you.' Sue brought a small jar out of her case and held it out to Vina. 'Lucy sent it to you,' she smiled.

'Vegemite,' Vina whooped with delight, 'that's fantastic. They have one over here called Marmite but it isn't nearly as tasty as our Vegemite. How did you get it from Lucy?'

'I forgot to tell you that last night. Lucy met me at Tullamarine when I was changing planes and she gave it to me. She said you wouldn't be enjoying your toast without Vegemite.'

'Bless her, I'll ring tomorrow to thank her. Do you fancy some fresh air?'

'Good idea. Do you have anywhere in mind for us to go?'

'Not really.'

Sue smiled. 'Then I have a suggestion. Will you take me to visit the Art Gallery? I'd like to see where you and the handsome Philip first met.'

'Sure.' Vina returned everything to the box and locked it again. 'You go and shower and we can eat in the restaurant at the Gallery when we get there.'

* * *

Vina wakened very early next morning, sensing a presence standing at her side. She knew that this was in her imagination but Jean's words in the diaries were still ringing in her ears. Was the ghost of her biological mother watching over her?

Sue at the other side of the room was still sleeping soundly.

Vina switched on her bedside lamp and propped herself up on her pillows to continue her reading from yesterday. She went through the diary right to the end and held her breath as she read the last entry, written the very day before Jean threw herself under the tramcar.

Oh God, if only that telegram hadn't come. Why did you let him survive? What am I going to do God? He'll kill me when he finds out I've been unfaithful, even though I thought he was dead when I met Bill.

Dear God, why did you take my darling Bill and leave the hateful Frank? I'm also worried about him hurting Nancy. She's only a baby, none of this is her fault.

Thank God Mum is with us, as I know she won't let him do anything to Nancy. Mum said nothing when she read the telegram but I could tell she was seething inside. I wish I could be strong like her.

Can he force me to go back and live with him? If only we were divorced, then he'd have no hold over me. Please God help me, show me what to do.

Jean's desperation came across the page loud and clear. What a state her mind must have been in when she was writing these lines and that must have worsened to lead her to die in such an awful way. Vina knew from the way Jean wrote that her mother had loved her dearly and only utter despair at her situation would have allowed her to take her own life. It was clear that Jean had total faith in her mother to take care of Nancy after her death and this must have given her some consolation.

Some time later when stirring noises began to come from Sue, Vina got up and went off for her shower. When she emerged again, Sue was up and sorting out what she was going to wear today. 'Morning, Sis, have you been up long?'

'Not very, but I'm ready for breakfast.'

'Me too. I can feel the first pangs starting up. Where are we off to today?'

'Thought I'd take you to meet Betty Black this afternoon. Are you alright with that?' Vina asked but the bathroom door had already closed behind Sue.

'Hello Betty,' Vina said when she phoned after breakfast, 'I've had a surprise visit from my sister, Sue, and I wondered if I could bring her to meet you today?'

'Delighted,' Betty agreed immediately. 'How lovely that she's come all this way to be with you. Will you manage to come for lunch, I'd love to have you both?'

'That's very kind, Betty. Will we say about twelve o'clock?'

'Ideal, Vina, see you later love.'

* * *

When Betty opened her door to them just before midday, Vina handed her a posy of flowers. 'We bought them in the florist's shop on Glenburgh High Street. They're in a bag of water to spare you having to arrange them in a vase.'

'Thank you, both of you, they're gorgeous.' Betty stood back to let them in and she hugged each sister in turn. She laid the flowers down on the marble fireplace and stood back to admire them. 'And how are you settling in at the guesthouse, Sue?' she asked.

'It's very comfortable and it's fab to spend some time with my big Sis.'

Betty smiled happily. 'Yes, it's lovely for you both. Now, I could make us lunch here but instead I'm going to take you both to the café in Glenburgh Town Hall. It opens on a Sunday for lunches and that way you'll see our Town Hall which has been refurbished in recent years.'

'I remember seeing this building the day Philip brought me over to Glenburgh for the first time,' Vina said when they arrived at the Town Hall. 'I thought then what a magnificent building it was.'

'Yes, the re-facing and cleaning of the stonework was done a few years ago.'

Betty took them into the well-designed café extension at the rear of the building. With its glass exterior, the café was bright and airy and it was here that the three women ate. Over lunch, Betty was keen to hear more about their lives, growing up in Penguin.

* * *

'It's Philip,' Vina said to Sue, who was rummaging in the

drawer for something, 'he wonders if we'd like to go with him to the Concert Hall tonight. It's a Welsh Male Voice Choir. Interested, or are you too tired after our visit to Betty today?'

'Not a bit of it, you know how I love choral music, Sis.'

'Did you hear that, Philip? Yes, we'd love to go with you. Okay, see you then,' she said and switched off her mobile. 'Right, Sue, we'd better get our skates on, Philip's going to pick us up at half past six.'

'Fab, race you for first shower,' Sue laughed, disappearing into the bathroom before Vina had time to blink.

* * *

Sue crashed out the minute she got into bed after their evening at the Concert Hall.

Sleep still eluded Vina and she picked up the diary. She read about Jean's joy of motherhood and how Nancy would smile up at her and raise her chubby arms to be lifted. There was a beautiful scenario of Nancy touching her toes and gurgling with delight. Routine entries returned once Jean went back to work in Hamilton's and Vina enjoyed reading again Jean's account of the V.E. day celebrations in Glenburgh.

Yippee, the war is over at last. I can hardly believe it after six long years. I joined in the celebrations on High Street today, everybody hugging and kissing and dancing around in the street. It felt like the whole town was there.

But, as before, she wept as she read the entry on Thursday 17th May.

A telegram came today. Frank is alive and is due home in a couple of weeks. Why did he have to survive the war? Why should he live and my darling Bill die? Couldn't the German prison guards have finished him off? I'm so scared of what he'll do to me when he finds out about Nancy. I know Mum won't let him harm the baby but I can't escape him. I am his wife after all, God help me.

Vina shivered as she read this entry, knowing that it was only about ten days later that Jean threw herself under the tramcar.

She remembered Betty telling her that Frank did indeed return to Glenburgh sometime in July of that year. He turned up on Agnes' doorstep but was most unconcerned about Jean's death. Agnes sent him packing and he'd never been seen again in Glenburgh.

The last entries in the diary were extremely depressed.

And with Jean's death, those entries that revealed so much of her sorrow and happiness, came to an end.

Very carefully Vina closed the diary for 1945. She placed it in the box beside the 1944 one and put out her lamp. Then she lay down in the hope of sleep overtaking her although sure that she'd be searching for it for some time yet.

Chapter Fifty-Three

After their evening at the Concert Hall, there came a few days of showing Sue some of the sights of the city, before they took the train up to Dundee on Wednesday to pay another visit to Hollytrees. Paul, Bill's carer, opened the door to them and threw a glance of recognition in Vina's direction.

'Hello again,' she said as she signed them both in. 'You might remember I visited Bill Prior, sorry Adam Prior, a couple of weeks back. This is my sister, Sue, who's recently come over from Australia to join me.'

Paul nodded. 'Yes, I remember you and I passed on your details to Adam's daughter, Mrs Bishop.'

'I haven't heard from her, do you know if she plans to get in touch?'

'She did mean to contact you, but she stayed on in Manchester for some time while her husband remained in hospital there. I understand he's been transferred to hospital here and she's back home now. I think she was finding it hard to believe that she had a sister although she does want to meet you and talk about things. I'm sure she'll be in touch soon.'

'Is her husband making a good recovery?'

'He is, although it will be a long way back for him. I don't think Mrs Bishop will be able to visit her dad as frequently as she did previously, because she'll have to divide her time between them both. She did call in here the day after she returned from Manchester but quite often Luke visits alone.'

'Luke?'

'Adam's grandson, Mrs Bishop's son.'

'Wow, I have a nephew, Sue,' Vina looked at her sister in wonderment.

Feeling it hot in the home, Vina pulled off her scarf, imagining she could smell Jean's scent as she did so. 'Do you think I could see Adam again? I have another picture to show him that might jog his memory.' She'd copied the picture of Bill in uniform so that she could leave it with him. 'I promise we won't tire him,' she said when Paul hesitated.

'Alright then, Mrs Bishop and Luke made no objection to your last visit.'

Sue smiled at Vina as they walked towards Adam's room. 'Your relatives keep appearing out of the woodwork, I wonder how many more there are?'

'No,' Paul smiled as he opened the bedroom door for them. 'Mrs Bishop only has one son so Luke is Adam's only grandchild.'

* * *

'How's he been?' Luke asked Paul when he went to visit Adam later that day. The last lecture of the afternoon had been cancelled, leaving Luke some free time before dinner to make a quick trip to Hollytrees.

'He's quite settled at the moment although I think he does miss your mother visiting. Even though he doesn't appear to recognise her, I think during his times of lucidity he wonders where she's gone.'

'She'll be here soon, Dad's coming on by leaps and bounds. We're now at the stage of trying not to let him do too much.'

Paul smiled. 'Always a good sign. He's made an excellent recovery, considering his injuries.'

'He has but of course there's still a long way to go and he'll be in plaster for many weeks yet. He's been given a wheelchair although I can see problems ahead with getting Dad to use it.'

Luke sat down and took Adam's hand. 'Great to see you Grandad. Mum sends her love.' He turned round when he heard Paul clearing his throat.

'That lady from Australia was here again today, with her sister this time. She left another photograph to see if it would help Adam to remember something from his past.' Paul lifted the two pictures Vina had left and handed them to Luke.

'Mrs West hopes to hear from your mother soon.'

Luke stared at the pictures for a few moments. 'I know this one of Grandad in uniform, we've a copy of that at home, but the other one means nothing to me. I've never seen any of those people before.' He laid them back down on the bedside cabinet. 'Mum will phone the woman soon Paul as I know she finds it all very intriguing, but she hasn't been able to think of anyone but Dad up till now.'

'I can well understand that. Right, I'll leave you and Adam in peace,' Paul said and left the room, closing the door quietly behind him.

Chapter Fifty-Four

When Philip answered his office phone first thing on Thursday morning, he knew straight away that she had good news. 'She's phoned, Philip. Molly, she phoned me, she wants to meet. Oh Philip, I can't wait to see her.'

'That's great, Vina. Have you arranged a time?'

'She's asked if I could go up to Dundee today. We're going to meet in the Park Hotel, the one I stayed in when I went up to Dundee the first time. I'm leaving shortly to get the bus into town and will take the train from Queen Street station.' Vina finally drew breath, allowing Philip the chance to ask a question.

'Will Sue go with you?'

'No, we felt that the first time I meet Molly I should be on my own.'

'Yes, probably best. Well, good luck and let me know how you get on.'

* * *

By the time she got into the station and purchased her ticket, Vina had only about five minutes to spare before the train was due to depart. She'd barely settled herself into her seat when the traffic light on the platform changed to green. Her compartment was empty apart from a young lad at the far end.

Once she'd shown her ticket to the conductor, she lay back on her headrest and closed her eyes. But it was no good; she was too excited to sleep. 'I'm going to meet my sister.' The words kept repeating in her mind. What would Molly be like, would she have taken after Bill or Margaret? Would she and Molly resemble one another? She wondered if Molly was having the same thoughts. She was at the door of the compartment waiting for it to open before the train had drawn into the station.

The cold air hit her the moment she stepped down on to the platform and she was grateful for the fleece-lined coat she'd bought in the House of Eden when the weather had turned so bitterly cold a couple of weeks ago. She'd really appreciated Gwen loaning her staff card for the purchase, resulting in a sizeable discount on the normal price.

Knowing her way this time, she got to the hotel about ten minutes early, and waited in the foyer for Molly to arrive. They'd given their description to one another but even if they hadn't Vina felt sure she'd know Molly immediately.

And she was right. When an auburn-haired lady, wearing a smart black trouser suit and a green polo-necked jersey, entered the hotel Vina went towards her. 'Molly,' she said to the newcomer, her tone unquestioning.

'Vina,' the woman replied in a rich, husky voice, her smile lighting up the foyer. She threw her arms around Vina.

'I've been so looking forward to meeting you.' Vina's words were muffled by Molly's tight embrace. There was no hesitation, no embarrassment, it was as though they'd known one another all their lives.

'Do you want to go into the restaurant for coffee?' Molly asked, 'or would you prefer to stay here?'

'I'm comfortable here.'

'Great, coffee or tea?'

'Coffee.'

Molly spoke to the receptionist, then parked herself in an armchair facing Vina, hanging her jacket over a nearby chair.

Vina smiled at her across the table. 'I've dreamed about meeting you for weeks now.'

'Sorry to be so long getting in touch but my life has been on hold lately.' A shadow passed across Molly's cheery face as she said this.

'How is your husband?'

'He's making steady progress. He's lucky to be alive.'

'It must have been such a worry, both for you and Luke. Paul at the nursing home told me about your son,' Vina explained.

'Yes it's been hard for Luke trying to fit in visiting his dad and his grandad with his college lectures. And supporting me too. He's been a good help to me during the past year.' Molly hesitated, and then said, 'Ted and I split up earlier this year. I hadn't seen him for months until his accident. Despite that though I stayed at the hospital until he was transferred to a hospital up here as I couldn't …. couldn't leave him on his own.'

'Of course not, especially when he's still recovering from his injuries.'

Molly nodded. 'He was lucky, it was mainly fractures and he's in plaster but the prognosis is good and shouldn't affect him getting back to work.'

'What line of work is he in?'

'He's a pathologist at Ninewells Hospital in Dundee. Started there as a junior and is now in charge. He's a workaholic and would go off his trolley if he couldn't function properly.'

'And is Luke following in his dad's footsteps?'

'No, he's doing an English and History degree, much to Ted's disappointment. I was proud of Luke for standing his ground.' Molly leaned back when the waitress appeared with the tray and placed their drinks down in front of them. She stopped speaking until the girl moved away again.

'Ted can be quite autocratic. Anyway enough about my family, I'm dying to hear about you and how you found out about Dad and me.'

'It's a long story but I'll try and give you the condensed version, otherwise we could still be here at midnight and I'll miss my train back to Glasgow.' Vina explained about her meeting with Betty Black and the tin box containing Jean's diaries. Molly listened intently, without interrupting. When Vina spoke of the telegram about Frank which had resulted in Jean's suicide, she saw Molly's eyes moisten and moved on swiftly.

It was when she came to the part of her adoption following her grandmother's death that Molly broke in. 'Is West your adoptive surname then?'

'Yes, my original name was Nancy Morrow, as Jean still had Frank's surname.'

'He's the abusive husband who was supposed to have died in Italy?'

'Yes, Jean and your dad, sorry our dad, planned to marry on his next leave but he didn't come back until after the war and Jean was dead by that time. Bill, sorry Adam, didn't know Jean was pregnant as he didn't receive her letter telling him of her condition.'

'It's such a sad story, but I'm glad to know that Dad didn't desert her, I'd have hated if that had been the case.'

'He didn't desert her. He didn't get her letter which went down with the Ontario. He was transferred to another ship before he was captured. I think he probably heard about Jean's death from his mother as there was a piece in the paper about the suicide and she'd recognise the name Jean Morrow. I realise now that neither Bill nor his parents knew anything about me.'

'I remember Granny Prior quite well. She died when I was 7 but I saw a lot of her, as she and Grandpa lived in Dundee quite near us. They'd moved up here after the war and Grandpa worked in one of the jute mills. I was also lucky to have my mother's parents too so I had four grandparents altogether when I was growing up.'

'That's great, I wasn't as lucky as all my adoptive grandparents had died at a young age.'

'How did you first find out that you were adopted?'

'A friend blurted it out during an argument when I was 12. I was heartbroken of course and gave my adoptive parents a hard time for a while but gradually I came to terms with it.'

'Tell me about your adoptive parents?' Molly asked, refilling both of their coffee cups.

Vina swallowed her last mouthful of coffee. 'They were lovely and the best parents I could have wished for. John, my Dad, was a dentist in Glasgow and I was 4 when he took up a post in Tasmania. Sadly, Dad died of a heart attack when he was only 49. I was 21 at the time and the twins were 18.' A shadow passed over Vina's face when she thought back to the dreadful shock her father's death had been to the family and, noticing her hands clenched tightly, Molly reached across the table and squeezed Vina's arm.

'It's good you had siblings when you were growing up.'

'Yes, Mum and Dad tried for years to have a baby before they adopted me but, when I was almost 3, Mum discovered that she was pregnant. She had twins, my brother Andy and my sister Sue.' She smiled. 'Sue's older by twenty minutes and she bosses Andy mercilessly.'

'Women,' Molly said and they both laughed again.

'Sue's flown over here for a couple of weeks to help me with my search.'

'And did your adoptive parents know about Jean and my Dad?'

'No, all they knew was that my biological mother had lived in Glenburgh, near Glasgow, and that I'd been looked after by my grandmother before I came to them. Mum knew nothing about Jean's suicide as everything's kept confidential in adoption cases.'

'So when did you decide to try and trace your biological family?'

'Not until after Mum's death last year. I wouldn't have tried to trace Jean while Mum was still alive. I was too scared of hurting her.'

'I can understand that but I also see why you'd want to find out. We all need to know about our roots, don't we? And how did you know where Dad was?'

'The three letters your Dad sent Jean made it obvious that he knew nothing about me. The Adoption Agency in Edinburgh, which is helping me with my search, was able to tell me that he'd been taken prisoner for the remainder of the war. I also found out that Jean and her mother moved, with me, to a bigger flat in Glenburgh, an address which Bill would not have known.'

'It's so sad what happened to them, and yet if they had got together, then Dad would not have met my mother after the war and I wouldn't have been here. Life's strange, isn't it?'

'But you are here and I'm glad about that. Sue's keen to meet you.'

'And I her. Did Dad recognise Jean from the picture

you left with him?'

'Not really, although he has called me Jean a couple of times. Betty Black told me that some of my mannerisms remind her of Jean.'

'Poor Dad is hardly able to recognise anyone these days, he doesn't even know me some days, or Luke, and he doted on his grandson.'

Once they were in the dining room and had ordered, Molly spoke again. 'You seem to have made good friends in Glasgow.'

'Yes, the ladies in the guesthouse are lovely and I've formed a close friendship with Helen. She comes from Orkney but works in a bank in Glasgow.'

'And you mentioned your friend Philip earlier?'

'I met him when I first arrived, at the art gallery. He's really kind, ferrying me around to places I need to go for my search. He's also taken me to concerts and I went with him to his friend's art exhibition at Chatelherault in October.'

Molly's eyes widened. 'I thought when I first came into the hotel today that I'd seen you before and I recognised your voice from somewhere. It must be from Chatelherault. I was there with my friend who knows someone in the art group.'

Vina shook her head. 'What a coincidence, I can't believe it. If our paths had crossed there, we wouldn't have had to wait until you came back from Manchester to get together.'

Molly suddenly snapped her fingers. 'I've got it, you and Philip gave us your seats in the cafè. I remember how much I admired the green jacket you were wearing.'

'How weird that we were so close and yet unaware that we were related.'

Lunch over, Molly walked to the station with Vina. 'You must come soon and have lunch at our house, so that you can meet Luke. It would also be great if you and I could go to Hollytrees and try and get some of the story through to Dad.'

'I'd like that. And you must meet Sue before she goes home.'

'Yes, and also Philip.'

Molly waved to the departing train and walked to the exit in thoughtful mood.

Chapter Fifty-Five

'It's great to hear your voice again, Molly,' Vina said, when her newly found sister phoned the following day about noon. The call had come in on the house phone.

'I forgot to say yesterday in all the excitement of meeting you that I was coming to Highfield today to stay with my friends Beth and Greg until Sunday night. With Ted being well looked after in Ninewells and Dad in Hollytrees, Beth persuaded me that I needed a change of scenery for a couple of days. My students have their Prelims looming up and are on study leave on a Friday so I got the early morning train down today.'

'Where did you say your friends live? Is it near here?'

'Near where we went to the art exhibition. Beth and I were at school together and did our teacher training in Glasgow. She met Greg during that time. I seem to have known her forever.' Molly's love for her friend was evident in her voice.

'I enjoyed our time together yesterday, haven't thought of anything else since.'

'I'm looking forward to telling Dad about the two of us meeting but I'm not sure how much he'll take in.'

'Will you have time to meet me again while you're at your friends' house?'

'That's why I'm phoning. I wondered if Beth and I could meet you and Sue in town tomorrow for coffee?

'Tomorrow would be fine for us. Sue has almost another week with me before she needs to return home.'

'Excellent, I was hoping to be introduced to her before she went back to Australia. Do you know the House of Eden in Buchanan Street?'

'I do, my friend Gwen is a buyer in there.'

'Could we meet there then? Say at two o'clock.'

'Fantastic, see you tomorrow Molly.' Vina was still smiling as she replaced the receiver on its cradle.

'Is she free to meet us?' Beth looked up from her knitting when Molly went back to the sitting room after her phone call.

'Yep, sounds really keen to meet you Beth and she's going to bring her sister, Sue, with her.'

'That's great, we can take the X11 bus. It uses a direct route with limited stops on the way into town.' Beth put down her knitting and got to her feet. 'Right, I'll just go and organise something to eat, mustn't neglect my guest,' she winked.

When Beth left the room, Molly picked up the knitting lying on the sofa. Beth had been making these scarves for months now. The multi-coloured yarn was called Can-Can and when it was knitted it fell into frills.

'I love the colours, and the frills,' she said, when Beth returned to tell her the meal was ready. She held up the royal blue and green scarf. 'Can't wait to wear it.'

'I'll finish it tonight while we're watching telly and then you can wear it tomorrow when we go to meet Vina.'

* * *

By the time Vina got back upstairs after taking her phone call, Sue was making up her bed. She arranged her pillows to her satisfaction and straightened up, clad in the thick polo-necked sweater she'd purchased in a shop in Muirbank the other day. She didn't want to carry such bulky clothes back home so told Vina she'd leave it with her to wear during the remainder of her stay in Scotland. Fortunately they were the same size.

'Was that Phil on the phone, Sis?'

'No, it was Molly and guess what, we are both going into town tomorrow afternoon to have coffee with her and her friend Beth. Beth lives in the Glasgow area and Molly is spending a few days with her and her husband. That is, if you're happy to go?' Vina added, remembering how Sue hated to be organised.

'I'm fine with it,' Sue smiled, 'in fact more than fine, I'd love to meet your other sister.' Their relationship was strong enough that she had no fear or jealousy about this new sister who had come on to the scene. 'What about today? Are we still going to have a trip on the open-topped Glasgow bus tour you told me about?'

Vina looked at her watch. 'Yep and if we head off now we'll be on time for you to get that guided tour of the City Chambers.'

* * *

When Vina and Sue got to the restaurant in the House of Eden next day, Molly and Beth were already seated at a table for four. 'We thought we'd bag a table in case the restaurant got busy,' Molly said, getting up and coming towards them.

Vina thought Molly looked glamorous in royal blue. Apart from red, Molly would suit any colour. She introduced Sue, and her biological and adoptive sisters hesitated only a second before hugging. Vina had been certain there would be no resentment between them but was relieved to have it confirmed.

Excitement caused them all to speak at once. When Molly moved aside and said, 'Vina, Sue, this is Beth', Vina remembered the friend sitting patiently at the table behind them.

'I'm so sorry, Beth, for our rudeness,' she apologised, shaking hands warmly.

'That's no problem,' Beth assured her, 'it's wonderful to be part of this truly fantastic get-together. I know Molly is thrilled to discover she has a sister.'

'Right, if we all settle down at the table, we can decide what we're going to order,' Molly indicated to the empty chairs awaiting the new arrivals.

'They do a gorgeous afternoon tea in here, don't they, Beth?'

Beth nodded. 'Sure do.'

'There's enough here to feed an army,' Vina said when the cake stands were brought to the table.

'We can always ask for a doggy bag. Are you enjoying your visit to Scotland?' Beth turned to Sue.

'Very much, although I wouldn't mind some higher temperatures occasionally,' she laughed, helping herself to a prawn sandwich.

'Wish I could say that you get used to the cold,' Beth

replied, passing the milk jug around the group. 'But I hate it myself, even though I've been born and brought up in Scotland. Is your climate in Tasmania as hot as it's said to be on mainland Australia?'

'Not really, we usually have a sea breeze to cool things.' While Beth and Sue discussed the weather in Penguin, Molly turned to Vina. 'I'm going back to Dundee tomorrow and I wondered if you were free to come with me to visit Dad next week. I thought maybe Friday? You could come back to our house for dinner afterwards and meet Luke. We've plenty of room if you'd like to stay overnight.'

'That would be ideal. I'm looking forward very much to meeting my new nephew and I'm keen to speak to Bill again and find out if he's remembered any more about his time with Jean.'

'I wouldn't place too much hope in that direction, love. Still it's worth a try.'

The next hour and a half flew by with lots of memories being dredged up. Vina and Sue spoke about their school days in Tasmania and the other two told of their long friendship, starting when they began school at the age of 5.

'What a magnificent scarf,' Vina said as they were getting ready to leave.

Molly gave them a twirl. 'It's lovely isn't it? Beth knitted it for me.'

'I've made a lot of them, they're really simple to knit,' Beth told Vina. 'I was thinking of Molly's suit when I chose these colours.'

'A perfect match,' Vina and Sue said simultaneously, then laughed. They'd often done that when they were growing up. Mum always said it was telepathy.

'It's been lovely to meet you Sue,' Molly took her arm as they were leaving the restaurant. 'Would you like to come with Vina next week when she comes up to Dundee? I thought maybe next Friday.'

'I can't, I'm due to fly back to Tassie next Thursday; it was literally a flying visit. I think anyway that it would be better for you and Vina to visit your dad on your own. Too many people could be confusing for him.'

'Yes, you're probably right but today has been a good chance for us all to meet. Take care of yourself Sue and have a good trip home.'

The four ladies parted company on Buchanan Street outside the store. Molly and Beth were heading up to the bus station to get the X11 back to Highfield while the other two were going for the Muirbank train.

Chapter Fifty-Six

Philip came out of the shower and pushed his used rugby togs into his sports bag. Dressed again, he slung the bag over his shoulder and made his way out of the warm dressing room and into the cold, frosty air. Although just after four o'clock, at this time of year it was dark as night. He looked up at the host of stars and smiled contentedly; he loved this sort of sky.

Some of his fellow coaches had already left the complex to have a Chinese meal and the usual few drinks at a nearby restaurant. Normally Philip would have joined them but tonight he'd a pile of stuff to get through for his meeting first thing on Monday. He knew the booze would be flowing after their boys' team win this afternoon and he needed a clear head for Monday's meeting so, Saturday night or not, he decided to give the restaurant a miss.

On the way over to the car Philip's thoughts were centred round Vina's meeting with Molly and her friend this afternoon. He'd been delighted to hear how well their first meeting on Thursday had gone, and it was great that they were meeting up again today. But the selfish part of him was concerned that now she'd found her biological family, she would return home soon. He couldn't bear to think of them living at opposite sides of the globe.

As he dumped his sports bag into the boot, it occurred to him how much Vina featured in his life by now. He wanted to tell her how much he loved her and ask her to marry him but drew back from actually saying it. He found it difficult to express his feelings, especially in matters of the heart. His lifelong fear of rejection was partly responsible for his reticence but his previous broken engagement didn't help either.

He switched on the ignition. The car park was almost empty by now so he got out on to the road fairly swiftly and headed straight for home.

He decided to speak to Vina soon before she returned

to Tasmania. If she left, he might never see her again. From what he could gather she was pretty well over the divorce from her husband and didn't appear to be romantically attached to anyone in Penguin. He supposed he could ask Sue about that but he hadn't up to now been on his own with her long enough to open up the conversation.

Engrossed in these thoughts, he jumped when the car behind him tooted as the light changed to green. He raised his hand in thanks and moved forward.

The phone was ringing when he got in. It was Vina. 'How did your rugby match go today?'

'Fine, our lads beat the other team soundly and are looking forward to a good scrap against our next opponents from the Borders.' The team was doing well in the amateur league at the moment and they had high hopes of a win next Saturday.

'Didn't think you'd be home yet. Thought you'd be out with the lads.'

'I declined, have some work to do tonight. Haven't started yet though.'

'I won't keep you on the phone then but just to let you know that Sue and I had a very successful meeting with Molly and her friend, Beth, this afternoon. I'm going up to Dundee next Friday and Molly and I will visit Hollytrees together.'

'Great stuff. I look forward to hearing more about it later. By the way, do you want me to drive you and Sue to the airport on Thursday evening?'

'That's really kind of you Philip but I don't want to feel I'm using you.'

'Of course you aren't, I'm offering to do it. You'll probably feel a bit sad when you see her off so we could go for a meal afterwards.'

'Thanks Philip that would be super.'

'Great. I won't arrange to meet any sooner as I know you'll be busy during your final few days with Sue but I'll see you both next Thursday. We can arrange a definite time for me to pick you up nearer Thursday.'

'Okay, I'll let you get on with your work now so you

don't have to continue into the wee small hours.'

'Shouldn't take me long. Thanks for phoning, Vina. Take care,' he said before the line went dead.

He sat looking at the phone for a few minutes before beginning work, wishing she was sitting opposite him at the table. He yearned for her nearness and decided to propose to her soon. If she agreed to marry him, he'd buy her an engagement ring before the wedding. Even though they weren't in the first flush of youth, he wanted to do something romantic to celebrate their engagement.

Chapter Fifty-Seven

'That's Philip now,' Vina called to Sue, when she saw the car pull up at the gate. She heard his feet crunching up the driveway as she opened the door. Monica came out of the kitchen as he carried Sue's case out to the car.

'Have you got everything?' Vina said to Sue as she came downstairs.

'Yep, and thanks to Phil we should be at the airport in loads of time. Thanks for everything, Monica,' she said, kissing the landlady's cheek.

Monica handed her a paperback. 'I've just finished this and it was really good. I could hardly put it down. Thought you might enjoy it on the long plane journey,' she said in a choked voice, gave Sue a quick hug and turned back to the kitchen abruptly.

The three of them sat in silence on the way to the airport, each with their own thoughts. Once parked, Philip found them a trolley and pushed Sue's luggage into the terminal building. Thankfully the queue was short and she was checked through speedily, allowing them time for a drink in the bar before her flight was called. It was a relief when the Gate number for her flight was announced. 'Thanks for the lift, Phil,' Sue said and turned to Vina, embracing her tightly. 'So glad you've tracked down Molly and Bill but don't forget us back in Penguin.'

'Of course I won't, how could I?'

Sue punched her arm playfully. 'Only joking, you numpty. Stick in there with old Phil, you make a good couple,' she whispered, and turned away, walking through the gate and down the long corridor ahead.

With Philip's arm around her, Vina waved to Sue until she disappeared from sight.

As they drove out of Glasgow Airport and on to the M8, Philip said, 'I thought we could try for a table at the new Riverside Hotel that opened a few months ago. I haven't been there myself but one of my colleagues took his wife for their anniversary a couple of weeks ago and he said the food and service were excellent.'

'It sounds great but will I be well enough dressed to go there?' Vina was wearing casual trousers, a heavy polo-necked sweater, and not a scrap of jewellery.

'You look superb as ever and I'm sure mid week people won't dress up. I could take you home to change but it would mean us eating very late on.'

'No, don't do that, as long as you feel I won't disgrace you then I'm happy to go as I am.'

'You certainly won't disgrace me,' he smiled.

When they got to the hotel, they stood outside to admire the lights reflected on the water from the luxury apartments situated on the opposite bank. Soothed by the sound of water lapping against the edge of the banking, they stood quietly and gazed up at the twinkling panoply above them.

The dining room was prepared for a party, a 40th birthday balloon on each table and birthday banners festooned across the walls.

'Can I help you sir?' a waiter came out from the kitchen area when he saw them standing there. 'Is it a table for two?'

'It was, but since you've a party due in we might leave it for another night.'

'There's no problem, Sir. We've another restaurant at the back of the hotel. If you come with me, I'll show you to a table.'

The room was small and intimate, the walls decorated in red and gold and there were red candles on the tables. There were only four other people dining that evening.

'You don't look over the river here,' the waiter said, pulling out Vina's chair for her, 'but it's peaceful and the same menu is served in both restaurants.'

'Okay?' Philip glanced at Vina.

'I like it in here,' she said.

Philip turned back to the waiter. 'Thanks, this will do

us nicely.'

'Can I get you something to drink while you are looking at the menu?'

Philip scanned the wine list and looked across at Vina. 'Red or white?'

'White please.'

'I think we'll have a bottle of Australian Chardonnay,' Philip said and winked at Vina.

The waiter laid the menus in front of them and sat a bottle of Chardonnay in an ice bucket beside the table. He filled their glasses and took their food order, a pasta dish for Vina and a steak for Philip.

Philip raised his glass to Vina's. 'Cheers,' he said.

'Cheers. What are we celebrating?'

'To good company.'

'I'll drink to that.'

It wasn't until they reached the coffee stage that Philip broached the subject that had been so much on his mind in recent days.

'We've had some great times together over recent weeks, haven't we, Vina?'

'We sure have. But I don't like the way you said that, makes it sound like our outings are coming to an end.'

'No,' Philip laughed, 'I didn't mean I wanted them to end, in fact, the opposite is the case. I want us to continue going out together.'

'Well I'm glad we're agreed on that score,' she smiled.

'Vina, I'm sure you're aware that I have begun to care more and more for you over the weeks we've been friends. Actually, that's wrong,' he stammered, cursing himself for putting this over so badly, 'I don't care for you, least I do care deeply but more than that, I love you.'

He stopped for a moment while she stared at him.

'Oh, Vina, I'm making such a mess of this but I'm … I've fallen in love with you and I really want to ask you to marry me. Oh God, you must think me an imbecile,' he finished, looking down at the table cover.

'I don't think anything of the sort, Philip, I love you too but was afraid that you didn't feel the same, just enjoyed having me for a friend while I'm here. What are we like?' she laughed. 'One's as unsure as the other about showing our feelings.'

'You'll marry me then?'

'Of course I will.'

'It'll mean you giving up your life in Penguin.'

'I know love, and I'll miss the twins and the rest of the family, but I want to be with you for the rest of my life and to do that I have to stay here. Your work's here and I don't want you to give that up when you enjoy it so much. I'm happy to stay, as I love Scotland. I was after all born here,' she reminded him.

'What about your unit in Penguin? You won't need it as we have my place.'

'I can sell it. Why don't we go over to Tassie next summer, UK summer that is, and we could stay in my unit while we're there. Afterwards I could put it up for auction.'

'I like the sound of that, I'd like to go to Penguin where you grew up.'

After the meal Philip dropped Vina at the guesthouse. 'Have a lovely time with Molly tomorrow, and don't forget to think about what we've discussed tonight.'

'I won't be able to think about anything else. Can I tell Molly our good news?'

'Of course.' He kissed her at the front door before, reluctantly, he let her go and she slipped quietly into the hallway.

Chapter Fifty-Eight

When Vina and Molly walked into Bill's room on Friday afternoon he was standing at the window looking out over the garden. The holly bushes were laden with berries and the light covering of powdery snow that had descended overnight gave the scene a Christmas card effect.

'Looks like we're having a good day,' Molly murmured. 'Dad taking an interest in things, a good sign.'

'It's the first time I've seen him out of his chair,' Vina whispered. 'Hello Bill,' she greeted him, going over to stand beside him. 'It's gorgeous out there, isn't it? When the weather improves you'll be able to have a walk in the garden.'

Bill didn't acknowledge her at first but when he did turn towards her he stared at her for a long time. Temporary recognition slowly dawned and he reached out a hand and drew it gently down Vina's face, tracing a path from her forehead, down her nose to her lips, then up over cheekbones to her ears. He moved to her eyes and sketched his way along the line of her eyebrows and under her lower lashes. She closed her eyes as he did this and when she opened them again he was smiling at her.

'He believes I'm Jean. Molly, do you think I'm causing more confusion by calling him Bill?'

'No, Dad is William Adam after all, it's just that I've never heard him addressed by his first name before. It's almost as if he's aware of our relationship,' Molly said to Vina quietly, 'perhaps he sees the slight resemblance.' The two women had decided that they did share some features in common, such as the wide bridge to their noses and the dimples round their mouths when they smiled.

Vina picked up Jean's picture from the bedside table.

'Have you had another look at this, Bill?' She held it up where he could see the picture clearly. 'Do you remember her and how much she loved you?'

For a few moments he stared at the face in the picture. 'Jean,' he said to the woman in the photo. He turned to Vina and repeated the name Jean.

Seeing tears rolling down his cheeks, Vina took the picture from him and put it back down at the side of the bed. She stroked his bony, blue-veined hand. 'I'm not Jean, but I am Jean's daughter,' she hesitated, 'and yours Bill.' She resisted the desire to call him Dad, not wanting to confuse him any more than he was already.

Molly cut in, planting a kiss on her father's forehead. 'You were in love with Jean when you were in the Navy, Dad, and were sad when you heard she was dead. What you didn't know was that she gave birth to your daughter, Vina, who's come here to visit you.' He kept staring at Vina and Molly carried on, hopeful that he was at least taking something in. 'After the war you met Mum and I was born. So you see, Dad, you have two daughters, Vina and me.'

The distress and confusion was clear on his face. 'Don't say any more, Molly, you'll only upset Bill and yourself.'

'No, I'm thrilled to have found you and I want to try and make Dad aware that he has another daughter. And it isn't as though he betrayed Mum because he knew Jean was dead before he courted Mum.'

Vina smiled and looked at Bill through moist eyes while she linked arms with her half-sister. 'I love Molly, Dad,' she finally used the word, 'and you too. I'm glad I've met you at last.' He returned her smile but, when he started to yawn, they told him they'd return to see him soon and headed back to the car.

* * *

'It's fantastic to meet you,' Vina smiled, shaking her nephew's hand.

'Do you want Aunt Vina or will Vina suffice?' Luke asked.

'If you call me Aunt Vina you'll make me feel ancient. My niece back in Tassie uses my first name only. We don't stand on ceremony in Australia.'

'How was Grandad today?' he asked Molly.

'Quite good, and he seemed to know who Vina was this time.'

'He also recognised Jean as someone he'd known in the past,' Vina chipped in. 'He seemed to sense too that Molly and I were both related to him.'

'Well that's a step forward,' Luke replied. 'Just when you're thinking Grandad has gone too far into the dementia to remember anything ever again, he rallies and becomes more lucid.'

'Sadly that's par for the course with dementia,' Molly said. 'Now, love, are you going to eat with us tonight or are you going out?'

'No, I've arranged to meet the lads at the pub, but I'll call round tomorrow so that I can get better acquainted with my new aunt,' he grinned.

'Bye then darling, have fun. Do you like Indian food, Vina?' she asked once he'd left.

'It's my favourite cuisine.'

'Good, then to save cooking I'll phone for a carry out. I'll go and get the menu from the kitchen.' Once they'd chosen and the phone call was made, they settled down to wait for the banquet to arrive.

'I have some more news for you,' Vina said.

'Good, I hope.'

'Well I think it's good and hope you'll agree. Philip and I have decided to be married,' she said quietly.

'Fantastic.'

Molly danced her sister around the room. 'We'll open a bottle of plonk to celebrate,' she said, once she'd come down from the ceiling.

Chapter Fifty-Nine

On Monday Philip had cut down on appointments and offered to take Vina for a drive and a late dinner. All he would say was that she needed to bring overnight things.

'Where are we going?' she asked when he picked her up at the guesthouse.

He tapped his nose. 'It's a surprise, but first of all I thought we'd look at engagement rings. That is if you haven't changed your mind.'

She gave him a playful poke in the ribs. 'You know I haven't. But where do you suggest we go?'

'The Argyle Arcade,' he said as they were coming over the Kingston Bridge into the city centre. 'Almost every shop in there is a jeweller's.'

'What about parking?'

'We can use the multi-storey at St Enoch's Centre. We could grab a coffee in one of the cafès before we go to the shops. Mostly fast food outlets and pretty noisy places there but we can have dinner in a posh establishment this evening.'

'Sounds good to me.'

'That's settled then.' Philip drove up the spiral ramp that led into the multi-storey car park, taking a ticket from the machine on the way in.

'It's difficult to choose, they're all so lovely,' Vina said when they were in the third jeweller's shop they'd come to in the Arcade. She held out her hand to let Philip see the ring she'd just tried on, a five stone diamond ring with a price to match.

'I like that one, Vina. It really suits your finger.'

'I've got very broad fingers, and although I liked the solitaire I tried earlier, the stone looked lost on my finger.'

'That's a truly magnificent ring,' the salesman said, 'it's an old Victorian setting.'

Vina looked at Philip and nodded. 'We'll have this one,' he said.

'Very good, Sir.'

'Glad we bought the wedding rings while we were in the shop,' Philip smiled at Vina in the car mirror, as they were travelling through the Clyde Tunnel, the quickest route from the south side to the west-end. Vina's face had taken on a yellowy glow from the lights on the walls of the tunnel.

'Yes, it was sensible. But I'm worried about what you've spent on my ring, Philip. I've never had such an expensive piece of jewellery in my entire life.'

'Don't worry love, I've still got plenty put by for a rainy day as the old saying goes. I wanted something special for you. And it's a one off, I don't plan to have another engagement,' he laughed, as they emerged from the tunnel and he took the turn-off heading west.

'I can hardly wait to wear it.'

'They said it would only take forty-eight hours to engrave so you'll have it by Wednesday. Did you tell Molly our news?'

'She was over the moon and she's thrilled about being a witness at the wedding. We had some wine to celebrate that I was in love,' she laughed. 'But seriously, it was great to be with her and Luke and I felt very welcome in their home.'

'And what about your visit to Bill?'

'He seemed more lucid, might even have known who I was.'

Philip pressed his hand over Vina's and left it there until a build up of traffic required his two hands back on the steering wheel. 'Any word from Sue since she got home?' he asked, following the line of traffic down a steep hill.

'I had a text from her, she had a good flight, with no delays.'

She caught Philip's eye and smiled at him, enjoying the smell of his after-shave, a musky scent. 'I love you Philip Dawson. I think I did from the moment you nearly knocked me over in the Art Gallery.'

'And I you.' They came to some road works, with a workman holding up a red STOP sign. When the man swivelled the board to GO, Philip was off like a shot.

'When will we have the wedding?' he asked, as they sped along the A82. 'I mean, what's the point in waiting?'

'No point at all.'

'Don't think there's sufficient time to organise a Christmas wedding? You need to let the Registrar know at least fourteen days before the big day. Or it may be twenty-one days. I must check on that.'

'I was married at Christmas last time,' she said quietly.

'We'll forget that then, unlucky. Early in the New Year,' he suggested.

'Molly has invited us up to Dundee to have Christmas dinner with them. She wants us to go up on Christmas Eve. What do you say if we have Christmas in Dundee and a wedding in mid January? We'll only be having a few friends at the wedding so it could easily be arranged at short notice.'

'Sounds sensible. It would give us time to arrange a wedding in the registry office in Park Circus. That is, unless you wanted a church wedding?'

'No, registry office is fine with me. Where's this Park Circus?'

'It lies high up on a hill overlooking the city. The registry office is at No 22, I believe the property used to belong to Walter Macfarlane, a foundry owner.'

'That's sounds ideal. And there's still time for Molly and me to get our outfits. Philip, why don't we have the meal afterwards at the Art Gallery?'

'Yes, we could. They do rent out rooms there for functions. The only problem might be the small number of guests. I think the gallery may only cater for very large parties, although we could enquire. I know they have a pleasant cafè cum restaurant in the basement, with a conservatory attached that looks over to Kelvingrove Park. Do you want to check it out?'

'Yes, let's, where else could hold so many memories for us than the place we first met? Where are we going, darling?' she asked, as she saw the sign for Loch Lomond.

'I've booked dinner, bed and breakfast at Cameron

House. It stands on the banks of Loch Lomond although you won't see the stunning view in the dark.'

'What about your work?'

'I asked Valerie to cancel my appointments for tomorrow.'

'Great.' Vina liked Philip's secretary, who was always pleasant and friendly. 'Have you stayed at Cameron House before?'

'No, this is the first time. I've played golf there and had dinner afterwards but never overnight. Here we are,' and he turned right into the grounds.

In the dim lights, Vina could make out the wooded area they were passing and the moon shining on the water to her left. It looked so romantic and she understood now why so many love songs mentioned Loch Lomond. 'I'm looking forward to seeing the area better in daylight. Fancy a ramble after breakfast?'

'Would be nice except we don't have the proper clothes and boots,' he laughed.

'I'd forgotten that.' She drew breath when she saw the well-lit hotel come into view. 'It's magnificent, Philip, what a magical place to celebrate our engagement. Even if I don't have my ring yet,' she said, her tone wistful.

As she followed Philip out of the car and into the hotel foyer, she thought again how lucky she'd been to meet such a wonderful man. The fates had been kind in guiding her to the Art Gallery that day.

Chapter Sixty

'I wanted to confirm that you and Philip are still able to stay with us at Christmas?' Molly asked Vina on the phone a few days later.

'We're looking forward to it, and I'm keen to let you meet Philip.' As she was speaking, Vina's engagement ring sparkled up at her in the light coming through the bedroom window.

'I haven't met him yet but I've seen your face light up when you speak about him, so I know he'll be a charmer.'

'Well I think so, but I doubt he'd agree. He's really quite shy.'

'We'll soon knock that out of him, won't we?' Molly laughed.

'How's Ted progressing?'

'He's being given really good treatment in the hospital, although of course he's moaning constantly. He's a typical man, thinks he should be cured in five minutes. However, he'll have to content himself for a few weeks yet until the plasters come off. He's walking about the ward on crutches.'

'No chance of a reconciliation for you two?'

'Too much water under the bridge for that, I could never trust him again.' Molly had told Vina about Ted's extramarital affairs but she'd kept quiet about the rape. The vision still haunted her.

'See you both on Christmas Eve,' Molly said before she hung up.

* * *

Vina had scarcely finished with Molly's call when her mobile rang again and this time it was Sue.

'Hi Sis, I thought I'd give you a ring before I go to bed. How are things over there? Any further progress with Bill?'

'When I went to Hollytrees with Molly, he was having

a good day and seemed to sense that we are all related although whether he has taken in the whole picture is difficult to say. As you know he has periods of lucidity and then times when he goes back into his own world.'

'And how's the handsome Phil?'

'I do have news on that front, Sis, Philip and I have become engaged.'

There was a moment's silence and then a huge scream of delight came over the line. 'Fantastic news, not that I'm too surprised as I sussed out the romance going on between you two. When did this happen?'

'I just got my ring yesterday. I was going to call you tonight but you've beat me to it.'

'I take it then you'll be staying over there?'

'Yes, Philip has his work here and I don't think he'd like the high temps in Oz, even though we're cooler in Tassie. I like Glasgow, so I'm happy to live here. I'll miss you and Andy of course but we can visit you fairly regularly.'

'I'm sad you won't be coming back here to live but I'm really happy for you both. Wait till I tell Andy, he'll be overjoyed. When will the wedding be?'

'We think Saturday 12th January, just a quiet do, with Molly and one of Philip's colleagues as witnesses. We'll come over to Tassie later for another celebration.'

'Sure, we must have a bash here too. Pity I couldn't fly back for the big day.'

'Don't even consider it, Sis, it's far too expensive,' Vina cautioned.

'Only joking, I'm afraid there wouldn't be sufficient dosh in the coffers to pay the fare,' Sue's tinkling laugh reached her over the airwaves. 'So you reckon you'll come over in about six months' time?'

'Probably in June. Philip couldn't stand the heat of the Aussie summer.'

'What about your unit?'

'I was thinking about that. Philip and I could live in it while we're over there and I can put it up for auction afterwards.'

'I'm sure you'll get a quick sale, Sis, as it's in a good location. Andy and I will keep an eye on it in the meantime. Door's open,' Vina heard her call out. 'Sorry, Sis, that's my new neighbour at the back door. Speak later,' she said before the line went dead.

Chapter Sixty-One

'Come in, great to have you with us,' Molly beamed at her guests when they arrived on Christmas Eve in the late afternoon. She ushered Vina and Philip into the warm kitchen, out of the biting cold coming in off the Tay. The thick mist that had enshrouded Dundee and the Fife coast for the past few days chilled the bones but at last the gloom had lifted and Christmas Eve dawned, still bitterly cold, but clear.

Once she had released herself from Vina's tight hug, she turned to embrace Philip. 'I've parked down there at the riverside,' he pointed to the car sitting at the sea wall overlooking the Tay, 'in case there wasn't room at your front gate.' Most of Molly's visitors used the steps up to the back door. Apart from delivery vans and other strangers, everyone else used the rear entrance to this back to front house.

'There probably would have been room at the front but not to worry, your car's quite safe down on the riverside. We'll be able to keep an eye on it from the kitchen window. Bring your things upstairs,' she said, leading the way.

'One bedroom or two?' she winked at Vina when they got up to the top landing. She saw their blushes and laughed. 'Only joking, you can make yourself comfortable in this room Philip and Vina you can have the same bedroom as before, the one next to mine.' Leaving them to unpack, she went back down to the kitchen. 'Don't be long,' she called from the bottom of the stairs, 'Dad is waiting for you in the front room. I brought him from Hollytrees this morning.'

Bill was in an armchair facing the door and he looked up when they entered the room. 'Hello, Dad,' Vina said, 'you'll remember Philip,' she added, knowing he wouldn't. 'No Luke today?' she asked Molly.

'There will just be the four of us for dinner tonight and Luke will join us tomorrow. Now let me have a look at your ring.' Vina took it off and handed it to Molly. 'Wow, it's magnificent,' she enthused, trying it on her own finger. I wish you both all the luck in the world,' and she handed it back to its owner.

'I think Dad sees your resemblance to Jean,' Molly directed Vina's eyes to the look on Bill's face.

'Yes, he's been calling me Jean from the first time he set eyes on me.'

'You know Vina now, don't you Dad? And this is Philip, her fiancé. Bless him, he's having a good day. He's quite content, much better than the last time he was here. Now, why don't you two settle down and talk to Dad while I organise some tea for us all. You must be ready for a drink after the long drive.'

Philip was trying to have some conversation with Bill when Molly returned with the tray. She handed round the cups of tea and Bill took his eagerly. 'You love your tea, don't you Dad?' Molly smiled at him, placing a small table at the side of his chair where he could rest his cup. Then she sat down on the sofa beside Vina.

'We'll need to get our outfits for the wedding soon, Vina. I'm so excited, never in my wildest dreams did I think I'd be a witness at my sister's wedding.'

* * *

'Happy Christmas everyone,' Luke called out next day, as he came through the kitchen into the front room, taking off his fleece in transit. He kissed Molly and Vina and shook hands with Philip. 'Hi old fella,' he patted his grandad's head. 'How are you today?'

'Dad's having a good day,' Molly said, 'and I think he's looking forward to his Christmas dinner.' Once they were all settled down and Luke had opened a bottle of bubbly and passed the glasses round, she raised her glass.

'Here's to us all and especially to the good news of Vina and Philip's engagement. Congratulations and all the best for the future.'

'Congratulations,' Luke said to the happy couple.

After the toast, Molly went over to the Christmas tree in front of the bay window. She picked up a couple of parcels wrapped in bright Christmas paper with large red bows from beneath the tree and handed them to Vina and Philip. 'Santa left them here for you,' she laughed, her shoulders hunching slightly as she did so, a mannerism Vina had become familiar with. Then she gave Luke and Bill their gifts.

Vina handed round the gifts she and Philip had brought and for the next five or ten minutes there was a great deal of rustling and ripping of paper, accompanied by shrieks of delight as the gifts were revealed.

Molly opened Bill's gift from Vina and Philip and brought out the thick, dark blue sweater. She held it against his chest. 'Vina bought you this, Dad, isn't it cosy?'

The old man looked down at the sweater and smiled.

'I thought the colour would reflect your lovely blue eyes, Dad,' Vina kissed his brow. He caught hold of her hand and drew his other hand gently down her cheek.

Molly got to her feet. 'Luke, could you check everyone's glass and then carve the turkey? Meanwhile I'll take our starters to the table.'

'Let me help you,' Vina offered.

'Everything's ready but come and chat to me while I'm putting it on the plates,' Molly said, and they left the room together.

'Will Ted be having his Christmas dinner in the ward?' Vina asked and when she turned round Molly was in tears. Next minute she was sobbing and blew her nose loudly. 'I'm sorry, I thought I could control it better, especially when we are celebrating Christmas and your engagement to Philip. Please forgive me, Vina.'

Vina pushed a box of tissues across the worktop to her sister. 'No love, it's better to get it out. He's hurt you so much and you need to release some of your pain.'

Molly smiled through her tears. 'I feel better for letting go and it's good to have you here to share my feelings.'

'And I'm here for you anytime. I maybe can't do anything to heal your hurt but I can at least listen.'

Vina stopped speaking when Luke came into the kitchen for another bottle of wine. It was obvious that he noticed his mother had been crying but he said nothing. By the time he came back into the kitchen to carve the turkey, Molly had fixed her make-up again.

'Right, we're ready to start,' Molly said a short time later. 'Could you help me carry through the plates, Vina?'

When they were finished eating, Vina pulled off her paper hat and got to her feet. 'That was a delicious meal, let me help you clear the table, Molly.'

But Molly held up her hand. 'No, just leave everything, Vina, until after we have coffee. Can you see Dad back into his seat in the front room while I switch on the coffee machine? Then we can listen to the Queen's speech while we have coffee.'

Just before three o'clock Molly appeared with the tray. She laid a dish of chocolate mints on the table nearest Bill, then she poured the coffee and handed round the mugs.

'By the way,' Vina said, once the Queen had finished, 'I forgot to say that Sue phoned me before I came downstairs this morning and she and Andy send their love.'

'That was kind of her. I like Sue, she seems such a straightforward person.'

Vina laughed. 'Yes, she certainly calls a spade a spade, always has done. But she has a heart of gold.'

'Were they all having a good time over there?'

'Yep, they'd spent the day on the beach and were about to have dinner after she'd phoned me.'

'Of course, it would be evening there, I always forget the time difference. Was she asking when you were going back?'

'She knows I'll be staying in Glasgow. She's really pleased for us and glad that we are going to have a trip to Tassie in June and have another celebration there.'

'That's a lovely idea, then they will feel part of the excitement too. I know how much they will miss you, Vina, but I'm selfish enough to be glad that you are staying on in this country. I was dreading you returning to Penguin.'

'What about a game of charades?' Luke suggested. 'It's been a family tradition at Christmas to play this after dinner so let's not break the habit of a lifetime.' There seemed to be general agreement to the idea so for the next hour and a half there was great hilarity trying to guess the miming that went on. Bill sat with a smile on his face, content to watch the antics of his family members.

Chapter Sixty-Two

Vina walked out of the cubicle where she'd been trying on outfits. This was the fourth one she'd tried on and, although the others had looked quite good on her, neither she nor Molly felt they had the wow factor they were seeking.

Molly sat outside the cubicle, the word 'wow' forming on her lips for the first time that afternoon, despite having been in a few shops before this one. 'You're lovely in that, Vina, in fact more than lovely, fantastic.'

'I think this has to be the one,' Vina beamed.

'I don't think you should even try on any more.'

Vina walked up and down the dressing room, giving Molly a view of the dress from different angles. 'Yes, this is it,' she repeated.

'Before you take it off, let's ask the assistant to bring us some fascinators for you to try.'

'Okay,' Vina said, when the fascinator had been chosen, 'it's your turn now.'

'I liked the outfit I saw in the previous shop we were in so can we go back there?'

'Do you mean the pale green or the blue?'

'I liked both but I preferred the blue,' Molly walked ahead of Vina to the exit, keen to get a second look at the dress.

* * *

'How wonderful to get off my feet,' Molly said, when they found themselves a table in a café in the Buchanan Galleries shopping mall where they'd bought the outfits. It was almost four o'clock and they'd been traipsing round shops for hours.

Vina studied the menu for a minute. 'I fancy some toasted cinnamon bread with my cuppa.'

'Make that two.' Molly sprawled back in her seat with their carrier bags around her feet. 'I really love that lace design on your dress, Vina. You'll be a gorgeous bride.'

Vina smiled. 'At 68 I'm a bit past being gorgeous,

looking good will suffice.'

'You'll be gorgeous I can assure you. I'm so looking forward to the wedding.'

'I am too, and more excited about it than I'd have thought. I really like that outfit of yours too, Molly. That shade of blue suits you with your auburn hair.'

'The only colour I don't suit is red. You will, being dark.'

'I suppose I do, although I don't wear red often. Can we have a pot of tea for two and toasted cinnamon bread, please?' Vina said to the waitress who'd come to take their order.

'Is it one bread or two?'

'Two slices each, please.'

Molly pushed her auburn mane back from her face and wiped her damp forehead with the back of her hand. 'I think we deserve some sustenance after all the walking about we've done, not forgetting the number of dresses we've tried on. Not that I'm complaining,' she added. 'I wouldn't have missed it for the world.'

'I'm surprised we got the outfits so easily. I really thought we'd have needed to look again another day before the wedding.'

Molly waited until the waitress had left their order and gone away before she replied. 'I'm glad I came down to Glasgow though, we don't have as large a selection of stores in Dundee.' She used some hand gel before touching her bread.

'Want some?' she held it out to Vina.

'Thanks,' Vina rubbed some on her hands. 'I always have that gel in my backpack when I go walking at home.'

Molly stirred some milk into her tea. 'I notice you said at home, wonder how long it'll take before you begin to look on Glasgow as your home.'

'I feel at home here already, but I guess I'll always be an Aussie deep down. You've got butter on your chin.'

Molly wiped the melted butter with her serviette. 'Just as well I'm not wearing my new outfit. How many guests will there be, Vina?'

'Let's see,' Vina began counting on her fingers. 'There's the four of us in the bridal party, the four from the guesthouse, Bill and Luke, that's ten. Then Valerie, Philip's secretary, Betty Brown, Frances from Find Your Family, that's thirteen. My friend Lucy from Melbourne is coming over, that makes fourteen. Then the wife of Philip's witness and two other partners from the firm and their wives brings the number up to nineteen.'

She stopped for a moment. 'Who have I left out? Oh yes, Philip's fellow rugby coaches and their wives or girlfriends. I've lost count but I think it's between thirty and forty.'

'That's quite a manageable number.'

'The room we're having in the registry office is The Avon Room. It's in the conservatory and seats twenty guests, so our closest people will attend the service there and the others will go straight to the Art Gallery. We've booked two large tables in the basement restaurant. The space would hold eighty people so it means we can spread out at the tables.'

'It's such a lovely setting for the wedding.'

'Yep. We'll have photographs taken in there as well as outside ones.'

Vina looked at her watch.

'Philip said he'd pick us up outside the Concert Hall after work so we need to get a move on. Use this to pay the bill while I go to the ladies' room,' she said, putting a £20 note down on the table.

Epilogue

Saturday 12th January, 2013

The wedding day dawned as bright as Vina's mood. If it hadn't been for the bare trees, it could have been April and the forecast was good for the remainder of the day.

Luke drove Vina to her wedding in his car. He'd used a valet service that morning and tied wedding ribbons on the front. Bill sat happily in the back beside Molly, dressed in his best navy blue suit, white shirt and blue and grey checked tie.

'Dad's having a good day,' Molly said, taking his hand, 'you know it's a big day for us all don't you?'

'You look very smart, Dad,' Vina told him, looking round.

He gave her a beaming smile and drummed his fingers on the back of Luke's seat. 'Lovely day,' he said when Luke helped him out of the car in Park Circus.

They made their way inside and were ushered into The Avon Room, where the guests had assembled. Philip and his best man got up and stood in front of the Registrar who was to conduct the ceremony.

Vina linked arms with her dad. 'Ready?' she smiled and he beamed back, unaware that he was about to give his daughter away. As the strains of 'Love Changes Everything' started, they walked towards Philip, followed by Molly and Luke. Once Vina was standing beside her groom, Luke and Bill slipped into a seat at the front.

The bride and groom had written their own vows and Vina stood beside Philip in her ivory silk and lace suit while he slipped the gleaming new wedding ring on to her finger. Afterwards the Registrar announced that they were husband and wife and Philip gave her the customary kiss.

Vina turned to take back her posy of flowers from Molly, looking magnificent in her petrol blue outfit.

They proceeded from Park Circus to the Art Gallery, where Philip had arranged for a short organ recital to entertain the guests while the wedding pictures were taken outside. He and Vina, plus their two witnesses, were pictured in front of the magnificent building where they'd first met and had other pictures taken on the banks of the River Kelvin with Glasgow University standing tall in the background. Some swans swimming regally on the surface of the river also featured in the photographs.

Back indoors a group photo was taken in the main hall, Luke standing close to his grandad, after which they moved to the basement for their meal. Being a Saturday, the café was busy, but their section was divided off from the public space, giving them privacy.

After a toast, everyone found their seat, a place card at each setting.

'I understand you're Frances, the counsellor who helped Vina in her search,' Betty Black said to the woman facing her at the table.

'Yes,' Frances smiled. 'I'm so glad there's been such a happy outcome for Vina, finding her family and acquiring a handsome husband in addition.'

'I'm delighted for her too. I'm Betty Black by the way, I was a neighbour and friend of Vina's mother, Jean.'

'Oh yes, Betty, Vina told me how much you'd been able to tell her about Jean,' Frances smiled at the elderly lady, 'it's great to put a face to the name.'

A guest sitting on Betty's left, joined in. 'I'm Helen, a friend of Vina's from the guesthouse,' and she introduced Monica, Gwen and Jenni.

Frances nodded towards another guest at the table behind them.

'Who's that woman wearing the beautiful red dress?'

'That's Lucy, Vina's friend from Melbourne,' Betty told her. 'They shared a flat together for years.'

Jenni looked round. 'I wonder who the blonde girl is sitting next to Lucy?'

'I'm not totally certain but I think she might be Philip's secretary, Valerie,' Helen told her. 'Vina's got to know her quite well during the time she and Philip have been dating.'

'Looks like we're going to have a speech by the bridegroom,' Betty signalled to the top of their table, where Philip was getting to his feet.

The speeches over, the new Mr and Mrs Dawson chatted to their guests before heading off for the airport.

The last person Vina spoke to was Bill. 'Bye Dad, see you when we get back,' she said, sorry although not surprised when there was no response. Then, as she turned away, hand in hand with Philip, the old man said, loudly and clearly, 'Bye Jean, I love you.'

The End.

About the author

Irene Lebeter worked as a secretary for forty-five years, in industry, Civil Service and latterly the NHS. Her childhood love of story writing has continued throughout her life and has led to professional creative writing in her retirement. A previous member of Priesthill Writing Forum, she is now a member of three writing groups, Strathkelvin, Ruadh Ghleann and Kelvingrove, and has completed a two-year creative writing course at Strathclyde University.

Irene has been an award winner in both novel and short story genres at the Annual Conference of the Scottish Association of Writers. She has been featured in the Federation of Writers' anthology 'Making Waves' as well as having multiple stories and non-fiction historical articles published in both UK and USA magazines.

'Vina's Quest' is her first novel.

About Author Way Limited

Author Way provides a broad range of good quality, previously unpublished works and makes them available to the public on multiple formats.

We have a fast growing number of authors who have completed or are in the process of completing their books and preparing them for publication and these will shortly be available.

Please keep checking our website to hear about the latest developments.

Author Way Limited

www.authorway.net

Printed in Great Britain
by Amazon.co.uk, Ltd.,
Marston Gate.